Also by June Faver

Welcome Back to Rambling, Texas

JUNE FAVER

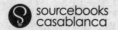

sourcebooks
casablanca

Published by Sourcebooks Casablanca, an imprint of Sourcebooks
P.O. Box 4410, Naperville, Illinois 60567-4410
(630) 961-3900
sourcebooks.com

Printed and bound in Canada.
MBP 10 9 8 7 6 5 4 3 2 1

♥ *To my neighbors in the Texas Hill Country. Thanks for the inspiration and friendship.* ♥

Chapter 1

REGGIE LEE STAFFORD GLANCED OUT THE WINDOW OF HER daddy's Hill Country convenience store just northwest of Austin, Texas. She looked out in time to see the silver BMW cruise slowly by. The top was down, and the driver looked as divine as the vehicle.

A bronzed god with longish blond sun-streaked hair, he radiated the attitude of a celebrity, hiding behind the lenses of his designer sunglasses. Driving with his elbow stuck out the window, he craned his neck to peer into the small store.

He gazed up at the fading sign that proudly proclaimed the establishment to be Stafford's Mercantile, a name Reggie's grandparents had selected in 1949 when they'd first opened their doors in Rambling, Texas, and when the wares had included yard goods and hardware.

Reggie leaned over the counter to stare back at the hunk in the sports car, surprised when he pulled into the parking lot and climbed out.

He shoved the keys in the pocket of his faded denims and continued to gaze through the plate-glass window with an air of indecision.

She noted that the denims were well filled with one-hundred-percent prime American beef. *Well, well, well. Eye candy from the city. My lucky day.* She surreptitiously glanced at her reflection in the mirror behind the counter and ran her fingers through her tousled hair. She took a deep breath as the stranger pushed through the entrance, clanking the metal cowbell against the glass. Her dimples flashed as she wrapped her soft Texas drawl around the words of greeting. "Good afternoon. How can I help you?"

The stranger pushed his sunglasses up on his head and grinned back at her. He laughed, a single derisive snort. "Is that really you, Regina Vagina? Still here after all these years?"

A claustrophobic strangling sensation reached up from her gut and threatened to suffocate the life out of her. "No-o-o!" she wailed. "Franklinstein!"

She stared in dismay at the grown-up version of the boy who had made her early adolescence a living hell. From the day he had arrived in town, Franklin Bell had been crossways with her, and he had remained so until the day he'd departed.

A clutch of something other than dismay seized her as he continued to inspect her with unmistakably mischievous green eyes. "You got anything cold to drink, Regina?" He pronounced her name as he always had, rhyming with *vagina*.

Color flamed her cheeks. "Any fool can see the whole back wall is lined with reach-in coolers," she bit out tersely. "Serve yourself."

Seemingly undaunted by her scathing remark, he had the nerve to chuckle before turning to inspect the contents of the coolers. All too soon, he returned with his selection and slid it across the counter toward her.

Reggie rang up his purchase and murmured, "That will be a dollar and sixty-nine cents." Her words came out all husky, and she pressed her lips together as she reached for the two singles he offered. Their fingers brushed, sending a tingling sensation to the pit of her stomach.

"You're looking good, Regina." His voice sounded smoky as his gaze lingered at the curve of her breast.

"Would you stop calling me that? We're not kids anymore, Franklin." She slammed his change down on the counter.

"Yes, ma'am," he said, seemingly contrite.

She took a deep breath and let it out all at once. "Reggie. My friends call me Reggie."

He gave her a strange little smile. "I know that. Only you would never let me be your friend." He twisted the lid off his soda and took a long guzzle.

"My friend!" she exploded. "You never wanted to be my friend. Your sole purpose in life was to make me miserable."

"If you say so." He smirked and took another swig.

She swallowed hard as she watched his mouth caress the soda bottle. She moistened her own dry lips, trying to appear casual. "Just passing through?"

"Not this time," he said. "I'm here to tie up some loose ends and take care of a little business."

Reggie sniffed. "What kind of business?"

He leaned his elbows on the counter and gazed up at her. "My great-aunt, Miss Rosie Bell Grady…she passed and left me all her considerable property."

Reggie glanced out the storefront at the silver Beemer sitting on the roasting-hot asphalt. "It doesn't look as if you need it."

He smiled, unperturbed by her withering commentary. "That could be, but I always liked this town. Believe it or not, I do have some fond memories of Rambling, Texas."

Reggie stifled a curt rejoinder. "I didn't see you at Miss Rosie's funeral."

His brash humor faded abruptly. "I was, uh…out of the country."

She eyed him with uncompromising candor. "I sincerely hope that your business dealings proceed without delay."

He pushed away from the counter. "So I can get the hell out of town as fast as possible?" He raised an eyebrow, glaring at her, although she refused to be baited. "Sorry to disappoint you, Regina, but I'll be staying on a while." He tilted the bottle and drained the contents.

"I swear, if you call me that one more time I'm going to climb across this counter and smack you one."

He opened his eyes wide in mock disbelief. "You would assault me on my very first day back in town?"

She glowered, crossing her arms over her chest. "Assault? You sound like a freakin' asshole lawyer or something."

"Guilty as charged."

Reggie experienced the choking sensation again. "Guh-rate!"

He replaced the bottle cap and flipped the empty into the trash container behind the counter. "See ya around, Regina."

———ᴠᴠᴠ———

That didn't go well. But it never did with Regina...Reggie, he reminded himself.

He didn't know why he thought she would treat him any differently than she had in the past. Always had hated him...always would. *Snotty bitch.* He sighed. *Beautiful, exciting, desirable snotty bitch.*

Frank dug the keys out of his pocket, and with a last glance over his shoulder at the storefront, he climbed into his car and turned the ignition.

Still, she had smiled at him before she realized who he was... and how much she hated him.

He pulled out of the parking space, knowing that Reggie was watching him.

Expelling the breath he'd been holding, he headed for Aunt Rosie's sprawling Victorian house down by the river.

Rambling was located in the beautiful Texas Hill Country, the so-called Heart of Texas. There were a lake and two rivers, so the area was a mecca for retirees and vacationers. For a prolonged period of time, visitors and residents alike took to the rivers to float with the currents on oversized inner tubes. Tubing on the river had been a real thing, and he presumed it still was.

The lake, on the other hand, offered the opportunity for motorboats to piss off the owners of sailboats, who preferred the much quieter and far less bumpy method of boating. There were also canoes and kayaks on the lake and rivers, so most people had a means of assaulting the water on a regular basis.

Frank had been an accomplished sailor, preferring the wind to power his boat, which had been moored at one of the marinas.

As he drove through the town, he recalled his first encounter with Reggie Lee Stafford, the dark-eyed beauty who had laughed when he'd stumbled, dropping his books at her feet.

"Watch it, new boy. You almost ran me down."

In truth, he'd stumbled when he'd done a double take to get another look at her dancing eyes and flash of dimples. But he'd blushed when she'd chided him and gathered his belongings in anger. That meeting had been the first of many disastrous encounters where Reggie Lee and her friends had taunted the "New Boy."

Later that day, when a teacher called on her in class using her full name, he'd seized upon the opportunity to get revenge. He'd enjoyed her discomfort when he'd first called her "Regina Vagina." His timing had been perfect. He'd chosen the moment just before class was dismissed and the teacher was distracted to call out to her, just loud enough to carry, "Hey, Regina Vagina. Why are you so stuck up?"

A wave of raucous laughter swept the classroom. Several of the boys who were to become his friends gave him a thumbs-up and nods of approval. It was the validation he needed. A way to fit in.

Reggie had turned red, and her eyes had teared. Grabbing her books, she'd rushed out of class, her covey of girlfriends clustered around her.

He'd felt a moment of remorse for hurting her feelings but had enjoyed bonding with the guys.

She'd retaliated in kind, dubbing him "Franklinstein," but her taunt had fallen short. Nothing could have equaled actually speaking aloud the female body part that so fascinated the entire male student body.

The wind whipped Frank's hair as he picked up speed outside the city limits. Within a few short minutes, he turned onto the shady lane that led to Aunt Rosie's house. It was lined with old pecan trees, their branches reaching across to each other like the arms of lovers forever separated by the winding dirt road.

Pulling up in front of the house, he turned off the ignition and sat for a moment before stepping out. The house had fallen into disrepair, but a feeling of warmth flooded his chest as he gazed up at the old structure.

The porch completely circled the house. He recalled the sound of his young footsteps as he ran irreverently around and around, playing games with other rowdy boys. He could still see Aunt Rosie rocking on the porch, with a bit of needlework or a crossword puzzle and pencil in her hands.

Climbing up on the porch, he set one of the dusty wicker rockers into motion, giving it a shove as he passed.

When he inserted the skeleton key in the old-fashioned lock, it turned with difficulty. He couldn't remember the house ever being locked, but the lawyer had mailed him a key along with a copy of Aunt Rosie's will. When he'd seen her spidery signature, he had been overwhelmed with sadness. He'd been traveling in Europe and hadn't known of her passing until after the funeral. Sucking in a deep breath, he blew it out, puffing his cheeks in the process. He would have to find out where she was buried and pay his overdue respects. *Another sin to atone for.*

The door opened with a creak, and he stepped across the threshold, entering a treasure trove of memories, mostly pleasant, some bittersweet.

His footsteps sounded hollow. They echoed off the wooden floors and up the stairs to rebound from the hard surface of the stained-glass window on the landing and back down to impact him again.

Walking back to the kitchen, he experienced a feeling of remorse when he saw the layer of dust on Aunt Rosie's usually immaculate surfaces. His throat tightened with sorrow.

I should have been here more.

He opened the back door, stepped out onto the porch, and gazed across the fields and the orchards. The air was heavy with the smell of fruit trees in blossom and the drone of honeybees harvesting nectar and going about their business of pollinating the blossoms. He drew great lungfuls of the fragrance deep into his chest.

This is mine now. He wasn't sure how he felt about owning so much land. He had scrupulously avoided entanglements, and this felt like a major commitment.

In the city, he leased a spacious condo, but he wasn't particularly attached to it. The furniture and even the paintings hanging on his walls were leased.

Frank stuck his hands in his pockets and sighed. Although he tried to live "in the moment" and be flexible enough that he could seize upon any opportunity that presented itself, he hoped that his legacy wouldn't require too much of his attention. Up until now, he'd been able to leave the country and travel whenever the notion hit him, and it hit him quite frequently.

He realized that owning this property would infringe upon his ability to go with the flow, change directions on a whim, celebrate his spontaneity. Now he was a landowner, and with that came certain responsibilities.

He knew that Aunt Rosie had derived some of her income from the harvest of fruit. Peaches and apples from the orchard and grapes from the vineyard. All suitable to be grown in the moderate climate and growing conditions.

Her other income had come from rental properties her husband had left her. They were located all around the small town. Most were residential, but there were several businesses as well.

She'd held the local Dairy Queen franchise, although there had always been a manager to handle the day-to-day transactions. And there was the vineyard, where they produced a superb pinot grigio. Also the small flower shop that handled all the local weddings and funerals.

A smile formed on Frank's lips. There was one more property. The *Rambling Gazette*.

After her husband died, Aunt Rosie inherited the building housing the weekly newspaper. As owner, she maintained a very loose control over the building, and in return for free rent, the publication guaranteed to maintain the building so Miss Rosie didn't have to deal with it, and the community got their news.

Now the building had passed to Frank. He released a deep chuckle. The *Rambling Gazette* where Miss Reggie Lee Stafford worked as reporter and columnist…when she wasn't babysitting her daddy's convenience store.

Frank had a feeling that he was going to enjoy checking out that old building. It was four stories of red brick, and as far as he knew, the *Gazette* only occupied the ground floor. It seemed he'd developed a sudden interest in the publishing business. What else did that old building contain?

––––––

Reggie Lee stared out the window of the store but saw nothing. She shivered as she recalled the look in Frank Bell's green eyes. He was definitely up to something…and it had to be no good.

From the first moment Franklin Bell had arrived in Rambling, he'd been nothing but trouble with a capital T.

She recalled when he'd been introduced to her ninth-grade class. She'd thought he was cute in a green-eyed, dark-blondish sort of way. Way cuter than the other boys. He'd come from some prep school in Arlington, up near Dallas. He was pretty stiff at first. He couldn't take a joke, and he'd almost gotten into a fight with Kenny Landers his first day.

His temper didn't improve in the weeks to follow. He'd rushed right smack into her the next day and hadn't even apologized. Just turned all shades of red as he'd gathered up his books and hustled off. Of course, a few people had laughed, but that was nothing. You have to be able to laugh at yourself once in a while.

As if!

Mr. Perfect Franklin Bell would never be able to laugh at himself. Not when he could be ridiculing others. Reggie Lee to be specific.

How could a lady as sweet as Miss Rosie Bell Grady even be

distantly related to Frank Bell? Their kinship was beyond Reggie Lee's wildest imagination. She couldn't conceive that they shared the same gene pool, except for the green eyes.

Miss Rosie had been the kindest person on the planet. If it weren't for her, Reggie might not have been given an opportunity to become a member of the *Gazette* staff at such a young age. Miss Rosie had suggested Reggie might like to submit something for the "younger crowd," as she'd put it. Miss Rosie must have put in a good word for her because this had led to Reggie being hired on to cover all school athletic events and later assigned to write a weekly column titled *Around Town*. Reggie also took her turn at writing obituaries and birth and wedding announcements.

Sadly, she had written Miss Rosie's obituary, cringing when she'd typed in the name of her nephew, Franklin Bell, as her sole living relative.

Miss Rosie's funeral had been attended by the governor of the state and a couple of past governors. Countless senators and congressmen came to pay their respects. But there was no member of the family to pay their respects to because her only surviving relative was out of the country and couldn't be bothered to fly back to say a final goodbye to the wonderful lady who had taken over the role of parenting him.

Reggie sniffed, remembering that the loss of his own parents was what had brought Frank to Rambling in the first place. Maybe he'd been depressed when he'd first arrived, but it had come across as a big fat chip on his shoulder.

Now he'd come back to claim all of Miss Rosie's property. The lovely old Victorian house. The verdant orchards and the vineyard. The businesses…

A cold lump settled in the pit of Reggie's stomach. The *Gazette*. Frank Bell had inherited the red-brick building that housed the *Gazette*. The building had stood in place over a hundred years. It was a monument to the community.

Frank Bell now owns the property. What will that smug bastard do to our building?

She envisioned her fellow staff members suddenly without a job. The community newspaper barely earned enough to keep the doors open, but it was desperately needed.

―∿∿―

A week went by. Reggie Lee saw Frank around town, but he apparently didn't see her. He zipped around in his silver Beemer, completely oblivious to the chaos he was spreading in her life. Just knowing that he could walk into the newspaper office on any given day and evict the entire newspaper and the staff kept her on edge. *He is such a jerk!*

Reggie sat at her desk at the *Gazette*, her fingers fixed on the keyboard of her computer. She needed to create a fluff piece about Sybil Carney's bridal shower hosted by her sorority sisters at the Grey Moss Inn, one of the longtime advertisers in the *Rambling Gazette*.

Frank Bell, the complete asshole, could destroy everything she had ever accomplished. That fact knotted her stomach and curled her fingers into fists.

Reggie swallowed the bile gathered at the back of her throat. If he thought he could just waltz into town and crush her dreams without a fight, he had another think coming. Reggie would fight back. She would—

Her shoulders drooped. What could she do? The boy who had been her sworn enemy all through school had grown to be a man, and as a man he held all the cards...at least all the good ones.

What would she do if...no, *when* he closed the newspaper and sold off the building? What would she do? She had only a high school diploma. All her life she'd lived in a small town. She hadn't dreamed any bigger.

Now what?

Her eyes darted to the framed photo on her desk. How would she support her daughter?

Chapter 2

Frank took a tour of the vineyard and sampled the wares. Evan Hauser had been one of his running buddies as a teen. Now Evan managed the whole operation from tending the vines to controlling the temperature of the storerooms.

Evan shook his head, a nervous grin on his lips. "Who would have thought?"

Frank paced around the showroom, set up with intimate tables where customers could sample and purchase wines. He stopped, gazing out the front window at the grapevine-carpeted hills.

"I don't remember the vineyard as being so spread out."

"It's been more than a dozen years since high school graduation, Frank. A lot of things have changed."

Frank turned to survey his old friend. He'd put on a little weight, and his hairline was starting to recede, but it was still Evan, the big guy who had kept Kenny Landers, the school bully, from killing him on a daily basis. Frank grinned. "You've worked here since graduation?"

Evan nodded. "Your aunt hired me and a few others for the summer, but I stayed on. She gave me more responsibilities as time went by. The last few years I've been running things for her...for you now." Evan spread his hands and shrugged his shoulders. "It's all I've ever done."

Frank ran his fingers through his hair. *Responsibilities.* He swallowed convulsively, trying to shake off the strangling sensation the word conjured up. "Doing a great job, Ev. Keep up the good work."

Evan beamed his relief. "Thanks, Frank. It's like a family here. My life's work is in those bottles."

Frank considered this statement. He wasn't sure exactly what his life's work was all about. He had finished law school to please Aunt Rosie and because he'd been good at it. He'd always loved a good argument, and he'd always loved to solve puzzles. He'd thought he would go into contract law, but before stepping into that somewhat dry and tedious role, he'd decided to indulge in his long-thwarted desire to travel. He'd made it as far as Stockholm, where he'd bought a small, run-down bar. He'd turned it into a thriving business, with crowds standing in line outside. One night, an impatient patron offered to buy the bar in a bid to gain immediate access. Frank blurted out an unimaginable figure, and the man met his price. Dazed, Frank walked away with a huge windfall profit in hand.

From that time until the present, Frank had searched out businesses that were running on fumes and purchased them from owners on the verge of bankruptcy. He had then invested his time and money in making them profitable and turning them around for an even more profitable sale.

He massaged the back of his neck. It felt tight, and his shoulders held the weight of his new responsibilities.

"It's great to have you back in town, Frank." Evan's grin went wall-to-wall. "I'm glad we'll be working together. I was worried about the vineyard after Miss Rosie passed away. I know the rest of the workers will be relieved to know it will stay in the family."

"Um, yeah. In the family," Frank echoed.

What would happen if he sold the vineyard and winery as he had intended? What would become of Evan's life's work?

—◠◠◠—

"A large order of chicken strips and fries." Reggie stood at the counter of the local Dairy Queen, holding tight to her daughter's hand. "Hang on a minute, Shannon."

"Ice cweam!" Shannon howled indignantly.

"You have to eat your food first."

"Finch fies!" Shannon stretched up to reach for the tray as the counter attendant scooted it toward Reggie. The tray started to slide as Shannon's fingers connected to its edge.

"Steady there." A man's hand shot out from the line behind them to grab the tray and right it before it fell.

Reggie turned to thank the man, her smile fading when she recognized Frank Bell.

He stood behind her gripping the tray as though frozen into a very attractive statue. He regarded her with interest, his green eyes taking in every detail of her appearance. He smiled and turned his attention to Shannon. "Well, hello there. Who is this little heartbreaker?" He squatted down to Shannon's level.

She grinned shyly before turning to press her face into Reggie's legs.

Frank remained on his haunches, grinning up at Reggie. "She looks just like you. She's a real beauty."

Reggie felt her color rising. "Thanks," she stammered, cringing in anticipation of his next snide remark. When he didn't snipe at her, she looked at him again. "This is my daughter, Shannon."

"I'm Frank," he directed his comments to the child. "Can you say my name?"

Shannon giggled prettily. "Fwank!"

He grinned back at her.

Reggie's gag reflex worked overtime as she saw her daughter being sucked into the dark vortex that was Franklin Bell's charm.

She bit back the caustic comment leaping from her tongue and reminded herself not to antagonize her employer. "We'd better eat before the fries turn to cardboard." She tugged on Shannon's hand

and headed for a booth, sending what she hoped was a nonthreat-ening expression over her shoulder.

She set the tray on a table and almost bumped into Frank as he pushed a high chair toward her. He held out his hands to Shannon, who lifted her arms.

Reggie's nails dug into her palms as Franklin Bell swung her daughter in the air before sliding her into the high chair. He seemed to have a genuine smile on his face. Not the smart-assed superior smirk he usually wore. Her heart fluttered when he met her gaze. It felt like he had caught her naked. He had no right to be in her life. To know anything about her life, for that matter. She wanted to grab Shannon and run away. Run to someplace behind high walls with a drawbridge to raise...and a dragon in the moat.

"Finch fies!" Shannon pointed to the tray of food.

Reggie swallowed and murmured under her breath, "Thanks, Frank." She slid into the booth and opened the Styrofoam containers.

"Sure." He winked at her and strode back to the counter.

She thought for a moment that he might return to sit at their table, but he waited for his order and took it with him. He walked out the door without looking back.

Reggie felt the tension leave her shoulders. She wasn't sure if she felt relief or disappointment.

"Man, what a bitch!" Frank slammed the car door. He had been as nice as pie, and she still had that uptight, stay-away-from-me vibe going on.

Her little girl was adorable. She looked like Reggie, if Reggie ever got that stick out of her ass.

Frank sighed and flexed his fingers around the wheel. *Not going to let her get to me this time.* "Damn! Why does she have to be so freaking beautiful?"

He took a sip from his soda and stuffed an onion ring in his mouth. In his many fantasies starring Reggie Lee Stafford, she'd never looked as pretty as she did when smiling at her little girl. The innate softness she wore like an aura turned to carbon steel whenever her eyes focused on him.

He had never considered Reggie as a mother, but the role seemed to suit her. He smiled and reached for another onion ring. He wondered who the father was. He hadn't seen a ring on Reggie's finger, but that didn't mean anything. Who was the sperm donor for the lovely little Shannon? Who was the lucky man to bed the Ice Princess?

He reviewed the list of likely candidates from high school. She had hung out with the rest of the popular kids. The ones who formed committees and ran for office. He couldn't recall any male to whom she had been particularly linked. No great love defined.

But there must have been someone.

Maybe it was time he paid her a visit...at work.

———

"Reggie Lee?" Her father's voice rose in timbre as she slipped inside the door and tiptoed across the hardwood floor.

She carried Shannon in her arms, her handbag slung over her shoulder. "Shh, Daddy. Shannon's asleep." Stumbling across the living room, she lowered her daughter to the sofa. She could feel her father's protective scrutiny.

Shannon stirred and then curled on her side, her angelic expression tugging at Reggie Lee's heartstrings. As upset as she was, she couldn't allow her feelings to affect Shannon. Her daughter didn't deserve that.

Henry Stafford peered at her over his glasses. "Are you all right?"

"I'm just peachy, Daddy. I saw Frank Bell today. He was at the Dairy Queen."

"That boy you used to fight with in high school?" He pushed his glasses up on his head. "He has a right to be there. It's a free country."

Reggie crossed her arms over her bosom. "No, he has no right to be anywhere in my world."

"Don't get your panties in a wad. I don't see how this Frank guy always manages to pull your strings."

She turned away, angry. "He doesn't pull my strings. He's just the most infuriating, most aggravating, most...most..."

Her father chuckled. "I see."

Reggie Lee shrugged, reluctant to admit how right he'd been. "Frank always manages to get under my skin."

"You always let him get under your skin." Henry sank into his favorite chair and reached for his glasses, settling them back on his nose. "It appears to me that this fellow has had your number from the start. I always thought maybe he liked you."

Reggie Lee made a noise in the back of her throat. "Franklin Bell hated me on sight."

Henry twinkled a grin at her. "So you say, but I was a boy once, and I remember teasing your mother before I figured out I was sweet on her."

She shook her head vehemently. "It wasn't like that." She recalled her mother laughing over Henry's infatuation and the way he'd teased her. "We just despised each other immediately."

Henry cleared his throat and unfolded his newspaper. "So you say."

"Daddy! Don't give me that smug expression. I do not like Frank Bell." She turned and stomped out of the room.

In the kitchen she filled a glass with ice and reached for the pitcher of sweet tea. She watched the amber liquid fill the glass and twisted off a sprig of mint from her window herb assortment. The tea ritual was a part of her. It calmed her. It centered her. It did not keep her from envisioning Frank's green eyes and the way they roamed over her body. She had always thought Frank's insolent overtures were born of loathing. She sipped her tea and considered her father's belief that Frank's attentions might have been due to some attraction.

"No!" The sound of her own voice in the quiet room startled her. "No," she whispered. There was no love lost between her and Frank. She set her glass on the tile countertop with a bang.

She recalled her first thoughts when she'd spied the grown-up version of Frank in his sports car. She'd entertained a rush of lust that she hadn't experienced in some time. Since her marriage ended, Reggie Lee had focused all her energies on raising Shannon, her job at the newspaper, and keeping house for her daddy. She hadn't spent much time or energy on her long-lost love life.

Of course, three of her best girlfriends had not married yet but held much more hopeful attitudes toward the prospect of marriage.

Her friend Lori Holloway was a children's book author and had moved to New York City. She was a big deal in the world of kiddie literature.

And Truly Nell Todd, the wonderfully wild and willful girl, had married a man who was quite well off and relocated to the big city.

Jill Garland, her best friend and the daughter of the local sheriff, had never married, but she flexed her maternal instincts as the owner of the local day care. If it weren't for Jill, Reggie Lee would have been at a loss for female friends.

Otherwise, Reggie Lee remained behind, abandoned and alone in the small town of Rambling, Texas, where it seemed that she would wither away without a true love...without a happily ever after.

Most of the good men in the area had married, and the single men in her age bracket weren't particularly attracted to nor attractive to Reggie Lee.

Pity that her own marriage had fallen apart. *I sure can pick 'em.*

She drew in a breath. Not that the marriage had been much to begin with. The demise of her lackluster marital state had not come as a surprise. What had surprised her was that Kenny hadn't seemed to want to continue his relationship with his daughter either. He had packed his belongings in his ten-year-old Impala and headed out of town.

―᠕᠕᠕―

Reggie Lee deleted the entire paragraph she had just written. She cleared her throat and sat up straighter, groping for words to make the life of Homer James Campbell seem important. He was the recently departed former school janitor who had retired after a long career with the school district. He'd had the intention of spending many years on the lake, sitting in his small rowboat with a can of worms and a cane pole. She flexed her fingers.

She typed... Homer James Campbell, a World War II veteran, passed away Wednesday after succumbing to a short illness...

She grimaced, her finger poised over the delete button. Surely there were words to summarize an entire life that didn't seem so totally banal. She heaved a deep sigh and shoved the rolling chair she was perched on away from the desk. "Oh!" She ran into something solid...something that also let out a surprised grunt.

Reggie Lee swiveled in her chair and was caught in the arms of Frank Bell.

A slow grin spread across his face. "Hard at work, I see."

Panic gripped her stomach. "Oh," she repeated. "I mean, yes. I'm working."

Frank stepped back, releasing her in the process. "So, what are you doing?"

"Obit. Old man Campbell died." She tried to smile, but the corners of her mouth trembled. She clamped her lips together.

"Old man Campbell." Frank frowned. "You mean the school janitor? He was pretty much ancient when I left town."

"Pretty old. He lived to be eighty-seven." Reggie wondered how long he was going to stand over her trying to intimidate her... succeeding. She pushed the rolling chair away and stood. Frank still towered over her, but not as much. She reached for some papers in her inbox. "If you'll excuse me, I have to deliver these right away."

The green eyes flicked over the unopened mail in her hand, and another grin said he knew she was lying. "I see." He stepped away. "I'll get with you later, then."

Reggie Lee nodded and slipped by him, almost fleeing to the editor's office. She closed the door behind her with such force it rattled the glass inset.

"Reggie Lee?"

"I—uh, he's here."

Phillip stared at her, his expression blank. "Who?"

Reggie Lee rolled her eyes. "Franklin Bell. He's here!" She delivered this news in a hoarse whisper. "Rosie Bell Grady's heir." She fought down the panic clawing at her throat. "He's here to destroy the paper."

Phillip shuffled the papers on his desk, his eyes darting around the cluttered space. "Well, he should have called."

Reggie stamped her foot. "He owns the place. He doesn't need to call for an appointment."

He glanced up at her, his eyes glazed with fear.

"Oh, never mind." Reggie Lee turned and marched out the door, having recovered her own courage when presented with such an impressive display of cowardice.

Frank Bell was perched on her desk, reading her monitor. "It's not bad. Just needs some punch."

Anger flared in her gut. "And are you an authority on journalistic style now?"

Frank raised an eyebrow. "I believe that's your area of expertise."

She sniffed. "Well, then…" She took her seat and rolled toward the keyboard. "If you'll excuse me, I must get back to work."

He placed his hand on her keyboard. "Perhaps you can show me around first. Give me a tour of the place." He seemed to be devouring her with his gaze. "I mean, since old man Campbell isn't in any hurry for his obituary."

She swallowed. "Surely you've been here before."

His lips twitched in an ironic little semblance of a smile. "How gracious. I haven't been in this building in over twelve years. I figured things might have changed a bit."

She sighed. "They have changed. I'm sorry if I was…abrupt." She swiveled her chair and rose to her feet. "The guided tour starts now. Follow me." She stood and strode purposefully toward Phillip's office. *Let him share in the joy.*

She led Frank into Phillip's office without knocking. "Franklin Bell, this is Phillip Jergens, editor of the *Gazette*. Phil, Frank is the new owner of the building." Reggie turned and crossed her arms over her chest. It gave her a molecule of satisfaction that Frank appeared to be seriously disconcerted.

Phil, for his part, looked dazed. He half stood and extended his hand. "Mr.—Mr. Bell. I'm… I'm delighted to meet you."

"Call me Frank." He grasped Phil's hand and pumped it.

She had to stifle the urge to laugh at Phil's expression. He looked like a large rat caught with his tail in the trap. He gestured to a chair opposite his desk. "Please sit down, Frank."

Frank pointed to the chair beside him and indicated Reggie was to sit. "Tell me about the newspaper. It was just pointed out to me that I am completely ignorant of the publishing business, so enlighten me."

Reggie sank onto the worn leather chair, biting her tongue to keep her acerbic words in check.

Frank sat and crossed his legs loosely at the ankle, completely at ease.

"Well…well…" Phil stumbled for words.

Reggie sighed and took over. "The *Gazette* is the only weekly newspaper in the county. We print the news, the social events, school functions, births, marriages, and deaths. Local crimes are reported as well as divorces and a letters to the editor op-ed column and, of course, the *Dear Irene* column." She heaved a deep breath. "The community depends on the *Rambling Gazette* for local news."

"What about advertisers? Who supports the paper?" Frank gazed at her with interest.

She moistened her lips. "Local businesses advertise regularly, and we have subscribers."

He arched a brow at her and then swung his gaze to Phil. "So, are you saying that the newspaper is a thriving business?"

Phil stammered, making unintelligible sounds.

"Tell me, then, who is your biggest advertiser?"

"The vineyard," Phil answered promptly. "And the Dairy Queen and flower shop."

Frank leaned forward, knitting his brows into a frown. "You're telling me that my aunt supported the local newspaper with advertising from her own businesses?"

Phil shrank visibly.

"We have other advertisers," Reggie said. "The Grey Moss Inn is a regular advertiser and the supermarket…and, uh…Stafford's runs a small weekly ad." Her cheeks were flaming as she sat with her lips pressed together.

"I see," Frank said. "The other enterprises that my aunt owned seem to be flourishing. Providing the newspaper with free rent seems to have been a charity of hers."

Phil's voice rose a whole octave. "Charity?" he squeaked.

"Tomorrow. I'll be here in the morning at ten, and you can

walk me through the building. Show me what's on the upper three floors...perhaps share the financials. I would like to feel confident about the newspaper's ability to support itself for the next quarter." He rose and extended his hand to Reggie as though to shake it. "Thank you for...the tour."

She shivered as he enveloped her hand in his. Instead of shaking it, he raised it to his lips, gazing into her eyes as he pressed a kiss against her fingers.

"I'll see you tomorrow." He gently placed her hand back in her lap and strode out.

"Oh, my," Phil moaned. "Oh, my."

Chapter 3

REGGIE COULDN'T SLEEP. SHE HAD FED SHANNON AND BATHED her and read her a story before tucking her into bed. Now she tossed and turned in her own bed, dreading the dawn when she would learn the fate of the *Gazette*.

It was worse than she had thought. He was going to close the newspaper. He would destroy the only source of local news for the entire county. A dozen of her fellow employees would be out of work, some of whom had worked at the *Gazette* for decades.

How could that selfish, arrogant asshole throw so many people into the unemployment line? *Because he's a selfish, arrogant asshole.*

She fluffed her pillow and turned over. *Not going to think about Frank Bell.*

She thought about Frank Bell. Thought about his green eyes staring at her hungrily. Thought about his lips brushing against her fingers. Thought about his voice as he'd crooned, "I'll see you tomorrow."

In the morning, Reggie Lee was at work at eight sharp. She went through her desk and cleaned out all the debris from her drawers. When Frank announced he was throwing the *Gazette* out of the old red-brick building, she would simply pick up her nameplate and the picture of Shannon and depart with as much dignity as she could gather. No tears. No goodbyes. No regrets.

She glanced at Phil's office. It remained dark. He was probably going over the financials in the bookkeeping office, making sure everything was in order.

She returned her attention to a sheaf of paper she found in the bottom of her left-hand lower drawer. These papers had been stuffed there since before her time, and she'd never bothered to purge them. Well, now was the time. Whoever took over this building could at least have a clean desk.

Shoving the papers into her wastebasket, she realized it was overfull, so she carried it to the dumpster behind the building. On her way, she noticed that Phil's parking space was empty. Well, he probably wanted to arrive just before his scheduled meeting with Frank. That way his nerves would be under control.

Maybe...

She returned to her desk and spent the next half hour sorting and purging. She finished Mr. Campbell's obituary with a flourish of brilliance, likening him to a guardian angel watching over the high school he had kept clean and repaired for thirty years. She saved the copy and sighed. *Now what?*

On an ordinary day, she would have been checking the churches for upcoming events as well as the school athletic schedules. She would have been filling her calendar with the important happenings scheduled around the county. These events were, she reasoned, important to somebody. The bride and groom, the parents christening their infant, the girls' basketball team. Somebody cared about what she wrote. Somebody clipped her articles and pasted them in a scrapbook.

She drummed her fingers on the scarred but clean desktop. The clock read nine forty. *Where the hell is Phil?*

She cringed when she glimpsed the BMW pull into a parking space in front of the plate-glass window.

Frank raked his fingers through his wind-blown hair and got out. He loped up the wooden steps and swung open the door, jangling the bell.

He caught her eye and grinned. "Good morning." He leaned over the counter and placed two bags on top. "I brought a peace offering."

Reggie drew a deep breath. *So he's going to play it cute and then cut the legs out from under me.* She pushed back from her desk and met him at the counter, her gaze cool, her jaw set. *Dang! He even smells rich.*

He opened the first bag and set a cup of hot coffee in front of her, taking another for himself.

She smiled in spite of her best intentions. The coffee aroma wafted to her nose and enticed her. She wrapped her fingers around the cardboard cup.

"And I have pastries." He held the other bag aloft. "Can we sit down and enjoy them?"

She nodded and motioned him around the counter. Wordlessly, she led him to the so-called employee break room. It was dark and dank, but it had a small table and three mismatched chairs. It also had a refrigerator, but no one took responsibility for cleaning it out, so she never stored anything inside.

She took a seat, and Frank drew one of the other chairs closer to her than she would have liked. Was he going to drop the bomb on her over coffee and pastries?

"I got cheese Danish, crullers, and oatmeal raisin cookies. What's your pleasure?" He pushed the bag close to her.

She made a show of opening the bag and peeking inside. She reached for a Danish. "Thanks," she murmured. She extended the open bag to him.

Frank reached inside without looking, his fingers grabbing the first thing they touched. "Cruller," he said, holding it aloft. He bit into it and took a sip of his coffee.

"This was nice of you, Frank," she said, conscious of how stiff she sounded. "Um...Phil isn't here yet." She kept her eyes averted, hoping that by avoiding eye contact she would stave off impending disaster.

"I'm in no hurry," he said. "I was hoping we could talk."

Reggie experienced a feathery feeling in her chest. *Talk?* What could they possibly talk about? The newspaper? How he planned to close it? Sell the building out from under them? Fire the entire staff?

She turned her face to him and was disconcerted to find him gazing at her like she was a cruller and he was about to munch into her.

"I was thinking, since I've been gone so long and you're an expert on the area, you might take a drive with me and show me what's changed in the last twelve years."

She took a sip of her coffee to preclude any comment on her part. *Hazelnut. Nice.*

"Maybe we could grab lunch at the Inn, or someplace else, if you prefer."

Reggie felt light-headed. Was Franklin Bell asking her on a date? *No, of course not.* He wanted her to show him around his domain. The monarch inspecting his realm.

"Sure," she said. "That would be nice." She picked up her coffee cup and took another sip.

She finished her Danish and glanced at the clock. *Ten fifteen.* Surely Phil had made it in by now. "We shouldn't keep Phil waiting." She rose, and Frank unfolded himself from the chair, standing way too close. He stared down at her, fencing her in for a moment, forcing her to look into his eyes and inhale his great scent. His gaze flicked to her mouth, and for an instant, she thought he was going to kiss her.

Abruptly, he stepped back and gestured for her to precede him out of the break room.

She struggled to keep her gait normal and not to bolt from the room. The sound of her heels on the wood floor should have alerted Phil to her presence, but she knocked anyway.

"Phil, it's Reggie and Frank." She twisted the knob and stepped into the still-dark office.

Flipping on the light, she gasped in amazement as she surveyed the immaculately clean office. Apparently, Phil had stayed late to empty out his workplace. A letter, addressed to F. Bell, sat atop the desk.

She turned to Frank uncertainly.

He walked to the desk and opened the letter. He read it over and placed it facedown atop the desk.

"It appears that Phillip Jergens has resigned his position effective immediately. And he named his replacement." He leaned across the desk to extend his hand. She grasped it as he said, "Congratulations on your appointment to the position of editor in chief."

Within the week, Frank went over the financials with Reggie Lee, and they determined that Phillip Jergens had been skimming for years. Phil had several "ghost employees" on the payroll who turned out to be his relatives. The bookkeeper had cranked out payroll per Phil's instructions, thinking the invisible employees were being paid for services rendered and never questioning their identity.

Calling the staff together, Frank explained what had happened to Phil; as owner of the building, he offered his support and wanted to help Reggie get settled into her new position. Considering his business acumen, all the staff members were amenable to his advice and expressed their appreciation for his support.

Frank stayed the first day to help Reggie move into her new office. She appeared to have been dumbfounded by her appointment to this position but had immediately accepted. He recognized her initial confusion followed by a surge of undisguised elation.

"There are others who have been here longer," she protested.

"That's not the criteria for this position. I think Phil was relying on you to carry on and hold the staff accountable. He wanted someone smart and trustworthy. Someone who can think on their feet and who is dedicated to the newspaper." He smiled down at her. "That's you."

She nodded and then presented him with a brilliant smile. The first time ever she had really smiled at him. Something about that smile of hers made him feel light-headed.

Frank didn't want them to prosecute old Phil. He hoped they would let him slink out of town quietly. No scandal to touch his great-aunt's beloved *Gazette*. *This one's for you, Aunt Rosie.*

Now he was making a daily foray into the newspaper office to check on the transition and to see if Reggie needed anything. He sat with her, and they went over the financials. She had some good ideas for encouraging advertisers with a reduced rate for multiple ads. He really didn't care what she did, as long as she kept talking to him and as long as she didn't cringe when he leaned close to inspect the paperwork she was diligently presenting for his approval. He loved those moments when he could inhale her fragrance and absently allow his fingertips to brush against her hair.

"I—I really appreciate you for helping me, Frank. I don't want to screw up." Her big brown eyes gazed up at him as he stood beside her desk. "I don't want to let the rest of the staff know that I don't know what I'm doing."

"Not to worry," he said. "I know nothing about the newspaper business, but I do know the nuts and bolts of running a successful business. I can help you get things lined out."

Her expression clutched at his emotions.

At the end of the first week, he asked, "How is morale around here?"

She gazed at him intently, as though trying to gauge his reaction. "Everyone is anxious. We're trying to please you and dig out of this hole we're in."

He smiled. He wanted to tell her that all she had to do to

please him was to stay close. "Don't try so hard," he admonished. "Things will get back to normal. Without those two extra paychecks, you're almost breaking even."

She grinned in apparent delight. "Really?"

"Really. How about that drive you were going to take with me? I want to see what's been going on since I left. Is this a good time?"

A tinge of color crept up her cheeks. "Sure. I guess it's as good a time as any." She reached in her new desk and took out her purse.

He held open the door and followed her out, taking pleasure in the smooth way her hips moved and the way her high heels made her calves tight. He gave himself a second to refocus and then opened his car door for her.

"Nice car," she breathed.

"Glad you like it. You should get one." He rounded the front bumper, climbed in, and started the engine. He had to rev it and then let it settle down to a purr before he pulled out of the parking lot.

"Oh, I would never buy a car like this. I have an SUV with a very high safety rating. My daughter comes first."

He glanced at her. "I would never buy a car like this either. I lease it."

She looked perplexed.

"If I get tired of it, I can return it and get something else."

A small frown puckered her smooth brow. "Do you get tired of cars frequently?"

He considered. "I guess so. I like to make changes. It keeps things interesting. Don't you like to change things up?"

She shook her head. "Not me. I like things to settle and develop. I like changes that come from nurturance, like a seed that grows and blooms. That gives me great satisfaction."

He changed the subject, sensing they were getting into an area that would cause dissension. "Is this place new?" He pointed to a fusty-looking little shop beside the flower shop.

She nodded. "That's Miss Mamie's Bridal Shop. She does all the important weddings around here."

"So much for Priscilla's of Boston and Vera Wang." He glanced at her for approval but saw that she looked confused. He drove down the main street, pointing out things that had not been there when he left.

In spite of his desire to remain free of all encumbrances, his brain was whirling with entrepreneurial churnings. He spotted a perfect location to open a coffeehouse and serve high-end flavored coffees and teas. There was adequate parking, and since it was at the end of the strip of businesses, he could design a drive-through window.

He turned to Reggie. "Invitations? Where do the brides get their invitations printed?"

"I don't know. Maybe they go into Austin or order them online."

"They should get them done at the *Gazette*. Don't you have the capacity to do printing?"

She bit her lower lip. "I'm not sure. I'll have to ask Marty Ketschmer, the guy who runs the presses."

He nodded. "Good for you. It might be a way to expand the business. How about going after other printing jobs? Menus for restaurants? Business cards?"

She brightened. "I see where you're going. So you're thinking of ways to increase revenue."

He winked at her, liking the way her eyes lit up when she looked at him.

They drove to the end of the city limits, and he turned to go down the street that ran parallel to the main street. Smaller shops and diners lined this street. A mechanic shop, a dollar store.

He slowed to gaze at every building. Why had he never noticed them before? His eyes lit on a small park where children played. Two women supervised the children; all of the little ones seemed to be preschool age.

"There's Shannon." Reggie pointed to a towheaded tot climbing the slide. She smiled as they passed.

"What's she doing there?" he asked, slowing to a crawl.

"She's in one of my best friends' day care center while I work. It's located in that little bungalow on the other side of the park. They bring the kids to play in the playground on nice days."

"That's good that you have someone you trust to take care of your child."

Reggie's genuine grin warmed his heart. "Yes. Jill Garland. You remember her? Long red hair? Her dad is the sheriff."

He nodded, though he couldn't recall the name. He could remember a redhead among Reggie's four or five female companions who seemed to run together as a herd.

"She is really involved in local environmental projects, and she loves little kids."

Frank listened to Reggie go on about her friend's good qualities. "Sounds interesting."

"She is. The name of her day care is Babes in the Woods. That fits, doesn't it?" She spread her arms to encompass the entire densely wooded area. "I think it's wonderful that we can live here with all the wildlife and greenery around us."

"Um—yes, I guess." Frank wasn't sure about all this eco-freak stuff. He was more comfortable with city streets and skyscrapers but said nothing to dampen her spirits. Her face was rapt while expounding on her friend's qualities.

"I—I'm glad you have a good place for Shannon to play."

Reggie shrugged. "Well, of course, I would prefer to be taking care of her myself, but it's nice to have a safe and secure preschool for her while I'm at work."

Frank felt a knot forming in his stomach. He hadn't realized how hard it was for Reggie to work and make sure her kid was taken care of. He had to admire that.

"Listen, Reggie," he said. "It's none of my business, but I am a little curious about Shannon. I mean, you don't ever mention her father, and I..."

"Divorced." Reggie shrugged. "I got dumped after Shannon was born."

"Sorry." He wondered how a man could run out on a woman as perfect as Reggie Lee and a treasure of a child like Shannon.

She was fiddling with her purse strap and gnawing her lower lip. "Kenny didn't plan on being a father right away, and I was too naive to know that."

That hit him like a sucker punch. "You were married to Kenny Landers?" He recalled the school bully and wondered what Reggie Lee could have possibly seen in him. He was such a crude oaf, and she was so...Reggie Lee...

"He joined the Army after you left. When he got out, he worked at the paper for a while, and I thought he hung the moon. When he left town again, he said he was going to look for a better job so he could provide for us, but then I got the divorce papers." She shrugged again. "I just let him go. I figured if he didn't want us, we wouldn't want him."

Frank concentrated on driving but kept his eye on Reggie. Her revelation had brought her mood way down. He reached out and gathered her hand in his. "Tough break."

"Shannon and I, we're okay," she said simply. Best of all, she didn't pull her hand away.

This feels way too much like a date.

Reggie was confused. She was having a leisurely lunch in a romantic restaurant with the man who had made her high school experience a living hell. And he was absolutely charming.

She laughed at the appropriate times but kept a wary eye on Frank, waiting for him to turn into Franklinstein. The atmosphere in the Grey Moss Inn was very romantic. It was softly lit and intimate even at the noon hour. The menu was phenomenal. Reggie tried to do justice to the food, but she was too nervous to properly enjoy it.

"Have some more wine." Frank gestured for the waiter, but Reggie protested.

"No, really. I'm a lightweight." She put her hand over her glass to keep the enthusiastic waiter from refilling it. She reflected that if she was a lightweight when it came to drinking wine, Frank was the heavyweight due to his many years living in Europe. "Besides, I have to get back to work."

"Eventually," Frank said and indicated that he was ready for a refill. "So tell me, since you now have free rein with the paper, what direction do you plan to take it?"

Free rein?

She had not really thought about changing anything. The *Gazette* had operated in the same way since she had first joined as a junior reporter when she was in high school. What would happen if she made big changes to the way the paper was run? She cleared her throat. "Well, I guess I would try to boost circulation by broadening the content to appeal to a wider segment of the community. You know? Write actual news stories."

Frank grinned at her. "Like the big boys?"

She felt her color rising. Was he just stringing her along? Waiting for her to say something stupid and fall on her face? "I think the residents of this community deserve a newspaper that is more than a glorified list of announcements."

He nodded. "And you think you can deliver that?"

She sucked in a deep breath and let it out all at once. "I would sure give it my best."

"Reggie, I appreciate your enthusiasm, but you're going to

need more than that. If you like, I can help you make a plan to take the *Gazette* from A to B and a timeline for getting you there." He cocked his head to one side. "Do you think we can develop a plan to make the *Gazette* a viable entity?" He gazed at her with what appeared to be open admiration.

Her heart was thumping against her ribs. If he had any idea what his flash of dimples did to her stomach, his substantial ego would soar. "Yes, I think we can."

He raised his glass and clinked it against hers.

Reggie took a sip of wine and surveyed Frank over the rim. "Tell me what you've been doing since high school. You said you were a lawyer?"

"Yes, I went to law school, mostly to please Aunt Rosie." He grinned sheepishly. "I seemed to have a penchant for the study of law, but not for the actual practice. After I passed the bar exam, I took off for Europe to reward myself. The longer I hung out, the less inviting the prospect of actually going into corporate law."

"I don't understand. You mean after all those years in school you just blew off your education?"

He shifted slightly, his gaze narrowing. "Exactly. I found something I was born to do."

"And that was...?"

"I have a certain knack for buying and rehabilitating floundering businesses. I know when to sell. Trust me, I've made huge profits just buying and selling."

She felt as though she couldn't draw a breath. Frank had spent years taking businesses apart and rebuilding them just so he could sell them off at a profit. What would he do with the red-brick building that housed the *Gazette*?

Just when she was beginning to feel a little more comfortable in Frank's presence, she learned he was just passing through.

Chapter 4

FRANK TOOK HER BACK TO THE NEWSPAPER, AND DROVE OFF feeling remarkably buoyant. His vastly improved mood was due to his lunch with Reggie Lee Stafford. It hadn't quite been a date, and yet it had.

He'd learned that she had taken back her maiden name. She was divorced from a major oaf, received no child support, and had sole custody of their daughter. She was showing him a lot more backbone than he had given her credit for. Reggie Lee Stafford was definitely more than just another pretty face.

The fact that he owned the *Gazette* building might be influencing Reggie's more compliant facade. He wouldn't fool himself into believing she actually liked him, but every now and again, he did see little flashes of attraction or at least a mild interest. Whatever was driving that was enough to keep driving him.

He had liked her since their school days, and the slim chance that she might return his affections someday kept him intrigued. He hadn't counted on liking her so much, and he hadn't counted on liking her little girl.

The BMW zipped along, almost without his direction. The roads twisted and climbed among the hills that gave the Texas Hill Country its name. Verdant rolling hills covered mostly with oak and pine masked the homes nestled beneath. There were communities with churches and small businesses tucked in nooks and crannies all around the lake.

The beauty of the area attracted a great many tourists, so

weekends and summers the traffic and activities increased significantly, yet the area was able to maintain the welcoming, small-town flavor that made it such a relaxing getaway.

Several rivers fed into the lake, offering additional waters to canoe and raft along with the river current, thereby avoiding the motorboats and water-skiers. Tubing on the river had been one of Frank's favorite pastimes, when he and his buddies rented inflated inner tubes and floated with the current. Okay, there may have been beer involved, but he cherished the memories of camaraderie with his buds.

He turned onto the road leading to the vineyard. Something about the sight of row after row of lush grapevines gave him a rush of pride. He was proud of his great-aunt for her vision, and he was proud of Evan for devoting his life to making her vision flourish.

His own life had been devoted to turning a fast buck. He had felt good about his accomplishments up until the time he had returned to Rambling. Now, his previous focus on chasing after the almighty dollar seemed shallow.

Perhaps he was considering the mindset of the beautiful Reggie Lee Stafford and her love of the environment, in particular the town of Rambling and surrounding area. He seemed to recall that Reggie Lee and her friend Jill had spearheaded a campaign to get the school to stop using plastic bottles in the vending machines, and they had succeeded. And it was the arty one—Lori Holloway—who had painted signs they plastered all over school. But Reggie Lee and Jill had been the ones who spearheaded the crusade.

Frank chuckled a little. Now he had the blonde crusader leading the charge at the *Gazette*. He figured she would put her heart and soul into anything she espoused. Too bad there was no room in her heart for him.

He stopped the car on the edge of the road and got out. Up close, he could admire the vibrant colors of the grapes and the texture of the twisted vines. He strolled into the row of vines, his handmade designer loafers sinking into the soft dirt. There was a fragrance in the air he couldn't place as well as the warm earth smell. The scents were like coming home. He expected to see Aunt Rosie step out from between the staked vines, wearing her straw hat and leather gloves.

"Frank?"

He turned to see Evan Hauser walking toward him, his hands shoved deep in the pockets of his jeans. "Hey, Ev. How's it going?"

"Great. I thought I recognized your car. Is something wrong?" His brow knitted into a worried frown. Evan was a gentle giant... unless on the football field...or perhaps other arenas he felt strongly about. Now his pleasant face was gnarled up in a grimace.

"Not a thing." Frank spread his hands to indicate the vines. "I just needed to clear my head."

Evan's brow relaxed. "This is a great place to do that."

"What kind of grapes are these?" Frank pointed to the nearby clusters, hanging dense and ripe.

"These are our own cross-pollinated grapes. They go into our Pinot Noir. We use a blend of two varieties to achieve our sublime taste."

"Hey, you don't have to sell me." Frank turned and continued walking deeper into the row of vines.

Evan grinned sheepishly and fell into step beside him. "Are you getting settled in at Miss Rosie's house? I guess it's your house now."

Frank shrugged. "It still feels like her house. I unpacked my bag in my old room. That's as settled in as I can get right now." He wondered briefly if he would ever again regain the feeling of being at home anywhere. Maybe Rambling was no longer his home.

"How does Rambling look to you after living in Europe? Are we just too redneck for a sophisticated man of the world?"

Frank slid him a sideways glance and realized he was being teased by an expert. He was glad Evan was getting over the fact that Frank was his employer. He longed to return to the casual friendship they had always enjoyed. "There are some things that look even better. I'm talking about Reggie Lee. I can't believe she hooked up with Kenny Landers." He shook his head.

"Tell me about it. When he came back from his stint in the Army, he was really buff, and he seemed to have gained some discipline." He shrugged. "But it didn't last. After he got Reggie, he reverted to type. Trust me, she's better off without him."

Frank fought down some primitive feelings of resentment. His memories of Kenny Landers were all bad. "He was the football hero."

"Yeah, but Reggie was the brilliant bookworm. She was popular, and she had the brains to go with her looks. Not like any of the airheads who used to hang all over Kenny." Evan spread his hands. "I mean, she was the one girl he could never impress."

Me neither. Frank picked up a pebble and weighed it in his palm. He thought about Reggie Lee as he had known her in high school. Skittish, aloof, her acerbic tongue had kept him from making friends with her. Of course, calling her Regina Vagina hadn't helped his cause. He took aim and slung the pebble down the road.

"She seems to be doing okay now," he observed.

Evan nodded enthusiastically. "She has a cute little girl. She goes to work at the paper. Works in her dad's store too. Goes to church and that's about it."

"It seems to make her happy."

Evan squinted at him and gave a throaty laugh. "You still got the hots for Reggie?"

"What do you mean, still?"

Evan gave him a little nudge. "C'mon, man. Everyone knew you liked her."

Frank made a scoffing noise. "Everyone but Reggie Lee."

"Well…" Evan spread his hands. "Maybe you carried things a bit far."

"Y'think?" Frank nudged a clod of dirt with the toe of his loafer. He wondered what else was going on in her life. "Reggie

Lee seems to be happy now. Some people don't have big dreams. Some people are content with the hand they're dealt."

Evan shrugged. "I think Reggie had plenty of big dreams. Having a kid must have put a damper on her plans."

Frank considered this. How would her life have changed if she had not married and given birth? Would she have remained in Rambling if she was less encumbered? Yet he had to admire that she stepped up to the challenge and didn't dump the kid on her parents and run off. He shoved his hands deep in his pockets.

Like his parents had dumped him on his great-aunt after he had been expelled from the posh Dallas prep school for fighting. They had thought that sending him to live in a small town with an elderly great-aunt would be the ultimate punishment. Little did they know how much he had enjoyed his freedom. When they were killed in a car accident a short time later, his great-aunt became his legal guardian.

Frank had made friends and, thanks to Evan, stayed out of fights. Other than Reggie and her snotty friends, he had been well liked. If things had been different between them, would he have left town? Would she have gone with him?

He shook off his idle thoughts and turned to Evan. "Any ideas on increasing productivity at the winery?"

Evan stopped in his tracks. He stammered something unintelligible. "I mean, are you dissatisfied with production?" If Frank had smacked him in the face, Evan could not have looked more astonished.

Frank slapped Evan on the shoulder. "Heck, no, man. I'm always looking for ways to up productivity. I figured, in your position, you might have some thoughts on making things even better. Is there some equipment you need? Another market to tap into?"

Evan looked perturbed. "Your aunt let me do whatever I thought would take us in the right direction. Since I took over as manager, I've more than doubled our revenues. We hit an all-time high this past year."

Frank raised both hands to calm his friend. "I realize that. And you've increased the volume of wine produced each year as well as the number of acres growing grapes. Altogether a fine job."

Evan stood with his hands fisted at his waist. "Then what's the problem?"

What indeed? "No problem, Ev. I just wanted to know if you had any ideas to knock around. I'm always open to new directions."

"I'll let you know." Evan kept his eyes cast down at the ground.

"C'mon, Ev. I'm not picking on you. I'm complimenting you. You're doing a great job here. I just want to encourage you to spread your wings. Let yourself go."

Evan flicked his gaze over Frank and nodded.

Oh boy!

Reggie Lee awoke snarled in the sheets. She had tossed and turned until she was thoroughly entangled. She tried to relax, but one thought kept racing through her brain. *I'm the editor of the* Rambling Gazette.

A flush of pleasure raced through her being. "I am the editor of the *Gazette*." Whispering it aloud didn't make it seem any less astonishing.

She stretched her arms overhead and pointed her toes, taking up the entire bed. She relished every little bit of time she had to reflect on her recent change of fortune.

Reggie had spent most of her life taking care of her family and helping others. In fact, just about anyone who asked for her help was rewarded with her enthusiastic consent. She took good care of her daughter. She helped her daddy in his store. She volunteered in the summer reading program at the local library. She participated on committees at her church. She crocheted tiny blankets for premature infants at the hospital. She was, by anyone's definition, a nice person.

If one were to describe a successful newspaper editor, *nice* was probably not an adjective one would choose. *Tough. Hard-boiled. Pugnacious. Staunch. Unswerving...* She grasped for other words to describe the editor she was not...yet. "I'm fair and reliable. Those are good qualities." *And I'm nice...*

Not what she wanted to be at the moment. She narrowed her gaze and assumed a haughty expression. She would have to toughen up if she was to fit into her new role as editor of the *Rambling Gazette*. How tough would she have to be?

She exhaled and sat up, feeling around with her feet for her fuzzy pink scuffs. "Very tough!" She would have to direct the sales staff and the reporters and the guys who were in charge of circulation. Most of all, she would have to develop her tough genes if she were going to stand up to the man who owned the building.

Frank Bell appeared to be an excellent businessman. The ideas he had flipped out of his brain off the cuff had been fabulous. And his ideas had given her ideas. How would she impress such a bright guy?

Stripping off her T-shirt, she stepped into the shower. The water woke her all the way up. She lathered her hair, rinsed, and applied a fragrant conditioner before her final rinse. She twisted the taps and wrapped a towel around her hair.

She groped for her terry robe and shuffled to her daughter's room. Shannon was awake and singing. Reggie greeted her with a kiss. "Morning Glory."

Shannon giggled. "Mommy! You got me wet!"

Reggie went through her familiar morning routine by rote, getting Shannon dressed, making breakfast, and wiping her breakfast off her daughter's face. Getting herself dressed was a rushed procedure but fairly easy; she made clothing decisions the night before, so throwing on her clothes was a snap. And finally buckling her daughter into her car seat for the short trip to day care. She parked in front of the quaint 1950s bungalow with the fenced yard and play equipment. There was a modest sign with the Babes in the Woods Day Care name. A name as quirky as the owner.

Jill Garland, the day care owner and one of her best friends, greeted her at the door. "Good morning, Shannon." She gave the little girl a brief hug as she was eager to run inside. "And good morning, Reggie. You're absolutely glowing. What's going on?"

Reggie gave a little squeal. "I'm so excited. I can hardly breathe."

Jill stood back with her hands fisted on her hips. "Well, spill it, girl."

"I'm the editor of the *Gazette*."

Jill stared at her with no change of expression.

"No, really. I am the new editor. I swear."

Jill's jaw dropped open. "No! What did you do? Kill off old Phil Jergens? Do you need an alibi? I'm sure I was with you. We were watching television."

Reggie laughed. "Relax, Jill. It's even weirder than that." She sucked in a breath and let it out all at once. "Remember Franklinstein?"

Jill gave an exaggerated shudder. "Do I! He was such a jerk." She leaned up against the doorframe, her arms crossed over her chest.

"Yeah, he was. But he inherited the *Gazette* building. He was kind of scary when he first came into the office, and he scared Phil into resigning." Reggie heaved a sigh. "Turns out old Phil, pillar of society, was skimming money."

Jill's eyes widened. "No way! I can't believe that. He was so—so stuffy and proper."

"That he was, but he had several nonexistent employees on the payroll...family members, as I understand it."

Jill covered her mouth with both hands. "That is something I never would have guessed. So how did you get to be editor?"

"In his resignation letter, Phil named me editor. So I guess I'm the boss now." Reggie giggled in delight.

Jill suddenly sobered. "That is a lot of responsibility, my friend. Trust me. Even as the owner of a much smaller business, it never lets up. I'm always 'Miss Jill' no matter where I am here in Rambling." She pointed a finger at Reggie Lee. "And you will always be 'the editor' no matter what. If someone doesn't like an editorial, it will be your fault. So be prepared."

"I'm pretty sure I can handle it. Well, maybe after I get used to the fact that I am the editor. How about that?" Reggie couldn't help but be amused by the look of shock on Jill's face.

"I'm just blown away. You've got to really gut up, girl." Jill kept shaking her head. "I thought Phil would stay behind that desk until he was mummified."

Reggie heaved a disgusted sigh. "I thought so too, but when Frank came in to check out the building he's inherited, he started making comments about the newspaper business and asking related questions about revenue and sales. Frank was going to return the next day to take a thorough tour of the property." Reggie shrugged. "I don't think anyone from the paper has been upstairs in years. The free rent Miss Rosie agreed to had the stipulation that the *Gazette* was responsible for the upkeep of the building."

Jill was frowning now. "I suppose the upkeep had been minimal?"

"I'm pretty sure the upkeep was nonexistent. That meant he could toss the *Gazette* out for not living up to its end of the agreement. Phil was really upset. When Frank found his resignation, I was surprised, but I suppose my initial thoughts were that Phil was old and tired. Turns out he was sucking out quite a bit of money."

Jill's mouth dropped opened in an exaggerated look of surprise. "I am truly blown away. He's a deacon in the church." She crossed her arms over her ample bosom. "And this is what Frank inherited? I'll bet he blew his top."

"Nope, he was quite calm about it and just expects me to make things better. Love you, girl, but I've got to get to the newspaper. Not setting a good example for the little people." She gave a little Queen Mum wave and stepped down off the porch. "See you later."

Jill let out a squawk. "You bet you will. I need the deets. Good luck with the little people. Hope they don't eat you alive."

Reggie waved goodbye and drove to the *Gazette*. Most of the staff had yet to arrive. She hesitated a moment before pulling into the space reserved for the editor. She sat in the car for a moment, her stomach entertaining a squadron of butterflies that seemed to be performing loop-de-loops. Heaving a deep sigh, she banished the butterflies before turning off the ignition and entering the building.

―――

Frank had slept in. Well, not really. He had lain in the bed that seemed far too small now but that had suited him just fine as a teen. He realized he was going to have to face the fact that the house needed to be dealt with. He would have to decide which room would be his, and he would need to order some new furniture to accommodate his adult self.

Yeah…a new mattress would be a welcome change…

It dawned on him that he was nesting. That idea should have alarmed him because Frank Bell was not a nester. He was…a nomad. A man of the world, meant to roam unfettered…free…

But this was his Aunt Rosie's house. The kind and generous woman who had embraced him as a rebellious and unwanted teen. The woman who had loved him when he was completely unlovable.

He would always keep her house as a memorial to the great lady. If he had roots, then they were right here in Rambling, Texas. Right here in this Victorian house. She was a beauty, but she needed a little tender loving care, and he was up for the job.

He thought perhaps his willingness to stick around for a while might have something to do with the beautiful, brown-eyed Reggie Lee Stafford. He may have turned her around by giving her encouragement to take on the editor job, but he had a feeling that she would dig in and find ways to improve the *Rambling Gazette*. She was a creative person, and being handed the reins of the newspaper should kick her imagination into overdrive. In their thorny past, he had always found that she rose to meet any and every challenge. *The girl has grit.*

Now, he had a challenge or two on his own plate.

The four-story building that housed the *Rambling Gazette* had been sadly neglected. He wouldn't be surprised to find rats and other varmints living upstairs. He wasn't looking forward to exploring the upper levels, but it had to be done.

And there were the repairs required to maintain the Victorian, but fixing up the lovely home would be much more pleasurable.

And there was the follow-up to the small matter of maintaining his friendship with Evan Hauser. It was important to Frank to make sure his longtime friend felt secure in his job and that the employer–employee relationship didn't cause any damage. Big, affable Evan had been a true friend and had been the one to keep Kenny Landers from slaughtering him on a daily basis. Maybe he could come up with a plan to reward Evan for his tenure and the progress he had made with the vineyard and winery. Maybe Evan might be willing to take on some tasks in Frank's overhaul of his new but old properties.

Frank had a slew of friendly acquaintances all over the East Coast of the United States and Western Europe. But real friends were few and far between. Better make sure to build the one true friendship he had in Rambling.

Yes, indeed. Frank was nesting.

—∿∿—

As the day wore on, Reggie took a few minutes to surf the internet. She had closed her office door, telling Gayle Sutton, the receptionist, that she was doing research. She was doing research all right... on Frank.

It hadn't been hard to find Franklin Bell online. There were a zillion images of him. In many he was dressed in formal wear at a charity event. He looked quite elegant in a tux. Not the same rebellious youth who had haunted her adolescence with asinine pranks. But who was he really?

His business activities were astounding. He had bought and sold businesses in England, France, and Germany.

Reggie took a moment to consider that fact. She wondered if he spoke other languages. She scrolled through other images, trying to get an idea of who Frank Bell had become.

Since he owned the building where she worked, she presumed they would be interacting with each other from time to time. Although he seemed to be quite pleasant at the moment, there was always the possibility that he would decide to sell the building. The *Gazette* paid no rent, by way of an unwritten agreement between Frank's great-aunt and the former editor. All bets were off now.

Reggie leaned back in her chair and tented her fingers. *How can I keep that from happening? How can I ensure that this building will always house the newspaper?*

Frank held the reins of her future as a newspaper editor.

She reached for a pitcher of ice water Gayle kept filled and poured herself a glass. It seemed that her throat had become dry as the Sahara. She glugged it down and returned to her research.

She found images of Frank on a yacht. The boat was moored in some exotic Mediterranean port or another and the photos showed Frank in a pair of shorts or swim trunks, showing off his lean, athletic body.

Reggie Lee swallowed hard as she stared at Frank shirtless.

He had a great body. Not like Kenny's puffy, over-muscled torso, but lean, with ripped muscles in his arms and shoulders and a set of washboard abs. Sucking in a deep breath and releasing it, she thought how easy it would be to fall for this man.

Not gonna happen.

She scrolled through the stories and pictures, thinking there was very little chance the mighty Frank Bell would be interested in a small-town girl such as herself. She was a mother, after all.

But she couldn't resist scrolling through the images again. Heaving a sigh, she turned off the computer and folded her hands on her desk.

"Well..." She heaved another sigh. "Well..."

Gayle Sutton sat at her desk, frustrated and on edge. She had worked at the *Gazette* for the past seven years, and things had always remained the same.

She was the receptionist. Gayle the receptionist. She had approached Phil once about expanding her role, but he had shut that down in a hurry. No, she would always remain Gail the receptionist.

But now what?

She had always taken pride in working for the newspaper.

She liked Reggie Lee Stafford, but that was in her position as a part-time reporter. What would she bring about in her new position as editor?

Gayle sighed and straightened her spine. Her job was to answer the phone and greet people who came in the door. She was qualified to take information for want ads and collect payment for them. For just about everything else, she was to call up another employee to deal with it.

But now, was there a chance that Reggie might be willing to give her the opportunity to grow in her job?

She was almost afraid to hope for a change.

On the other hand, perhaps the always-pleasant Reggie would change with her new responsibilities and become a beast to work for. Maybe she would be worse than Phil, who had merely ignored her.

Gayle huffed out a frustrated sigh. She was stuck. No matter what Reggie demanded of her, she would be bound to perform the task without complaint. The plight of the small-town girl with no particular education or skills.

The little bell over the door jingled to indicate someone had just entered.

Gayle went to the counter to greet Paul Harmon, the middle school history teacher. He was so shy that dealing with him was usually almost painful.

"Hi, Mr. Harmon. How are you today?"

Sure enough, he blinked, and the tips of his ears turned red. "I, uh...I just wanted to, uh..."

She folded her hands on top of the counter and smiled, hoping to give him confidence. *No impatience here...I've got all day...*

"Well, I want to run an ad." He was actually very nice-looking in a starched-and-ironed sort of way. His thick brown hair was always parted neatly on the same side, and he always appeared to have just stepped out of the barbershop.

"Excellent! Let me take your information." She pulled out a pad used for that purpose. "What kind of ad is it?"

"Kind?" He looked bewildered.

"You know. Are you selling something? Or hiring someone?"

He pressed his lips together as though considering. "Um, I lost something...or someone."

"Someone?" Gayle peered at him. "Shouldn't you call the sheriff's office for a missing person?"

"Oh, not that kind of person," he protested. "My dog...my dog is missing."

Gayle's face morphed into one of concern. She was a sucker

for animals of all kinds and hated to think that this man's dog was lost somewhere. "Oh, I'm so sorry. What kind of dog is it?"

He looked bewildered. "Kind? Just a dog...a small dog."

She looked at him expectantly.

Another blush. "Well, you know..." He made hand gestures to indicate the dog wasn't very big.

"A small dog?"

"Yes." He regarded her with kind-looking brown eyes framed by large black glasses.

"Now we're getting somewhere. A small dog..."

When he didn't respond, she remained pleasant, although her patience was thinning. "Is it a boy or a girl dog, Mr. Harmon?"

"Um, could you knock off the Mr. Harmon? I get that all day at school." He shrugged. "Just call me Paul...please."

"Sure thing, Paul. Now how about sex?"

That jolted him into a whole different dimension. He gazed at her wide-eyed.

"No, I mean, what sex is your dog? Male or female?" Okay, it was her turn to blush.

He chuckled a little. "Uh, female." He was really cute when he grinned.

She grinned back at him and then sighed. "Okay, so it's a small female dog. What color is she?"

He swallowed hard.

What was so difficult about describing his dog? Maybe she was being unknowingly domineering? Time to be sweeter. She tilted her head to one side and smiled. "Is she brown? Or white? Or maybe black?"

"Yes," he said, looking hopeful.

Gayle stared at him. "Your dog is black, brown, and white?"

He nodded furiously. "Absolutely. She has spots."

She stifled the urge to roll her eyes. "And my last question... What is her name?"

"Oh, uh…" He looked totally flummoxed. "Violet. Her name is Violet."

Gayle added his phone number, scribbled words on the pad to create a lost dog ad, and quoted him a price.

Paul gave her his credit card, and when the transaction was done, he raised a hand to bid her goodbye. He appeared to be a little sad, but Gayle figured he was missing his dog.

"Hope you get her back," she called as he headed for the door.

Gayle heaved a sigh. Back to contemplating her position in the newly shaken-up hierarchy of employees.

—᠁—

Frank strolled around the entire exterior perimeter of the house, his footfalls sounding on the wooden porch. *My place now.* He stopped to lean against the railing and look out over the property. The idea of being a landowner was growing on him…especially since he would never be able to sell the winery without destroying his friend Evan's life work.

And his emotions were so entangled in the Victorian "Painted Lady" that his great-aunt had loved so much, he couldn't imagine anyone else moving in.

He heaved a gigantic sigh, crossing his arms over his broad chest. It was quite a large house and would be perfect for a family. He wondered if he would ever have children to run up and down the staircase or circle around the porch. Perhaps he wasn't good daddy material. He wasn't sure he could make a lifelong commitment to one woman and to the prospect of fathering small humans.

Nah! Not my bag.

And yet the image of Reggie's young daughter popped into his head. He thought he could take on a beautiful duo like those two.

He had decided to give Reggie plenty of space. He didn't want her to think he was micromanaging her. And he wanted to see what she could do on her own. She was, after all, the editor of the *Rambling Gazette*. He was certain she would grow into the job.

To keep out of her way, he would have to have a plan because the desire to glue himself to her was almost irresistible. He could call friends in New York and make arrangements to fly up to see them. About a week should do it.

Then he could come back and ask her how it was going. That should be cool enough. He recalled all too well how it felt to be the recipient of Miss Reggie Lee's acerbic commentary. He wanted to keep things easy between them.

Sighing, he went through his morning tai chi routine. A simple pleasure, but it kept him limber and reminded him of his other martial arts accomplishments. A man who had owned bars had to be able to take care of himself and put down trouble should it walk through the door.

After his twenty minutes of exercise, he plopped down in one of the wicker rocking chairs, sending a cloud of dust rising in the air. Smiling to himself, he remembered Aunt Rosie rocking in this very chair and asking him about school. He'd even told her about Reggie Lee Stafford. She had laughed and told him that she'd bet Reggie Lee liked him.

He knew better.

His brows knitted together as he realized he really didn't want to leave Reggie just when they were finally talking. He didn't want to risk letting the door close again.

This was a brand-new experience for him. He was used to turning away when things got too cozy. No strings. No entanglements. No responsibilities.

It wasn't as though he had left a string of broken hearts in his wake. He had always made it clear at the onset that he wasn't the forever type of guy. And he made sure his female friends had a good time while it lasted.

But this was Reggie Lee Stafford, his dream girl. The girl who had scorned and abused him and was now at least willing to talk to him without sneering. Some adolescent part of him wanted retribution for all her taunting, but the rest of him just wanted to thaw her out.

A picture flashed through his brain of Reggie's daughter, Shannon. He couldn't imagine a more perfect child. Thankfully, she looked nothing like Kenny Landers.

And discovering the sweet, vulnerable side of Reggie was creating havoc with his libido. He was having trouble sleeping at night. He tossed and turned, imagining holding her in his arms, thinking about how her skin would feel pressed against his, how her hair would look spread out on a pillow.

He stretched out his legs and propped his feet on the porch railing. It was loose. He rocked it back and forth. And the paint was flaking. Maybe he could pick up some sandpaper and a few tools when he drove into town a little later. Maybe a gallon or so of paint and a scraper.

He had the skills to make the repairs to Aunt Rosie's house... *my house*. He had learned a lot when he had purchased his first run-down bar. He knew how to spruce things up, at least for the short haul. But this was his house now. He wanted to fix it right. Maybe the guys at the hardware store could offer a little advice.

He stood up and reached for the keys in his pocket. Maybe he could fix up the house and manage to stay out from under Reggie's feet while she spread her wings at the *Gazette*. *Good plan.*

—⁓—

That was the plan.

Too bad it didn't work. When he'd driven into town, little had he dreamed that he would find Reggie Lee at the hardware store.

She looked up and flushed when their eyes met. "Are you stalking me?"

Guilty. "This isn't where I imagined you would spend your time." He gestured to the tools she had assembled on the counter.

"I'm not on my time," she said. "I'm on *Gazette* time. Arnie said he needed a ratcheting screwdriver to adjust the something or another on the offset. I thought I would get it for him so the offset printer would be ready to roll when we go to press."

"And you thought you might need a chisel too?" He stifled a chuckle.

"Oh, I, um… This is for me. The back door at my dad's doesn't close right. The strike plate needs to be reset so the dead bolt closes in the right place. As it is, there's a big gap, and the hot or cold air leaks in."

"I didn't realize you were so multifaceted. You could do double duty in maintenance."

She grinned. "I'm just trying to be green here."

He cocked his head. "That's a great idea, Reggie. You could write a column with tips and advice for saving energy and cutting costs around the house. Everyone would like that."

The dark-brown eyes warmed. "And you think I could write it?"

He made a scoffing noise in the back of his throat. "Piece of cake. You can gather lots of information off the internet."

"Hmm… Sounds like fun. Thanks for the good idea, Frank."

For some incomprehensible reason, he felt a rush of warmth flood his chest. Was it the note of pleasure in her voice? Or the flash of dimples when she grinned? Perhaps it was the admiration that shone for one brief moment in her gaze? Whatever the source, it was at that instant that Frank Bell admitted the truth to himself: *I am falling in love with Regina Vagina.* He cleared his throat. "Glad you approve."

She gathered her purchases and her handbag. "If you're not stalking me, what are you shopping for today?"

"I'm thinking about updating Aunt Rosie's house. My house. There are a lot of things that need to be repaired."

"That sounds like a challenge." The dimples quirked again. "In fact, that sounds like a series of articles to me. There are a lot of people around here who were friends and admirers of Miss

Rosie. I'm sure they would take an interest in the refurbishment of her home." She gave him a long look. "That is, if you would allow me to invade your inner sanctum and write a story about your property. It's such a beautiful house."

"Ah—I, um…" He was dumbstruck. Not his usual state. He hadn't considered refurbishing the entire house. Just piddling around with a few little repairs to keep him busy. Her vision sounded way too much like a long-range project. One that might take months, no, years to complete. *Responsibility. Commitment.* "Great idea."

"It will make a fabulous layout. I can see before-and-after photos." She clapped her hands together. "In color!"

He felt his airway constricting. "Right," he wheezed.

She was beaming. "I have always loved that house. You could make it a showplace."

He sucked in air. "Really? It sounds like you might be the one to—advise me. You want to help me with the project?"

Her eyes opened wide. "Are you serious? I'd love to work with you on the refurb. I love historical houses."

Her eager expression was setting off fireworks in his brain. If he played it right, he could work closely with Reggie Lee and not arouse her suspicions.

He struggled to keep a straight face. "I would appreciate your help. I don't know anything about decorating a historical house." He lifted his shoulders in a helpless gesture. "I sure don't want to mess up Aunt Rosie's home."

"Don't worry. It will turn out beautifully."

As he watched her cute behind sashay out of the hardware store, he heaved a deep sigh. *This is going to be expensive.*

Chapter 5

REGGIE LEE WAS THRILLED.

Her hands were shaking when she tried to insert her key into the ignition of her SUV. She finally managed to get the car started but sat inside gripping the steering wheel.

She had been excited when Frank had suggested that she write a column with energy-saving tips. That was one of her pet themes anyway. "Going Green," she said, trying it on as a title. "Greening the Hill Country." She shook her head. "Green…? Green…?" *Lame. Totally lame.* "Green Mansions. Green Sleeves. Green with Envy. Green Around the Gills."

She turned the steering wheel and slowly eased out of the parking space. She could always come up with a title, or Frank would probably have some suggestions. She liked his suggestions. She couldn't believe how rapidly her opinion of him was changing. From adolescent albatross to adult entrepreneurial genius. And if he were truly planning on refurbishing the Grady house, that meant he was planning on staying around for a while. A smile quirked her mouth.

Reggie couldn't think of a project she would like to take on more than the Grady house. She had held many long conversations with Miss Rosie during the years she had worked for the *Gazette*. From the time Reggie had been a high school cub reporter until Miss Rosie became ill, she had always been an eager listener to the older woman's stories about the history of the house.

Horace Pace Grady's father had built the house, and when Horace had chosen the young and lovely Miss Rosie Bell to become his bride and moved her into the family home, she had expected to produce future generations of Gradys. She hadn't planned on remaining childless, but that was before in vitro fertilization, and her husband hadn't been interested in adoption. He had been more interested in business acquisitions than family.

When her only nephew and his wife had been overwhelmed by the responsibilities involved in raising a teenage boy, she had gleefully taken the child on. And when they had been killed in an accident, she'd mourned them deeply. But when she subsequently became the guardian of their only son, she was overjoyed. Miss Rosie had shared with Reggie Lee that Frank became the son she had always wanted. He was smart and handsome. He had good manners and was respectful. She couldn't have asked for anything more.

At this point, Reggie would bite her tongue, failing to enlighten the dear lady as to the "Regina Vagina" taunts. It was a sin of omission.

But she had always enjoyed visiting Miss Rosie and taking tea in her lovely home. Now Reggie had an opportunity to help restore the house to its former glory, and she was excited about the project.

Reggie considered her present situation: a divorced single parent who couldn't afford to provide her child with a home on her own, so she had gone running home to daddy. Not that she didn't appreciate it. She felt safe and secure in her childhood home, and her dad was an upstanding male image for Shannon, but he kept the house as a shrine to her mother, refusing to update any of the decor. Like every little girl, Reggie Lee had played house and dreamed of the home she would have someday. In the meantime, she would help Frank fix up Miss Rosie's house and enjoy the fleeting fantasy that it belonged to her.

Good thing because it's unlikely that I will ever have a house of my own.

She pulled into the editor's parking space in front of the newspaper office and turned off the motor. This was the only tangible result of her promotion. She still hadn't completely moved into Phil's office yet. Maybe it was time. She stepped out of the car, strode up the stairs, and pushed the door open, ready to take on the challenges.

When she stepped inside, she was greeted with the sound of raised voices.

"I told you I want to take over *The Social Scene*!" Rhea McAllister shook her finger at Milton Mayweather. "It's a perfect complement to my *Dear Irene* column." *The Social Scene* had been one of Reggie Lee's columns, reporting events around the area.

He made a derisive sound and folded his arms over his paunchy middle. "Don't be ridiculous! I'm the obvious choice. I'm an excellent photographer, and besides, I've been here longer."

"Don't you be ridiculous!" Rhea stomped her foot. "I've been here longer than Reggie Lee, and she was just promoted to editor."

A hush fell over the newsroom as everyone turned to stare at Reggie. She felt her cheeks go scarlet. Clearing her throat, she tried to recover her composure. "Is there a problem?" She raised her chin and gave each of the combatants a cool stare.

The onlookers were immediately galvanized into motion, discovering they had things to do. Phones were answered whether or not anyone was on the line. Chairs were scooted back, and fingers flew over keyboards.

Rhea and Milton glared at each other and then turned away with mumbled assurances that nothing was wrong.

Reggie stood like a statue for a moment and let her gaze control the room. She turned to the receptionist, Gayle. "Any calls for me?"

Gayle fumbled through the notes and turned over a half-empty cup of coffee, saturating the papers on her desk. She shook the papers over the trashcan and mopped at her desktop with a handful of tissue. "So sorry." Big blue eyes looked anguished.

Reggie frowned and accepted the wad of damp, smeary sticky notes between thumb and finger. She headed for her new office and draped the wet notes over the side of her trashcan to dry out.

She hoped there wasn't anything vital recorded there since the ink appeared to be running and the notes were gummy with the sweetened brew. She went to Phil's private restroom to wash her hands and stood staring at herself in the mirror. It hit her like a bolt of lightning. *This is my office. My bathroom. My staff, dammit!*

She swallowed and ran her dampened fingers through her tangled hair. She focused on controlling the desire to give in to tears. It was time to really move into her new office and take charge.

—◦◦◦—

Gayle was mortified. Now that Reggie was her boss, it seemed that everything Gayle attempted went wrong. She had carefully stacked Reggie's phone messages together and then spilled her double mocha latte on them.

Reggie looked like thunder when she accepted the sodden mess and stormed off to her office.

Gayle sat back down at her desk. She'd never thought her life would end up like this. The lowest-level employee. Less valued than the janitor.

Maybe it was time to rethink her occupational possibilities. Unfortunately, in the small town of Rambling, there were few employment opportunities for someone with only a high school education...someone who had spent the last eight years answering phones, taking messages, and writing ads for lost pets.

She was pretty sure she would make a lousy waitress. And the only preschool in the area was fully staffed by the owner and a helper.

What else could she do? Clean houses? Mow grass?

She had always thought she would become a journalist. She had taken journalism in high school and thought she would be able to start in a clerical position at the *Gazette* and work her way up.

The only problem was there was no turnover. Not until now. And there had been no growth, so no need for adding positions.

Gayle heaved a huge sigh and propped her chin on her fist.

Well, there was a little switcheroo going on now. Phil was gone. Reggie Lee had moved into his office. And people were fighting over who would acquire Reggie's old column.

Gayle would have loved to throw her hat in the ring but figured after spilling her coffee on Reggie's messages, it was not a good time to attract her notice. Better to just remain invisible. At least she had a job.

A little paycheck is better than no paycheck.

Frank stood staring down at the headstone.

Rose Ellen Bell Grady. Beloved Wife of Horace Pace Grady.

The kind and generous woman who had taken him in when he was a rebellious teen was in her final resting place beside the husband who had preceded her. The woman who had loved him when he was not exactly lovable. The only person who had truly cared for him in his youth.

She had been quite beautiful as a young woman, when she had caught the eye of the wealthy bachelor, Horace Grady. Their marriage had been like a fairy tale, to hear her tell it. Frank recalled the sweet smile on her face whenever she told her great-nephew about her strong, intelligent husband. Horace was an astute businessman who had a special knack for acquiring real estate. That real estate had supported Aunt Rosie after her husband was gone...and Frank inherited it upon her passing.

Frank squatted down on one knee to touch the garland of roses carved into the rose-colored granite headstone. "Aunt Rosie, I'm so sorry," he whispered.

After all she had done for him, he had been too busy to attend to her needs. Truly, he had called her often, telling her about his business acquisitions. She had shared very little with him, just reciting a few routine facts that he would expect of her. She had told him about the vineyard and the various other fruits growing in her orchard. She had informed him about the weather, the rain or lack thereof.

But she had never complained. Aunt Rosie had never mentioned any physical problems or decline in health, but she had never failed to inquire about Frank's health and well-being and offer motherly advice.

And yet he had been unavailable when she needed him. He had taken off for a spur-of-the-moment trip with friends, and there had been no particular plan in place beforehand.

But, a week later when they had returned, he had learned of his great-aunt's demise and subsequent burial in the cemetery where most all residents of Rambling, Texas, wound up.

Now, he was in Rambling, trying to deal with the properties that Miss Rosie had bequeathed to him. He felt that he needed to make it up to her. To atone for his absence.

He huffed out a deep breath. He couldn't mismanage the properties that he had inherited. If he was truly Rosie Bell Grady's blood relative, he would stay and make sure that all of the businesses were prospering. He owed it to her and to her memory. He wanted to respect her desire to support the community by providing jobs for some of the residents.

Frank rose to a standing position, still gazing at the headstone. "I'll do it, Aunt Rosie. I'll make sure that all of your properties are well taken care of and that they thrive."

~~~

Reggie Lee sank into the rose-colored plush recliner. It had been her mother's. She raised the footrest and heaved a deep sigh, glad that the day was over.

Shannon was sprawled on the area rug; a coloring book and a cigar box filled with crayons had her full attention.

Her father cast an appraising glance at her over the rims of his glasses. He sat in the adjacent recliner, as he had for many years alongside her mother. He shook his paper and turned the page.

She closed her eyes, pretending she hadn't noticed his concerned expression.

He cleared his throat.

Oh, brother! So much for ignoring him. She opened her eyes and turned to face him. "Yes, Dad. What words of wisdom do you have for me?"

"Brat!" He shook his paper again and gave her a mock glare. "I was just wondering how your new job at the paper was going. You look like you're worn out."

She emitted a loud sigh. "How very observant of you. I do feel like I've been run over by a truck. A big one."

"Well, I hope you got a big fat raise to go with all the responsibilities." He folded the section of the paper he had been perusing and set it on the side table. "You did talk money, didn't you?"

"Please, Dad. Not now." She blinked several times and pushed back in the recliner, going almost horizontal. Why hadn't she thought to find out if a raise came with her promotion?

I'm such an idiot! Why didn't I ask about money? Reggie felt like giving herself a head slap, except her dad was sending her his X-ray stare that could see straight through to her soul. She composed her features into a serene visage and closed her eyes. She heard the newspaper rustle again.

She tried to think of an offhand way to broach the subject of money. Couldn't. She supposed she could just come out and ask the bookkeeper what her salary would be. But she was the boss, and she was supposed to be in charge. Surely a woman who had accepted the position of editor of the newspaper would find out what the job paid before accepting all that responsibility? She could just see the expression on the bookkeeper's face if Reggie asked about her rate of pay.

Or she could just wait until Friday, the next scheduled payday. She exhaled heavily. *I guess I can wait. Maybe the title is enough.*

Henry Stafford could tell his beloved daughter was having some sort of trouble with her job. He hadn't ever thought she could have moved up to the position of editor of the *Gazette*. He went out to the garage and turned on the light. No point in making Reggie upset. She needed to keep a clear head to deal with the guy who owned the building. That Frank boy who she'd complained about in high school.

He grabbed a soft lint-free cloth and lovingly ran it over the highly waxed finish of his 1969 Pontiac GTO. His pride and joy after his daughter and granddaughter. The finish was a deep-blue metallic flake, and he kept it spotless. The car's name was Priscilla, and she was badass.

Most weekends he got together with his old friends and rolled out in Priscilla, looking cool. They called themselves the Rambling Cruisers Classic Car Club. But it was really just the boys getting together to talk cars and plan events. Sometimes they traveled in a caravan to other towns for classic car shows and contests where they vied for points.

He popped the hood and gazed at the highly polished chrome. "Pretty girl," he murmured.

Henry knew that he had it all. He owned his home. He owned Stafford's Mercantile, which had been in his family since his father first opened it in 1949. In time, he would pass it along to his only daughter, Regina Lee Stafford. Henry was pretty much satisfied with his life...but he had one unfulfilled desire. He wished he had taken a tire tool to Kenny Landers's head for hurting his daughter. And Henry was dead sure he was not about to let it happen again.

He considered this Frank Bell, the boy who had made his little girl cry on many occasions when she was a teen. Henry was damned if he was going to let her shed one more tear over this bozo.

Henry hoped Reggie had landed the position of editor through her own merits, but if Frank Bell had anything to do with her promotion because he expected sexual favors, he had another damned think coming.

He knew the community needed the newspaper, but if it came down to a choice between his daughter's happiness and security and the *Gazette*, he would choose Reggie Lee every time. Hell, Henry would take out a loan and find another location for the newspaper if he had to. Let Frank Bell figure out what to do with his building with no tenants.

Oh, yeah…he remembered the newspaper wasn't paying any rent. His shoulders sagged.

He had been rubbing Priscilla's fender so hard he had dulled the waxed finish. "Sorry, baby."

Frank couldn't sleep. He lay on his back, listening to the old house noises and thinking about Reggie Lee. Her beautiful face haunted him.

He was conflicted. Being back in Rambling brought back lots of memories, some sweet and some bitter. He recalled all the kind things his great-aunt had done for him, how she encouraged and supported him. He relived some of his past exploits with Evan and the rest of his boyhood pals. But the strongest memories were of his interactions with the enigmatic Reggie Lee Stafford.

It surprised him that she'd never realized how much he had liked her.

Guess I was too subtle for her. He scowled, recalling their verbal skirmishes. He wondered if things would have been different between them if she had known that he was covering his shyness and insecurity with rudeness and audacity.

He would never know, but there was a chance he could have a do-over, that he could set things straight between them.

And then what? He rubbed his hands over his face. He wasn't exactly the settling-down-in-one-place kind of guy.

He wasn't sure he had the capacity to stay in one place for any period of time. He blew out a breath. But if anyone could make him want to settle down, it was Reggie Lee. He envisioned himself walking with her, carrying Shannon as he held Reggie's hand. The picture in his mind was a little frightening. It was a little too perfect.

He turned over and plumped his pillow. *Not going to get to sleep this way.* He sought another mental image. He pictured the vineyard. The fertile hillsides covered with different varieties of grapevines. He recalled the tasting room and the storage area, where casks of wine aged at the perfect temperature. The flower shop and the Dairy Queen seemed to be thriving. His only business liability was the red-brick building housing the *Gazette*. He would be paying taxes on the property with no income to offset his expenditures. Maybe it would be a tax write-off. Maybe not. Whatever the cost, it would be worth it if he could keep figuring out ways to work with his high school crush.

Reggie's face appeared in his consciousness as he had last seen her. Relaxed and smiling. He had never thought he would see that expression directed at him. And she was excited about her new position and about working on the Victorian house.

He turned over again.

Not sure how this is going to play out. What if she paints the house pink?

He considered that possibility for a few seconds and then decided he could live with it...no matter what color she painted his house.

The next morning, Reggie Lee called the staff of the *Gazette* together for her first meeting as editor. Her stomach was aflutter, and her palms were sweating. She rationalized that if these people were complete strangers, she might be able to handle it. But it was harder to suddenly rise from her previous post to assume a position of authority, to earn the respect of her former comrades who were staring at her with expressions reflecting varying shades of skepticism. Almost all of her employees were older than she and had more experience. They chattered among themselves, ignoring her when she took her place at the head of the conference table.

She cleared her throat, but they didn't pay any attention to her.

Stan Merkel caught her eye and let out a shrill whistle. "Quiet down, everyone. The boss wants to talk."

An ear-splitting hush filled the room. The silence seemed to press in on her eardrums. She tried to flash a smile as everyone turned to stare at her.

"Good morning."

A few people mumbled greetings in return.

She tried to swallow, but her throat was unexpectedly dry. "I wanted to tell everyone how happy I am to be here. I know that many of you outrank me in terms of seniority and experience, but I hope I can bring my enthusiasm to this position. I know that you all have some ideas to make things run smoother, and I hope you will be willing to share your thoughts."

Rhea McAllister waved her hand and, when Reggie Lee nodded at her, said, "I just want to know who is going to take over your *Social Scene* column. I think everyone knows who is most qualified to write it." She glared at the others as though daring them to refute her words.

Reggie Lee swallowed hard. "As a matter of fact, I have made a decision. I would like to offer *The Social Scene* to Milton Mayweather. I feel that his ability as a photographer as well as a reporter will enable Jim to focus on broadening his range." She smiled brightly at Jim Flores, the official photographer of the *Gazette*. Milton beamed from where he sat at the opposite end of the table. "As far as my other duties, I was hoping that you would take over the obituaries, Rhea."

Rhea stood up and slammed her palms down on the table.

"Well! This is just ridiculous. I should be covering *The Social Scene*. Anyone with an ounce of sense could see that." She shoved her chair back, and it rolled to a stop against the wall. Rhea flounced out, slamming the door behind her so hard the glass panel rattled.

Another deafening silence ensued, followed by a cacophony of voices.

Reggie Lee held up her hand. "Is there anyone who would like to take on the obituaries?" She swept them with her gaze and saw a lot of averted eyes. "Oh, come on. Someone has to do it."

"*Ahem...*"

She turned quickly to see Gayle, the receptionist, sheepishly raise her hand. "I sure would like to try it."

"Gayle?" She tried not to look incredulous. "You want to write?"

Gayle nodded. "I've always wanted to be a writer. It would be my dream come true. Can you give me a chance?"

Reggie took a deep breath. "Sure. I appreciate your positive attitude. Is there anyone else who has something to offer? We need to attract new advertisers and increase our circulation. Any ideas?"

"Who are you going to get to write the *Dear Irene* column?" Wally Barnes asked. He had been staring out the window.

"That's Rhea's column, Wally." Reggie Lee fisted her hands on her hips.

"I don't think so," he said. "She cleaned out her desk, and now she's getting in her car." He pointed to the window behind Reggie Lee.

She turned in time to see Rhea pull out of the parking lot, her tires spinning rocks and dirt as she sped away. A squeezing sensation in her stomach made her choose to drop into her chair. Otherwise she might have dropped to her knees. "That's all. Let's get back to work."

The others scurried out of the conference room, exchanging glances.

Reggie Lee felt desolate and alone. She dug her nails into her palms to keep from screaming or breaking down in tears. *Great way to start my career as an editor.*

Other than Gayle, Reggie Lee was now the only other female on the *Gazette* staff. There was no one on staff to write *Dear Irene* now. And the column was due tomorrow. *Maybe one of the guys? No, too much testosterone.*

Reggie Lee hid out in her office until the rest of the staff had departed. When she checked Rhea's desk, she discovered that the letters from readers asking for advice from dear old wise Irene were also missing. So there was nothing. No place from which to start.

Except square one.

Gayle was ecstatic. She was the only one.

Being assigned to write the obituaries might not have appealed to anyone else, but Gayle was thrilled to have any writing assignment.

Everyone else had broken into small groups, and they were murmuring among themselves. At the end of the day, Gayle had hung around a little while hoping to have a chance to chat with Reggie Lee Stafford...but she did not come out of her office. Disappointed, Gayle went home to curl up on her couch, her tablet in hand.

She read through the obituaries that Ms. Stafford had written. It seemed that she had taken the time to get to know a little bit about each and every deceased person and included some personal information for each.

Gayle's brow furrowed. Reggie Lee would be a hard act to follow. *But I can do this.* She thought perhaps she could practice by writing obituaries for people she knew.

First, she killed off her kindergarten teacher, Miss Loraine Lewis, who had shamed her when she had not made it to the bathroom in a timely manner.

> Miss Lily Liver passed away after experiencing a tragic accident in which she was electrocuted when her tendency for incontinence caused her to dribble over a live wire. She will be missed by her large collection of cats.

Gayle giggled and thought about her new responsibilities. *I must be serious about this.* She sighed, and then she killed off Beverly Watkins, the church organist.

> Blabberlee Napkins, organist at her church, died tragically when she plopped her mammoth butt down on the bench in front of the church organ, which set off a 6.2-magnitude earthquake, causing the giant pipe organ to dislodge several large brass pipes, which fell on her head. Unfortunately, her abundant hairstyle did not save her. Alas, she is pumping her organ in the hereafter.

She tapped her pen against her cheek, considering who else she might metaphorically murder.

Oh, yeah... Red Carmichael... That guy at the car dealership who treated her like an idiot and had tried to sell her a lemon because he assumed she knew nothing about cars.

> Reporting on the unfortunate demise of Dread Carmonger, who met his fate after selling an Edsel to Hellon Wheels, who works at the shooting range. Miss Wheels, a woman of action, decided to give Mr. Carmonger a demonstration of her marksmanship. Fortunately for Miss Wheels, many of Mr. Carmonger's former clients were on the jury and declined to convict.

Gayle put her tablet on the coffee table and stepped out onto the porch. The sky was still light, but the moon was out. She leaned up against one of the posts supporting the porch and folded her arms across her chest. It was muggy, and she could smell something pleasantly floral, but the mugginess felt as though the air was sticking to her skin.

"Oh, hello."

Gayle snapped out of her reverie and saw Paul Harmon standing on the sidewalk. "Um, hi, Mr. Harmon. I didn't see you there."

He waved shyly. "It's Paul."

"Oh, yes… Paul. What are you doing?"

He shrugged. "Just taking a walk."

She looked at him critically. "I didn't know you lived around here, Paul."

He shrugged again. "No, I live over on Rosebud Lane."

Gayle spread her hands. "That was a long walk. Rosebud is on the other side of town and up on the hill." She grimaced, not imagining why he would take such a long walk.

"Oh, I was…uh, I was looking for my dog."

"Violet?"

"Yes, Violet." He nodded furiously. "Well, I'll just be on my way, then. Here, Violet." He whistled a bit as he walked away.

Gayle stood watching him. He was a tall, slim, studious-looking man. She recalled that he taught history at the middle school. Yes, he looked the part but also looked a little sad…maybe lonely… Probably because he missed his dog.

She wondered if he had a wife and maybe a few children. That should cheer him up. Or maybe he had a girlfriend.

Gayle went back inside, escaping the humidity, still thinking about Paul Harmon. Ready to get back to practicing her obituaries.

Frank slowed down and cruised by the *Gazette* offices. There was a light on inside. He spied Reggie Lee's car sitting alone in the parking lot.

He circled the block and came to park next to her. The front door was locked. He used his key. Most of the lights were off, but he saw Reggie Lee sitting at one of the desks in the large office shared by most of the staff. She was staring at the monitor with her fingers idle on the keyboard.

"Reggie," he called softly. No response. He moved closer, frowning. She looked like she was frozen to the keyboard. "Reggie Lee!" He said it louder this time.

She started, turning in her chair and emitting a yelp. "Oh my God! You scared me. What are you doing here at this time of night, Frank?"

"The question is, what are you doing here at this time of night?" He gazed down at her, wondering what had caused her to stay so late.

"Oh, well... I, uh..." She blushed. A crimson stain rose from her neck and painted her cheeks.

"What's the matter, Reggie?" he asked softly, trying to sound matter-of-fact when he caught the concern in his own voice.

She sighed and shrugged. "I lost one of the regular columnists today. She slammed out of here because I assigned someone else to take over my old column, *The Social Scene*." She pressed her lips together. "It was *Dear Irene*. She just walked out."

He shook his head. "Who is that?"

"It's the name of the column. *Dear Irene* has been several people over the years, but the current one walked off today." She wrung her hands together. "I don't know what to do." She looked so distraught he almost gathered her in his arms.

Yeah, I'd like that, but she would probably deck me. "It can't be all that bad. Just assign it to someone else."

"Noooo. I can't do that. I'm the only other woman on the staff, besides Gayle, the receptionist, and I just assigned her to write the obits. She's never written anything before, but I thought I would give her a chance." She stopped in the middle of her tirade and gazed at him uncertainly. "There's no one but me. I have to write the column and fill it with lots of sage motherly advice. And I have to have it ready by the deadline. We go to press tomorrow at noon, and I have nothing…nothing."

He looked around. "Well, can't you just write something? I mean, how hard can it be?"

A strangled whimper escaped her throat. "Yeah, I should be able to do that, except Rhea took the letters with her."

"Letters?"

"The letters that people wrote in, asking for advice from *Dear Irene*." Her lower lip trembled. "They're missing. I don't know how to give advice when I don't even know the questions." She looked like she was close to tears.

"I see." He stroked his hand over his face, regretting his decision not to shave today. "Can you show me some of the past *Dear Irene* columns?"

She nodded and rolled her chair to another desk. In a drawer were the neatly folded issues of the *Gazette*. She extracted a handful from the stack and wordlessly handed them to him.

Frank opened the first one and spread it on the desk. "Let's see now…" He scanned the pages until he found the column labeled *Dear Irene*. "The first one is asking for help in telling the neighbor that his dog is tearing up her flower beds. The second one sounds like a young person asking for advice about a girl he likes, and the third is a woman who wants to end a long-standing feud with her sister-in-law." He turned to Reggie Lee. "I'm sure you could offer some clever advice about these problems."

She nodded. "I suppose."

"Or you could just not run the column this week." He cocked his head to one side and eyed her speculatively.

"Oh, no. I couldn't do that." She looked stricken. "People love that column. I couldn't disappoint our readership." She gnawed her lower lip. "And the space is already blocked out for the column."

He smiled at her. "Let's get busy then." He took off his jacket and rolled up his shirtsleeves. "I'm going to read over these past columns and write the letters. You can come up with the answers."

"You mean, fake them?"

"That's exactly what I mean. If you want the readers to have a column, we have no other choice."

She nodded and rolled her chair back to the desk she was using. "You're right. We have to do this."

With a little thought, he was able to compose a couple of letters that sounded plausible as having come from local citizens. He passed the first one to Reggie Lee and watched her smile.

"This doesn't sound half bad." She turned to face him. "Thank you, Frank. I really appreciate your help."

He grunted. "You can pay me back with some elbow grease."

She raised her brows.

"My house. You're going to help me with the redo thing, aren't you?"

She brightened immediately. "Oh, yes. I'm very interested in your project. I can't wait to get started."

He smiled with more assurance than he felt. He wasn't certain about the redecorating or remodeling or whatever she had in mind. But gazing into her big dark eyes, he was sure of one thing. He wanted Reggie Lee Stafford.

She took the letters he had fabricated and began to write what he supposed would be the *Dear Irene* column. After a few keystrokes, she turned back to Frank.

"You don't need to stay. I can finish the column now. Thanks for your help."

He folded his arms across his chest and shook his head. "Not getting rid of me. It's almost eleven o'clock, and I wouldn't feel right leaving you here alone."

She flapped her hand in a shooing motion. "Don't be silly. I'll be fine."

"Not leaving."

"Are you seriously worried about me?"

"Maybe," he said. "I'm just a careful kind of guy. So turn around and get busy. I need my beauty sleep."

She flashed a grin and complied. "Yes, sir."

He strolled around the office and pretended to be inspecting the place, but he kept a surreptitious eye on her. When she logged off and rolled her chair back, he turned to catch her scrunching her shoulders up to her ears and then rotating them.

He reached out to stroke the skin on her neck. "You have a lot of tension. Let me give you a hand."

She sucked in a breath and seemed to freeze at his touch.

He lightly massaged the back of her neck and her shoulders. He felt her taut muscles relax beneath his fingers. He wanted to let her know he was crazy about her, but this wasn't the time to do it. *Just take it easy.* "Better?"

She sighed. "Better. Thanks."

"Let's get out of here. I think you've done enough for one day." He crossed to open the door for her and held it for her to pass. He switched off the lights and locked up. When he turned, he expected that she would have been halfway to her car, but she was standing behind him.

He almost leaned down to kiss her but held himself in check. He took her arm and walked her across the pea-gravel parking lot to her car.

She surprised him by giving him a hurried hug and a kiss on the cheek. "Thanks for everything, Frank." She climbed into her car and started the motor.

He stood like a statue, raising a hand in response to her breezy wave as she drove away. It took a moment for him to figure out that the drumming he heard was the sound of his heart pulsing in his ears.

Chapter 6

AFTER THE GAZETTE WAS PUBLISHED AND DISTRIBUTED THE NEXT afternoon, Reggie Lee was more than a little anxious. Writing the *Dear Irene* column hadn't been so difficult with Frank supplying the letters. She wondered if her advice was appropriate. She wondered if it made sense. Most of all, she wondered if the readership would notice that there had been a change of "Irenes."

And if the readers were able to accept the new Irene, would she be able to keep it up? Or was there someone out in the world who yearned to become the next Irene? Maybe Reggie would just be the interim Irene?

She paced around her office while torturing herself with self-doubt. What had she been thinking when she accepted the position of editor? Moreover, what had Phil been thinking when he'd appointed her to the job? That question seemed to burn a hole in her gut. But, since he was long gone, she had no way of contacting her former boss.

She folded her arms across her chest and perched on the edge of her desk. What *had* she been thinking? She supposed that some of her initial confidence had to do with Frank's encouragement. But he hadn't seen her since high school. How did he have any idea what she would be up for? He was a relative stranger now.

Reggie heaved a deep sigh. Frank was supposed to be an astute businessman. What made him think she could handle this job?

Reggie's throat tightened up. *This is my one big chance. I can't blow it.* No matter what, she would make sure she evolved in this position. This was a once-in-a-lifetime opportunity.

That thought hit her like a slap. She actually cared what the *Gazette* staff thought. She wanted the community to be proud of her. This was her hometown, and her daughter would grow up here. She wanted her to be glad her mother was sitting behind the editor's desk.

And then there was Frank.

She picked up a ballpoint pen and clicked it several times in rapid succession. *Is that all there is? Do I really care what he thinks? Is it personal or professional?*

"No!" She jumped when her voice rebounded back off the hard surfaces. "No," she whispered. "It's strictly professional."

But last night she had hugged him and given him a peck on the cheek. She had been feeling...grateful. *That's it! I was grateful when he helped me out.* She gnawed on her lower lip and began to click the ballpoint pen again.

Gayle had approached her boss's closed door twice already but chickened out before she could muster the nerve to venture a knock. *It's now or never.* She raised her fist to knock but lowered it immediately and turned around, pressing her lips together in frustration.

I am so pitiful.

Gayle heaved a sigh and returned to her desk near the front. She drummed her fingers on the scarred wood surface, chastising herself for lacking a spine.

She rose to greet a woman who had come in to place an ad for her garage sale the following week, and the next person to come through the door was someone she knew.

Jill Garland was the sheriff's daughter, and she also owned a day care center for mostly preschoolers, but Gayle knew a few kids of working moms were dropped off there by the bus for after-school care. It must be tough to be a working parent.

She knew Jill from high school. She and Reggie Lee had been seniors when Gayle was a sophomore. It had seemed to Gayle that these popular girls ran the school.

"Hi, Ms. Garland," Gayle said.

Jill was a stunning redhead with green eyes. She would have made heads turn for her beauty alone, but she had a take-charge manner that garnered attention as well.

"Hi. It's Gayle, right?" Green eyes examined her closely. "I remember you."

Gayle smiled, flattered to be remembered. "Yeah, from school."

"But you've been working here awhile, too." Jill flashed her million-dollar grin. "I wanted to see Reggie, if she's available."

Gayle half turned and punched in Reggie's extension on the phone. "Ms. Stafford? Ms. Garland is here to see you." She hung up, motioned for Jill to come around the counter, and then led her to the big, scary door Gayle had been afraid to broach. She scowled at her own cowardice and knocked on the doorframe. She opened it when Reggie called out.

When the door opened wide, Reggie was standing behind her desk, waving with both hands. "Come on in, you two."

Yes, Gayle was stunned, but she dutifully slipped in behind Jill.

"Sit right down, ladies." Reggie was smiling as she gestured to the two chairs in front of her desk.

Gayle quietly took a seat, hoping her smile looked genuine and didn't reveal her acute anxiety.

"You sure do look good behind that desk," Jill commented.

"I sure don't feel comfortable yet." Reggie heaved a sigh. "But it's good to see a friendly face."

Jill gestured to Gayle. "Well, you've got Gayle. At least you have one person under the age of fifty to work with."

Reggie laughed. "I hadn't thought of it that way, but I guess you're right. Everyone here has been on the staff since Miss Rosie hired them... Some were here when her husband was the publisher."

"In that case, the two of you have to keep the interest of those in the community who are not geriatric." Jill looked from one to the other for approval.

"Sure, I'll do my part." Gayle surprised herself by speaking up. "I mean, I'll be happy to do whatever you think I should."

Reggie gazed at her thoughtfully.

"What I had in mind," Jill said, "was to see if you might be interested in doing a story on my childcare center."

Reggie straightened her spine, leaning toward Jill. "What's the news?"

"You know, I've always had a few students who ride the bus after school, and I just give them a snack and let them play...but I'm making some changes. Miss Betty Jo, my part-time helper, is a retired schoolteacher, and she wants to expand the after-school program and take the school-age kids under her wing. We'll still offer snacks, but Miss Betty Jo will also supervise homework so parents don't have to deal with it when they pick up the children."

Gayle let out a little gasp. "Oh, that's a great idea."

"Well, there you go." Reggie gestured to Gayle. "Looks like Gayle is the eager reporter who will come out and cover your story."

"M—me? You want me to write the story?" Gayle felt a tightness in her chest.

"Sure," Reggie said. "You, not being geriatric, will have a different slant on it than the other reporters."

"That sounds great," Jill said. "Come tomorrow afternoon and I'll treat you to a healthy snack. Maybe you can write about the good meals too." She gave Gayle a wink.

Gayle tried to find words, but there were none. Not good for a wannabe reporter. She nodded furiously.

"I'm sure Gayle will come up with something amazing." Reggie sat back in her big, cushy, oversized chair.

"Thank you. Thank you. I'll do a great job."

"I'll see you tomorrow at about 1:30 at my center," Jill said. "You know it? Babes in the Woods?"

"Yes. I'll see you then." Gayle tried to contain her glee, but she wanted to squeal.

Jill gathered her purse and left with as much energy as she'd entered with.

"Thank you, thank you, thank you," Gayle said.

"Just take lots of notes and write a good story. You can bring it to me when you get it done, and I'll go over it."

Gayle's chest felt as though it was full of feathers. "Oh, I was going to see if you could look at the obit I wrote for Miss Kincaid, the lady who worked at the post office."

"I read it," Reggie said. "Very nice. Very sensitive. The family will appreciate it."

Gayle felt as though she was floating as she left Reggie's office. *She thought the obituary was sensitive.* Now all Gayle had to do was show up at the day care center and write up a little story about the after-school care. The butterflies in her stomach were flying in formation.

Frank slept late. He opened his eyes gingerly. Sunlight streamed in through the sheer curtains. He stretched and spread out all over the bed. The mattress wasn't particularly comfortable, and it was too short for him now.

Somehow, he hadn't been able to move Aunt Rosie's personal belongings out of the master bedroom, so he was still sleeping in the room he had occupied as a kid. He felt certain it had been larger back then.

He stared up at the ceiling. It had yellowed with age. There was a brownish stain. Probably the old roof leaked. No telling what else was wrong. *This house is a money pit.* No matter how many cherished memories he held onto, the truth was that it would cost him dearly to fix the house up, and for what? He had never intended to stay in Rambling. Why should he invest in something he wouldn't be living in anyway?

Untangling himself from the sheets, he set his feet on the bare wood floor. The worn oak felt cool beneath his feet. He stood and stretched again, scratched his stomach, and headed for the door. He made his way to the bathroom and relieved himself. The porcelain on the claw-foot bathtub was in good shape. He found himself assessing the fixtures with the eye of an owner.

He finished washing up and examined his face in the mirror. He hadn't shaved the past couple of days and was looking pretty ragged. A haircut was overdue as well.

When he had cleaned himself up and walked back down the hall, he paused beside Aunt Rosie's door. He twisted the ornate brass knob, darkened with age and lack of care, and stepped inside.

A pang of unaccustomed nostalgia shot through him. The room was filled with the collectibles and bric-a-brac his great-aunt had held dear. Her fragrance filled his senses, and he found himself struggling to keep the tears at bay.

"Sorry, Aunt Rosie," he said aloud. "Sorry I wasn't here for you." He took a deep breath and let it out carefully. With determination he went to the bed and ran his hand over her silken coverlet. He gazed at the collection on her bedside table. A lacy crocheted doily was topped with a small gathering of articles: a crystal carafe with a water glass turned upside down to form a lid, an old-fashioned radio, a box of tissues, and a single photograph in a silver frame. The frame held Frank's school photograph taken in the ninth grade. He wasn't smiling in the picture, and he could remember why he wasn't. That had been the day Reggie Lee had dubbed him *Franklinstein.*

—~~—

She saw the silver BMW slide to a soft landing in the parking lot. *The eagle has landed.*

Don't be ridiculous! It's just Frank, my personal nemesis.

She straightened her back and placed her fingers on the keyboard of her laptop. She should look busy...like an editor...like a busy editor.

Must look professional.

I am professional.

But I have to look professional...

She was aware her pulse rate had quickened. Her stomach clenched, and her breathing grew shallow. She gave herself a second to regain focus. *I can do this.*

All this for Franklinstein?

She jumped when she heard a knock on her door. She tried to speak, but her voice was gravelly. Clearing her throat, she called for the person to come in.

Milton threw the door open and approached her desk. He tossed the mail near her elbow. "Here's today's batch. Bigger than usual." He turned to leave.

"Wait! What is all this?"

"*Dear Irene.* That's you now." He stopped at the door and gave her a half smile. "Enjoy."

As Milton was leaving, Frank appeared in the open doorway. "What are you enjoying this morning?"

She smiled, flustered. "The *Dear Irene* mail. I guess we were a hit."

He placed a cardboard cup from the coffee shop drive-through on her desk. "It's hot and sweet," he said. "Like you."

"Oh, um..." she stammered.

"Lighten up, Reggie. It was just a little humor."

She took in a breath and let it out slowly. "I knew that." But they both knew she hadn't. She flashed a totally insincere grin.

"Aren't you going to open your mail?"

"But all this… I mean, it's just so much. We usually only get a couple of letters per week and a few emails, of course."

He leaned closer, his voice low and conspiratorial. "Maybe it's hate mail."

"Well, I certainly hope not." She reached in the top drawer for a letter opener and ripped the first one open.

Dear Irene,

I really enjoyed this past week's column. You seem to be so much more attuned to the problems Mike and Bev wrote in about. Maybe more compassionate than usual. This gave me the courage to write about the problem I'm having with my neighbor. He's hard of hearing and leaves his dog outside at night. Then he falls asleep in front of the television. The poor dog barks, and I can't get to sleep. I don't want to cause a problem, but how do I let my neighbor know it's bothering me without putting a strain on our relationship?

Sincerely,
Lucille

"Hmm… This sounds simple enough," she said.

"Simple for you, but not poor Lucille."

She had to smile at that.

He tossed another letter toward her. "Try this one."

She slit it open and found another complimentary letter telling her that she had approached Mike's problem with kindness and that her suggestions were right on.

"Well, that was nice," she said.

"Good job."

She found herself glowing under his praise. She swallowed hard. This was not the way she had planned to deal with him. She wasn't some simpering schoolgirl melting into his green eyes.

She sat up straighter and cleared her throat. "And what brings you to the *Gazette* today?" She cringed at her own words, knowing he had a right to be there every day if he saw fit. *He owns the building...*

"I thought of some things that might help your bottom line." A wide grin spread across his face. "I had some ideas for your sales staff. Are they here today or out in the field?"

"Sales staff? You mean Elvis Nordheim? He sells the ad space."

A twitch of his lips that might have been a smile glimmered for a moment and disappeared. He sat down on the edge of her desk and leaned toward her. "Well, do you want to have a meeting with old Elvis?"

Reggie nodded and punched his extension into her phone. "Elvis, could you come into my office for a moment? Mr. Bell wants to meet with you." The silence on the other end of the line was like a vacuum sucking at her ear. "Elvis? Are you there?"

"Yes... I'm here... I mean, I'll be right there." He hung up abruptly.

She moistened her lips and smiled at Frank, wondering what he had in mind for Elvis and if this would result in the loss of yet another longtime employee.

When a timid knock on the door heralded Elvis's arrival, she called for him to enter. The door swung open, and a pale, terrified version of Elvis Nordheim stepped into the office.

She pointed to one of the cushy leather chairs in front of her desk. "Have a seat, Elvis."

Elvis was probably not forty yet, but his large, owlish glasses and receding hairline gave him a perpetually "middle-aged" appearance. The collar of his somewhat wrinkled white shirt was open, revealing a rather unattractive Adam's apple in his ropy neck. His arms, hanging out of the short sleeves, seemed too long for his body, but that was probably because his pants were too big and belted way too high. He managed a tentative smile as he shuffled toward the chair.

Frank stepped forward, offering his hand. "Frank Bell," he said.

Elvis stared at the hand before grasping it. His lips moved, but she couldn't make out his response.

"Elvis has been with the *Gazette* for almost fifteen years," she offered brightly, not sure if this tenure would matter much to a man who leased everything. Did he value loyalty, or was he focused only on immediate results? There was a silence that followed her statement. Neither man spoke. She cleared her throat. "Elvis is responsible for maintaining all the accounts."

Frank nodded. "Is that so?" He turned to Elvis with a cheery expression. "I was driving around yesterday, just checking out some of the changes that have occurred since I left town, and I thought of some things that might beef up sales…"

There was no response from Elvis. He sat, as though paralyzed, his eyes glazed with fright.

"Maybe you might want to show me a list of all the current accounts? I'd like to know who your advertisers are."

Elvis nodded and mumbled something unintelligible, his Adam's apple bobbing up and down.

"No hurry," Frank said. "Maybe by later today…"

A strangled sound gurgled out of his throat. He leaped up and made for the door, nodding and mumbling as he traversed the distance. The glass panel in the door rattled as he closed it behind himself.

Frank looked at her, appearing puzzled. "Was it something I said?"

She made a scoffing noise and folded her arms across her chest.

"I think you scared the daylights out of him. Please stop terrorizing the staff. I can't do all the jobs by myself."

He surprised her by flashing a boyish grin. "Yeah, you probably could." He returned to his position perched on the edge of her desk. "Don't you think the paper would function better with staff that was a little more...alive?"

"Elvis is alive." She heard the defensive note in her own voice.

He snorted. "Barely. Not exactly what one thinks of as an extrovert salesman type."

"Well..." She cast about for some strong defensive argument but found none. "Well, he's been working here for almost fifteen years."

Frank arched an eyebrow at her. "I see." He shrugged and slid off her desk. "I'm just trying to support you, Reggie. I'm not going to stick around for this, but when he brings you the list, why don't you challenge him to bring in one brand-new account by the end of the week? That's reasonable, isn't it?"

She nodded grudgingly. "I suppose."

"And I'll leave so I don't terrify your staff." He winked at her and grinned as though this was the funniest thing in the world. "By the way, you look...great today."

She felt herself coloring and stammered her thanks. As he slipped out the door, it was as though he took all the oxygen with him. She watched from her office window as he stepped outside the building. He stretched his broad chest, and the expanse of muscles showing off under the knit shirt caused her to gape.

"Oh, my!" Her breath caught in her throat.

He walked purposefully to his car and then hopped in without opening the door.

Reggie wondered why every encounter with Frank Bell left her feeling both irritated in his presence and empty after he left.

Frank cruised through town again. He had already made a list of potential advertisers, but he didn't want to offer it to the ultra-sensitive Elvis.

Frank kind of liked that Reggie was so protective of her staff... But she still saw him as the enemy. He wished he could break through that wall she had erected around herself.

Or maybe it's just me. Maybe she built the wall around me. This seemed appropriate since everyone else seemed to be on her good side and only he was out in the cold.

He was glad he'd been on hand to witness her opening her fan letters. She needed to know that she had talent, that she could make a difference in people's lives.

He drew a deep breath and blew it out. She had plenty of compassion for the weak and downtrodden... For the defenseless, she would rise up like a mama tiger protecting her young.

A smile flicked across his face. *She needs to see me as a sympathetic character, not as her oppressor. How can I get there from here?*

How could a girl who would marry the school bully possibly think of Frank as terrifying? He unconsciously shook his head.

How can I make her like me? He blew out another deep breath. *How can I make her stop hating me?*

A slim scrap of an idea was coming into focus on the back of Frank's brain. If he could pull this off, maybe he could get Reggie Lee herself to tell him how to get through her defenses.

Later that afternoon, when Elvis presented her with the full record of all their advertisers, Reggie Lee had to admit that it was a pitifully small list. And there were no recent additions, many advertisers having accounts for almost all of Elvis's fifteen years. Apparently he just made the rounds to drink coffee with the advertisers and see if they had any changes in their weekly promotions.

Her stomach quaked as she contemplated how best to tell him he needed to get on the ball.

He sat across from her, still looking a bit nervous but a lot more centered than he had earlier when Frank was holding court.

"Um, I want you to find a new account by the end of the week," she said.

"Yeah, like that will ever happen." He rolled his eyes.

"Elvis, I'm not kidding. You need to go out and sign up a new account by Friday."

He gripped the armrests. Leaning forward, his eyes seemed to bulge out at her from behind his glasses. "What if I can't? Am I going to be fired?"

"I'm just challenging you to go out and find one new account." She realized she had used Frank's words, but they did seem to define the situation better than any she could come up with. "I know that mostly you just call up our longtime advertisers to take their renewals, but this is serious, Elvis. You need to get out there and find a new customer right away. We're trying to turn this business around."

He appeared to be strangling.

"You can do it, Elvis. This is your job. It's what you do." She smiled at him brightly…too brightly. "You're the point man."

"I—I don't know. I've had the same accounts forever. How can I…?" He left off abruptly.

"It's going to be okay. Just find one new account. There are quite a few new businesses in town. I'm sure you can find one that will advertise with us."

He gazed at her as though she had suggested he grow another head.

She grinned and gave him a thumbs-up.

He climbed out of the depths of the leather chair and stood, an uncertain frown on his face. Then he surprised her by flashing a grim smile and giving a thumbs-up in return.

She wanted to hug him. "Go for it, Elvis!"

He straightened his narrow shoulders and marched out of her office.

Reggie Lee's hands still shook when she reached for the stack of unopened letters. *This being-the-boss thing isn't so tough.*

"Excuse me!"

Gayle looked up from her computer screen to see a young couple at the front desk. The man had a baby in a pouch attached to his chest.

She pushed her chair back and approached them with a wide smile. She had not seen them in town before. "Good afternoon. May I help you?"

"I sure hope so," the young woman said. "We're looking for an apartment and haven't seen anything here in town."

The young man leaned his elbows on the countertop. "We have driven all over, street by street. Are there any apartment buildings in the town of Rambling?"

Gayle sucked in a breath. "Um, not really. Mrs. Henson turned her garage into a real garage apartment, but I think she's had the same renter for about a hundred years."

To her dismay, the young woman burst into tears.

"What kind of town doesn't have any apartments? We can't even find a place to live." Her voice rose a whole octave as other *Gazette* employees stopped what they were doing to stare.

Gayle grabbed a couple of tissues off her desk and offered them to the woman. "I'm so sorry. If you'll leave your contact information, I'll do some research and see if I can find you a place. What are you looking for?"

While the woman mopped up her face, her husband provided some details. He was with the Texas Fish and Wildlife Agency and had just been assigned to this district.

"I think there is a trailer park in the next town to the south. It's only about ten miles away." Gayle cringed when the young woman burst into a new round of tears.

"A trailer park! I don't want to live in a trailer park."

The man put his arm around her and led her from the *Gazette* office.

Gayle made a silent vow to find the young couple a place to live...and not in a trailer park.

Frank pulled into the national franchise coffee shop where he stopped to purchase coffee each morning. He was becoming a regular here. He wondered why they didn't advertise in the *Gazette*, but it wasn't his job to find out. *Give old Elvis a chance.*

He nodded to the barista, who rattled off his usual order. He paid and took his coffee to a table by the window. Definitely a thriving business.

He set his laptop on the table and logged on to the Wi-Fi. He logged in to an account he kept for making anonymous inquiries and began to compose his letter.

Dear Irene,
You're my only hope. I'm so miserable, I'm head over heels...

He snickered as he tried to picture her face when she read his letter. Smiling to himself, he continued. When he was done, he read it over and tweaked it a bit.

This should get her attention. His finger hovered over the key for a moment, and then he hit send.

Done! Now all I have to do is be patient and wait.

He picked up the paper container and sipped the hot brew. Unfortunately, patience was not one of Frank Bell's virtues. He questioned his own motives and wasn't sure of the answers. He wasn't quite certain why he was trying to get close to a woman who had hated him since early adolescence. He didn't know why it was important for him to win her over, but it was. He envisioned her dark eyes and pouty-baby lips. Lips he dreamed about kissing. He dreamed about her mane of blonde hair, loose and tangled after a strenuous bout of lovemaking.

He snapped to attention, realizing his surroundings and what he had just thought. He wanted to bed the lovely Reggie Lee Stafford. *What was that all about? Was that all?* Somehow, he knew there was more, but he refused to explore that issue. He would concentrate on making Reggie Lee his official girlfriend... his lover. He would court her and win her heart and her luscious body...and she would tell him exactly how to seduce her.

Chapter 7

THE NEXT MORNING, REGGIE LEE WAS RUNNING LATE.

Shannon had dumped over her entire bowl of Cheerios and milk. She had to be cleaned up and re-dressed.

Reggie's dad was grumpy because his magazine got drenched.

Reggie Lee hadn't had time to do much with herself except run a brush through her hair before buckling Shannon into her car seat and heading for the day care center. Once there, Shannon had turned clingy, clasping Reggie around the knees and bawling.

"Shannon, Mommy will be back after work. You love to play with Miss Jill and the children." But her words fell on deaf ears and wailing lungs. By the time Miss Jill was able to distract her and allow Reggie Lee to slip out, she was seriously late to work.

She tried to keep breathing as she neared the *Gazette* office, but when she pulled into the parking lot, her heart nearly stopped. Frank Bell's silver BMW sat parked close to the front door.

Oh, no! Not today. I definitely can't take a dose of Frank Bell on top of everything else. She turned off the ignition and sucked in a deep breath. *I am the editor of this paper. I will not be intimidated.*

When she pushed through the front door, she found a circle of her employees clustered around Frank, who was in the middle of regaling them with some story.

When he saw her, he quipped, "Better look busy. The boss is here." There was a titter of laughter, and everyone drifted away, leaving Frank and Elvis sitting together.

"Thanks for the tip, Frank," Elvis said. "I'll call on that coffee shop first thing."

Reggie did a double take. What had happened to terrified Elvis, the one who couldn't speak intelligibly in front of the man who owned the building? Now they were chatting as though they were old pals.

"Good morning, gentlemen," she breathed.

Elvis grinned, giving her a wink and a thumbs-up.

Frank stood up. His gaze flicked over her figure before reaching her eyes. He reached for a bag containing coffee from that same coffee shop where he always stopped.

Weasel. She didn't know what his game was, but she sure wasn't going to let him set Elvis up for failure. Did the coffee shop manager have the authority to advertise in the local newspaper? Elvis deserved some respect. After all, Elvis had worked there fifteen years.

Reggie Lee pasted on a smile. "Were you looking for me?" she asked with forced pleasantness.

He winked. "Nah, I just dropped by to intimidate your employees."

Obviously. "Well, you're doing a good job. They looked terrified." She turned and led the way to her office with Frank following close behind.

"I'm not a scary guy, Reggie," he whispered.

Oh, yeah. Right. She bit her lower lip. "Oh, I am so late. I had a rough start with Shannon this morning."

His expression sobered. "Reggie, I don't think you're on a time clock here. You're the boss." He handed her a cup of coffee.

"Thanks," she murmured. "And thanks for giving Elvis the lead on the coffee shop."

He shrugged away her thanks. "I just figured they should give me a return on the money I'm investing with them."

"Good idea." Heart thumping wildly, she sat down and rolled her chair under her desk. How could he be so considerate this early in the morning?

He saluted her with his cardboard cup. "You put in plenty of time on the job."

Reggie Lee heaved a deep sigh. "Tell me about it. Being a single parent is also a tough job, but my dad has about had it. I've relied on him to pick up the slack since I became editor." She shook her head. "I need to get things under control here at the paper so I can provide some sort of consistency for Shannon... and for my dad."

"Good idea. Kids need some kind of routine... I mean, don't they?" He gazed at her, his brow furrowed.

In spite of herself, she had to giggle. The idea that Frank Bell could give her advice on child rearing was ridiculous. "Uh, yeah. They do. I'm trying my best. But somehow the time just gets away from me."

"How about you get your receptionist to give you a warning when you need to start wrapping up so you can pick your little girl up on time?" He shrugged. "That's what I would do, but what do I know?"

Reggie blew out a breath. "Apparently you know more than I do." She pushed the intercom button. "Gayle, could you give me a heads-up at about a quarter of five? I need to pick up my little daughter on time for a change."

"Sure thing, Ms. Stafford."

Reggie leaned back in her chair, inspecting the old ceiling for stains. "I don't want to be one of those bosses who think they don't have to show up and keep regular hours."

"Reggie, you're doing all you can to figure out your new job here."

She straightened and met his gaze. He didn't seem to be putting her on.

He spread his hands. "Besides, I know for a fact that you were here quite late preparing the *Dear Irene* column."

She swallowed hard. *Oh, yeah. I was here, and I kissed you.*

"Did you get through all the *Dear Irene* letters?"

She shook her head. "Sorry to say I haven't made much progress."

He flashed a grin. "I can help you with that."

"Who are you? My secretary?"

"I can be." His voice rolled out, smooth as satin, almost caressing her, sending a whisper of shivers along her skin.

Reggie sucked in a breath. "Sure, help yourself." She pointed to the stack of unopened letters holding down one corner of her desk.

"What about the ones online? Who answers those?"

She sighed. "I guess that will be me."

"I can help. If you want, I can at least open the emails."

"Thanks. That would help." She logged into the *Gazette* email account and clicked on the *Dear Irene* tab. Seven recent emails stared at her. She stood and offered him her chair. "Knock yourself out."

She was on an emotional roller coaster. She was delighted that Frank was being so helpful, especially to Elvis. But she was also feeling peevish and out of sorts. Probably due to the chaos of her morning.

Frank seemed to be oblivious to her rancor. He was impeccably groomed as usual. Somehow, even if he was dressed in faded denims, he still looked good enough to eat.

Reggie quickly dismissed that thought, blushing even though she was fairly certain Frank couldn't read her thoughts. Or could he? She swept him with a surreptitious glance.

A little smile played around his lips.

Hmm...

Frank stole a glance at Reggie as she prepared to tackle the *Dear Irene* letters. She reached for the stack of correspondence and the letter opener and slit open the first one. "Dear Irene," she read. "I hate my mother. She's just too strict..."

Frank laughed. "Don't all teenage girls hate their mothers?"

"At one time or another," she agreed and reached for another envelope.

He looked at the computer screen and scrolled down the page of messages. "Listen to this one," he said. "Dear Irene... You're my only hope. I'm so miserable, I'm head over heels..." He snorted. "What a loser!"

She cocked her head to one side and came to stand behind him. The scent of her perfume or lotion caused his senses to reel. She leaned over his shoulder to peer at the screen. "Awww...the poor guy. He's in love with a coworker."

Her hair swept forward, brushing his cheek. He squelched the urge to stroke her hair. Kiss her neck...earn more of her loathing.

He inhaled another lungful of her fragrance and discreetly rolled the desk chair back. "Here—you sit down and read. I need to be going anyway."

She lifted her gaze as he stood beside her. His tentative grasp on his emotions strained to the breaking point as he fought down the urge to plant a big one on her. *Not now. Keep it cool...* He held the chair for her and pushed it closer when she sat down. "See you later."

She nodded absently. "When do you want to start on your house project?" She turned back around to gaze up at him. "I should really have some 'before' pictures. I'd like to take Milton, the photographer, out to your place...the Grady house. How about tomorrow?"

"Sure. I'll try to peel a layer of dust off for the pics."

Reggie laughed. "I'm sure it's not that bad."

He decided to go for broke. "Why don't you come hang out with me this weekend? Bring Shannon with you? I'd love to really show you through the house, and we can talk about projects."

She flashed a big grin. "Are you sure you want me to bring

Shannon? You can't imagine what a little terror she can be in a new place."

"Not a problem. I love kids." As soon as the words left his mouth, he experienced a sick twisting in his gut. *Kids? Me? What am I doing here?*

Her expression softened. "That sounds really nice, Frank. I'm sure Shannon will love it."

He walked out in a daze. What was happening to him? Cool international bachelor types do not love kids. He hit the front door and stepped out into the cool breeze. *But Shannon is a sweetheart. Who could resist her? Not me.*

He climbed into his car and inserted his key in the ignition, wondering if he should take a road trip, anything to put some distance between himself and the crazy emotions churning his gut.

———∞———

Reggie watched him drive away. *I wonder if I've been mistaken about him. High school was a long time ago. Maybe he's changed? Maybe he's matured? Maybe I'm crazy?*

She swiveled back to her desk and the partially read email. *This is so sweet.* She continued reading.

> I'm in love with a coworker, but she doesn't seem to like me at all. I've been as nice as I know how to be, but she's cool and distant. I'm not exactly a Romeo, but I think about her all the time. I know she's been burned in the past, but I'm not that guy. How can I warm her up and win her heart?
>
> Mr. Nice Guy

A warm, tingly feeling filled her insides. She wanted to help Mr. Nice Guy find love with his coworker. She wanted him to win the lady's heart... She sighed.

I want to meet my own Mr. Nice Guy. A picture of Frank Bell's grinning face swam through her brain. She shook her head. *I said Mr. Nice Guy.*

She put her fingers on the keyboard and began typing.

Dear Mr. Nice Guy,

   If your company doesn't have rules against employee dating, you might want to surprise her with some thoughtful small present. Nothing big, but something to let her know you're thinking of her. Or invite her to do something simple and non-personal. If she's responsive, take the next step slowly. Don't scare her away.

                                                         Irene

She read it over, smiled in satisfaction, and printed it out for publication. She would choose a few more for this week's edition, but for now she was content to feel all warm and squishy about this sweet man... *Mr. Nice Guy.*

She thought about the daily coffee she had become accustomed to receiving from Frank. She was now expecting him to show up each morning, paper cup in hand. She shook her head, wondering how that had happened. *Franklinstein.* She pictured his handsome, intelligent face. *Eeeuw!* She figuratively shook herself and pushed back from the desk. *I called Franklinstein handsome! When did that happen?* She blew out a long breath. *Well, he is hot... And he loves kids. He can't be all bad.*

And she would be taking Shannon out to the beautiful Grady estate on Saturday.

The Victorian house had always thrilled her. In the past, when she had gone to visit Miss Rosie Bell Grady, she had secretly coveted the lovely home, imagining herself coming down the curved mahogany staircase. She loved the chintz slipcovers and the tatted doilies, the shiny marble tabletop and the highly polished sideboard. She loved the way sunlight filtered in through the sheer lace curtains. Reggie sighed. At least she would get a chance to be involved in the renovations to Miss Rosie's house. She would make sure it retained its charm and status as a historical house.

She smiled to herself in anticipation of being able to make an impact. She hoped Frank would appreciate her tastes. A man who leased everything might have strong opinions on renovating a historical house. *Well…I'll just have to educate him.*

When Gayle buzzed her on the intercom to let her know it was a quarter of five, Reggie thanked her and picked up her purse. Before leaving the building, she stopped by the bookkeeper's tidy little office. "Hi, Roy."

He looked up, squinting at her over the top of his glasses that he perpetually wore on the tip of his nose. "Hey, little lady. How you doin'?"

"I'm good. How are you?" She gestured to the paper strewn around his desk as he sat hunched over his keyboard.

He shrugged. "Good as can be expected. What can I do for you?"

Reggie sucked in a deep breath, hoping her shaking hands weren't revealing how nervous she was. She gripped her purse with both hands. "I was wondering if you could print out a list of all employees and their current pay rate. I want to be sure I'm not missing anyone who is due a raise."

Roy nodded, the fluorescent light overhead mirrored in a strip of light across his shiny bald head. "Good for you. Phil had to be hit over the head to bother to give a raise." He returned to the task he was working on. "You can clear off that chair and take a seat." He gestured toward a rickety-looking chair stacked high with papers and ledgers.

Reggie examined it from afar. "Um, I'm good."

Roy typed on his keyboard for a while, searched through digital files, and finally clicked on something that started the printer sitting on a file cabinet beside his desk. "Here ya go." He shoved

his chair back and stood beside the printer while it finished crank-
ing out pages. When it was done, he neatly patted them into shape
and handed them off to Reggie.

"Thank you so very much." She tried to steady her hand as she
reached for the papers.

Roy flashed a toothy grin. "Now, if my name happens to come
up as one of the employees in need of a raise, I would be truly
grateful."

"Um, yes. We'll see." She made a hasty retreat, waved at Gayle,
who was also trying to leave, but beat her out the door. Once in
her car, Reggie exited the parking lot and drove a couple of blocks
before pulling over.

She was breathing hard when she unfolded the papers. She
used her finger to sort through the list of names that were not in
alphabetical order but apparently arranged in some mystical order
dreamed up by Roy.

Her name was listed twice. Once for when she was listed as a
reporter and the date she ceased to be one...and again right under
Phil's name with the same date that he stopped being editor and
she began...and she was given the same salary as good old Phil.
Apparently it was the prescribed editor salary, and it made her
pucker her lips in a silent wow. She had never dreamed there was
that much money in the world.

Reggie closed her eyes and leaned back against the headrest,
clasping the papers to her chest. A single tear trickled down her
cheek. This was it. She had arrived at her own special nirvana. A
place where she would earn the same salary as a man.

She thought about all the things she could buy with that
money. Christmas would be outstanding this year. And she would
get her own house...a place for Shannon to grow and thrive.

She opened her eyes and sat up straight, taking a few deep
breaths and blowing them out noisily. What she needed to do was
to continue to live with her dad, appreciate that he was willing to

help her raise Shannon, and put the major part of her raise in an account for Shannon's future. A college fund. That felt right.

Reggie slipped the car into drive and proceeded at a very calm rate of speed. So very happy she could have floated to pick up Shannon.

—⁓—

When Frank checked the email in the seldom-used account, he was surprised to find a response from "Irene." His heart had leaped up, thinking it was from Reggie Lee, but no... It was an automated response from the *Dear Irene* email saying "We've received your letter for the *Dear Irene* column, and we thank you. It's not possible to print every letter that we receive, but if yours is selected, it will appear in the paper." There was a disclaimer telling him that by sending his letter to the *Dear Irene* column he was giving tacit permission for the letter to be printed in full or in part.

He swallowed his disappointment. Of course she wouldn't send him an email. Now he had to wait and hope that she might post something in the weekly paper, but he was encouraged that she had read it when he was in her office. Maybe he had used the right bait. Maybe he could reel her in.

He pushed back from the computer, his desk chair almost hitting the opposite wall. *What do I care? This is Reggie Lee Stafford, the girl who hates me. When she finds out it's me, she will kick me to the curb.*

But why should she? If I follow her instructions, maybe the ice queen will thaw out... Why do I care?

He stared at the monitor for some time, contemplating that last question.

I do care. I really do care about her. Am I falling in love with Regina Vagina? He blew out a deeply frustrated breath. *When was I not in love with her?*

Frank straightened his spine. He knew what he wanted, and

he was willing to acknowledge it to himself. How did he go about getting her? He was a man who went after what he wanted in the most direct way possible, but he knew if he used his usual ball-peen hammer approach, she would walk—no, run away.

He'd made plenty of mistakes with her from the first day they'd met. Well, he wasn't that kid anymore. He was a successful grown man and had finally come to terms with the fact he was in love with Reggie Lee. He wanted to make a life with her. He wanted to take her and her daughter with him when he left this town. *I'll show her the world...my world. I can provide a much better life for both of them.*

Frank experienced a warm feeling flooding his chest when he thought about waking up with her in his arms. He envisioned her in his New York condominium. He wanted to show her the Europe he had come to love. Surely she could appreciate the things he could provide for her and her daughter.

Gayle's insides were quaking. She sat in her car outside Babes in the Woods Day Care, her fingers gripping the steering wheel. This was her big chance, and she didn't want to blow it.

She couldn't believe that Reggie had given her this opportunity. First she had let her try her hand at writing the obituaries, which had been Reggie's responsibility before she was appointed to the position of editor.

Gayle closed her eyes and tried taking in huge gulps of air, filling her lungs completely and blowing all the air out slowly through her pursed lips. That was supposed to lower heart rate and help one get centered.

Okay, I can do this.

She stepped out of the car and locked it, clutching a pen and notepad to her chest. She had considered using her tablet but thought the old-fashioned approach would be better.

Gayle stood outside the gate, examining the exterior before crossing into the property.

The building itself was adorable. It was a really attractive old bungalow with a porch and actual ivy growing up on one side. The landscaping was minimal but neat, as most of the yard had been turned into a play area.

There was a swing set and a sandbox. A low slide was on one side of the swing set. Everything appeared to be very well kept. The most charming feature was a wooden structure, obviously meant to inspire creativity and imagination. It could have been a play-house or a pirate ship, depending on what the child envisioned.

Heaving a sigh, Gayle opened the gate and walked inside, securing it behind herself. *Don't want any little kiddies to escape.*

Stepping onto the porch, she inhaled a wonderful fragrance and realized the plant growing on the side of the house was actually jasmine. The beautiful tiny white flowers were supported by a trellis affixed to the side of the house near the door. Her footsteps sounded loud as she crossed the wooden porch, and before she could knock, the front door was thrown open by a small woman with a thick head of almost-white hair on the blondish side.

"Hello," she said. "Come right in. We've been expecting you." She pushed a pair of large, red-framed glasses up on her short nose.

"Um, okay." Gayle had been startled, but the woman who stood grinning up at her appeared to be friendly.

"I'm Betty Jo Nevins, Jill's pre-K teacher. I retired from the school district last year, but I'm having a great time teaching the younger ones." She flashed a grin.

There were young children in the front room busy with various activities. Tiny tables and chairs were arranged around the space, with some kind of floor game that almost appeared to be like a quilt or rug on the floor. Several children were holding it down and examining the squares.

"Miss Betty Jo!" One little boy came running up with a piece of paper on which he had used crayons. "Look what I made for you." He stood with eyes shining and a big grin on his face.

Betty Jo's face morphed into one of surprise and awe. "Oh José. I love it! You know red is my favorite color." She gave him a hug. "I'm going to post it on the bulletin board right now. I really love it." She hustled to the other side of the room and tacked the drawing onto a large corkboard. "Beautiful!" she exclaimed.

When Gayle turned, there was a little blonde girl gazing up at her with large and solemn blue eyes. "Hi," Gayle said.

The girl blinked and turned away, scampering to join another child at one of the tables.

"That's Reggie Lee Stafford's daughter," Betty Jo said. "Doesn't she look just like her mom?"

"Wow. I'll say. Like she was cloned."

"I taught Reggie years ago. Such a lovely young woman." Betty Jo sighed and went to see what the two little ones were doing.

When she returned, she took Gayle by the arm and steered her to another room. If the front room had been a living room, then this one must have been the dining room. There was a large sideboard built into the wall and framing a set of four casement windows.

This room also had tables and chairs, but these were a bit larger. And the children scattered around the room were a bit older but still quite young.

Gayle, who was not routinely around young children, gave herself a moment to draw a deep breath and expel it. *Of course there are young kids at the preschool center. Duh!*

"Hey, Gayle." Jill Garland greeted her. She was in the room beyond that was quite a massive kitchen. There was an impressive industrial-looking setup with large chrome appliances and equipment. "I'm just bringing out snacks. Everything is on a timetable." She had arranged what looked like lemon gelatin in paper cups with an assortment of fresh fruit on the side. Everything was on a serving trolley with little plastic utensils.

Betty Jo appeared and took charge of the trolley, rolling it to the front room to provide snacks for the young ones.

Jill picked up a tray and carried it to the room with the older children. "These children are the four- and five-year-olds, and Betty Jo has the two- and three-year-old kids."

"Um, I thought five years was the age for kindergarten," Gayle said.

"It all depends on their birthday. They have to be five by the time school starts, or they have to wait until the following year."

Jill pointed to a small adult-size table and chair and placed a snack on top. "Take a seat and check out the gelatin."

Children were scrambling to sit at the small tables, looking excitedly at the treats Jill was passing out.

Gayle sat down and examined the items before her. There was lemon gelatin in a cup, plus three apple slices, some seedless grapes, and half a banana. Feeling a bit self-conscious, she picked up the plastic spoon and scooped some gelatin into her mouth. She had not eaten much gelatin as a child. She never knew what to do with it. Did one chew it? Let it melt? Or perhaps squish it through one's teeth? She managed to mash it up and swallow it before reaching for an apple slice.

Jill made the rounds again and offered her a cup of apple juice.

"Thanks. Uh, I have to ask... Why are the grapes cut in half?"

Jill chuckled. "To lessen the risk of choking. If they're left whole, the child might choke trying to swallow it, but cut in half they taste the sweetness and chew them up."

"Oh, there is so much about children that I don't know." Gayle shrugged. "I guess it's a good thing I don't have any."

Jill patted her on the shoulder. "I'm sure you will, in time. I haven't found the man I want to spend my life with, so having my own kids is on the back burner for me too...for now."

"Yeah, I know that feeling." Gayle shook her head. "Living in a small community, it's kind of hard to find your true love."

Jill tilted her head to one side. "Tell me about it. The boys I dated in high school were such fun dorks, but there was never a romance...and then I inherited my grandmother's house." She gestured to her surroundings. "I always loved this place and thought the community needed a good day care."

"Well, you've made a great name for yourself. The community sure loves what you do."

Jill smiled. "We try."

"This is a lovely house," Gayle said. "Didn't you ever consider moving into it yourself?"

Jill looked around. "I have so many memories embedded in this home. My grandmother was a great influence on me. My parents worked, and she was my after-school day care." Jill's eyes teared up. "Gran always had a snack for me and a place to do my homework. And she would read to me as well."

Gayle smiled, thinking what a sweet image sprang into her mind. "And so you want to include more after-school students?"

Jill nodded. "Yes, now that Miss Betty Jo has come on full-time, we can go ahead and offer the tutoring with a licensed teacher on board. I'm so thrilled to have her working with the children."

"So, it's just the two of you?"

"I hired another helper who will be coming after school. She is a high school senior and will be majoring in early childhood development when she graduates."

"That sounds great."

"She will actually be getting some college credits, so I'll have to do some documentation too." Jill was beaming.

"Sounds like a great plan," Gayle said. "Would you like this story I'm writing to focus on the after-school care?"

"Yes, please. I'm only licensed to take care of a certain number of preschoolers, and we're always at capacity. People come in and sign their kids up almost at birth."

Gayle munched a grape half. "But you can take more school-age kids?"

"Yes, with Betty Jo's credentials." Jill spread her hands. "I'm perfectly content with the number of children we have in our day care, but as the daughter of working parents, I wanted to offer a safe after-school program to the working parents of Rambling."

"It's a great community," Gayle said. "We're so fortunate to live in this very close-knit town."

Jill nodded. "I can't imagine how anyone could leave...but two of my closest friends from high school moved far away. Do you remember Lori Holloway? She moved to New York City. She's a children's picture book author and perfectly at home in that monster big city."

"Whoa!" Gayle considered the Lori she had not known well but admired from afar. "You and your friends worked on the school newspaper, didn't you?"

Jill grinned. "Sure did. Reggie Lee and Lori took it to heart. I was just in it for the camaraderie. Loved hanging with my gal pals."

"What were you into?" Gayle asked.

"I was a jock. I played basketball and ran track...and my girls came to cheer me on."

Gayle considered how nice it would feel to have friends that close. She had been shy and a total introvert. "Must have been nice to have such good friends."

"Reggie is still tight with me...and I call the others sometimes." She shrugged. "It's good to catch up."

"Thank you for this opportunity to cover your story. I appreciate it." Gayle gathered her tray and started to take it to the kitchen, but Jill took it from her.

"I thank you for coming here to see what we're all about."

Gayle took her leave and left the building, clutching her note-book and pen. It was only when she stood outside her car that she realized she had locked her purse and car keys inside.

She felt like a total idiot. Stamping her feet, she gritted her teeth and returned to the day care center.

Jill let her back in and gave her a hug. "Not to worry. Everyone has locked their keys in the car once or twice. Let me call my daddy."

Gayle covered her mouth with both hands. "Oh, no! Don't bother the sheriff."

Jill laughed. "My daddy is the one to call in situations like this. He's the man." Jill had a brief conversation with her father, and in a short time a tall, uniformed deputy rolled up in a cruiser, got out, and used a slim jim to open her car.

"Thank you," Gayle said.

"No problem, ma'am." He climbed back in his vehicle and drove away.

Gayle waved at Jill, who watched from the porch, and climbed into her own vehicle, grateful that she had been assigned to cover Jill's story and hoped she would be able to do justice to the com-passion Jill felt for the community.

That was the core of the story that Gayle wrote. She sat at her kitchen table and typed out the story she had developed. She reread it several times and tweaked it a little. When she realized she was grinning, she felt enormously satisfied. *I can do this!* But she decided that she would read it over again at work the next day before turning it in.

Fingers crossed.

The next afternoon, Reggie Lee was in her car, headed to the Grady estate with Milton Mayweather, the *Gazette*'s photogra-pher, riding shotgun. Milton rode with the window open, looking for all intents and purposes like a big, shaggy dog with his face pointed into the wind. Milton's longish hair and gray beard were blowing back. He wore his big shades and had a smile on his face. Perhaps he was looking forward to this assignment as much as she was.

Impossible.

Reggie realized that her own face was wearing a smile as well.

When she pulled up close to the Grady house, a shiver rolled down her spine. She recalled all her visits to Miss Rosie when she was in high school, and now, her incredibly handsome nephew was standing on the porch with his shirt off.

She swallowed hard and drew in a breath. *A thing of beauty is a joy forever. Well, a joy to behold, even for the moment.*

Frank Bell was, to put it mildly, ripped. He seemed to be hammering something at the top of one of the columns, and with each swing of the tool, an exquisite array of rippling muscles danced for her.

She had never actually seen such perfection firsthand. He was lean, but his musculature was well defined. She swallowed again, a swirl of pure lust raging low in her belly.

"Well, would you look at that?" Milton intoned. "Mr. Pretty Boy can swing a mean hammer."

"Um, yeah. He sure can."

Milton grabbed a couple of shots of Frank through the open window before he got out of the car.

Dayum! Pretty Boy is right. Reggie scrambled to open her door and follow Milton up to the house.

"Hey, folks," Frank called, giving a wave with the hammer. "Come on up."

When Reggie stepped onto the porch, she saw that Frank was standing on a step stool. "What are you doing?"

"I noticed almost all the columns and railings are loose. I was just hammering some shims in to steady them." He stepped down and tossed the hammer in a toolbox before reaching for a faded T-shirt. He pulled it on over his head, giving another impressive display of dancing muscles. He raked his fingers through his hair and then gestured toward the door. "Let's go inside. Can I get you something to drink?"

"Sure," Milton said. "Whatcha got?"

Frank grinned. "I haven't stocked the bar, but Aunt Rosie had quite a stash of sherry, and I made tea." He ushered them through the front door.

"Geez!" Milton stared up the mahogany staircase, gazing at the stained-glass window at the landing. "Just look at this place." He lifted his camera and took a series of shots. "Is it okay if I just look around first?"

"Knock yourself out," Frank said. "Everything is just the way Aunt Rosie left it, except for the first room on the left upstairs. I've been staying in the room I had as a boy." He turned to Reggie, and she felt a flush rise from her chest and crawl up her neck.

"I would love some tea," she said hurriedly, hoping to divert his attention.

"Why don't you have a seat in the parlor and I'll bring it to you?" He gestured to Miss Rosie's pretty front room, filled with velvet- and chintz-covered furniture, lace curtains, and bric-a-brac.

"Um, sure. I'll just...wait in here." She waved toward the room he indicated, feeling totally absurd. Watching Frank's retreating form, she was acutely aware of the lean muscles striding away with an athletic gait. The worn T-shirt and faded denims displayed his assets to advantage. *Oh, I'm in so much trouble here.*

She sucked in a breath and blew it out forcefully. *The house. I'm here for the house.*

In the parlor, she gazed around at the room filled with lovely treasures. A tall étagère held a collection of music boxes. Reggie carefully opened one of the glass doors and picked up an intricate carousel with beautiful hand-painted horses. Unable to resist, she wound the stem and felt the sting of tears when the tinkling strains of "Clair de Lune" floated around her. It was so beautiful and so delicate. She clutched it, afraid she might break it.

"Do you like that?" Frank had come to stand in the doorway, gazing at her with interest.

"Oh, it's lovely. I'm sorry. I shouldn't have touched it." She started to put it back, but he set a tray on the small table and invited her to be seated on the curved chaise longue. "I brought that music box to Aunt Rosie from Brussels. She was really pleased, and that pleased me."

She perched on the edge, still clutching the music box. She hadn't expected him to bring hot tea, but he pulled up a chair across from her and set a delicate, eggshell-thin china cup on a matching saucer.

"How do you like your tea? I have milk, honey, and lemon."

"Ooh," she crooned. "I love a proper English tea. Milk and honey, please." Reggie was aware she was grinning like a fool, but she couldn't stop. Carefully, she set the music box on the table.

She watched as he poured tea from the fine bone-china teapot and added her favorite ingredients. His hands were large but well-shaped. She noted they looked as natural handing her a teacup on a delicate saucer as they had wielding a hammer.

"Thank you," she murmured.

"Biscuit?" Frank offered a plate of shortbread cookies.

Reggie took one and placed it on the saucer. "This is very nice, Frank."

"You're very nice, Reggie." His voice dropped to a lower register, and when she glanced up into his eyes, she was snared by the tenderness of his expression. He lifted his teacup and took a sip, still holding her in thrall.

Oh, no! I want him. I want Franklin Bell. I want to be naked with him. I want those strong arms around me. She hurriedly took a sip of her very hot tea and set the cup back in the saucer.

He smiled, and she felt lust coiling around her gut again. Just admitting to herself that she wanted him seemed to have unleashed her long-pent-up passions.

"How's your tea? Did I get it right?"

She breathed out a sigh. "Perfect. It's just perfect."

"Well, what do you think?" His penetrating gaze had her off-kilter.

"About what?"

"The room. This was one of Aunt Rosie's favorite places in the house. How would you propose we proceed with it?"

She glanced around, feeling inadequate. "It's a lovely room."

"But the wallpaper is faded, and there are a couple of places it's pulling away at the seams."

"Um, yes. I see."

Truly, she had not noticed. Her attention had been firmly attached to the man sitting across from her. The man who used to be the bane of her existence. The man who was now trying to be her friend. The man she suddenly wanted to jump on.

"We can go shopping for new wallpaper," she suggested.

"And I think most of the upholstered pieces have seen better days."

"Yes, some of the fabric is worn in places, but they are still fine pieces. Perhaps you can have them reupholstered."

"Sounds like a plan, but you have to help me choose the wallpaper and material. I don't have an eye for this sort of thing." He flashed a grin. "I mean, if you left it to me, I might install a big flat-screen television and haul in black-leather recliners."

"Oh, no!" She sat up straight and then realized he was teasing her. Flashing a grin of her own, she laughed. "I don't see black leather in this room."

"Maybe we'll have to go to market and you can select the right colors to make this place pop."

"That sounds wonderful. I would love to do that." She thought perhaps he was thinking of the big Design Center in Dallas.

"Great! I'll make travel arrangements. What about Shannon?"

"Not a problem," she assured him. "Dad loves to watch her, and he can take her to day care when he's at the store."

Frank drained his cup and set it on the tray. "Then it's settled. I can't tell you how much I appreciate your help." He sat across from her, beaming as though she had given him a great gift.

"Think nothing of it. I'm really excited about this project." Reggie tried to tear her attention away from Frank's magnetic gaze. She looked around the room and tried to memorize the patterns she saw there. "Oh, I just realized what this room is all about."

Frank leaned toward her. "What?"

"This is the Rose Room, for your Aunt Rosie."

A smile spread across his face. "Of course. She always said this was her favorite place in the house. She loved roses, and the grounds are covered with beautiful rosebushes. There are climbers on the gazebo in back."

"Well, I hope you're in agreement that this should stay the Rose Room. We can paint and paper and reupholster, but we have to maintain the essence of this room…for Miss Rosie."

"Agreed." He winked at her, sending her libido into orbit.

Reggie spent the next several hours going on a grand tour of the house. She had seen it before, but this time she was looking at it from the perspective of someone who would remodel it.

Milton had made his own tour, capturing a lot of "before" images to feed the ongoing story. He now sat in that same parlor Reggie and Frank had vacated, sampling Aunt Rosie's sherry in a tiny cut-crystal cordial glass.

The tour had wound around the upper floor, with a quick peek in the attic, which was filled with even more antiques, mostly mahogany or cherry wood.

Somehow, walking around with Frank was even more intimate than sitting across from him. Several times, his arm had brushed hers as he reached around to open or close a door. And once, she collided with him when she turned too suddenly. He held her for a moment, staring into her eyes as he steadied her.

"Careful," he whispered.

She swayed toward him and had the distinct impression he was going to kiss her, but at that moment, Milton yelled up the stairs.

"Hey, Reggie Lee. It's getting late. My wife will have dinner on the table pretty soon."

She jerked away. "Coming." She smiled at Frank and made a break for the staircase. When she arrived at the bottom, she turned to gaze up at Frank, her heart pounding in her chest. She wasn't sure if her escape was a good thing or a bad thing.

Chapter 8

THE NEXT DAY, WHEN REGGIE ARRIVED AT THE OFFICE, SHE gathered the magazines she had used to research ideas for updating Frank's house without destroying the Victorian charm. She had notebooks where she had doodled and made notes. Thus armed, she pushed through the front door to deposit her load on the front counter.

She found Gayle, the receptionist, waiting for her. Her eyes were shining, and it would be impossible for anyone to produce a bigger grin. "This is for you," she said in a breathy voice. She hefted a square, beribboned box onto the counter.

"Uh, thank you, but you shouldn't have." Reggie stared at the gift-wrapped box with trepidation. It wasn't her birthday, and she couldn't think of any occasion warranting a gift. She swallowed hard, re-gathered her magazines and notebooks, and continued on her path to her office.

Gayle followed her, placing the box reverently on Reggie's desk. "It's not from me. It's from him."

Reggie sucked in a breath. "Him?" She put her purse in a drawer and sank into her chair.

"Mr. Bell. He brought it by earlier."

Reggie could see that Gayle was about to hyperventilate with excitement. Her eyes were sparkling, and her cheeks were tinged with a very attractive pink.

Reggie pressed her own lips together. Her reaction seemed to be the opposite of Gayle's, since Reggie couldn't seem to catch her breath. *Frank Bell brought this for me. Oh, what should I do?* She swallowed hard. *Open it, silly girl. Open it.*

With trembling fingers, she reached for the box. Gayle sank into a chair on the opposite side of the desk, her gaze fastened on the box.

When Reggie lifted the lid, she gasped. There, nestled in tissue paper, was the carousel music box Frank had brought his aunt from Brussels. Her hands flew to cover her mouth. "Oh, my!"

"That's beautiful," Gayle said. "What a thoughtful gift. He must really like you."

Reggie wanted to agree but didn't want to start any office gossip. "I'm sure it's just because I'm going to help him with the house remodel... I mean, I love old houses." She gazed earnestly into Gayle's eyes. "We're just friends."

Gayle smiled an incredibly knowing smile and nodded. "I'm sure."

Reggie removed the music box from the tissue and set it on the desk in front of her. She wound it up and pulled out the knob on the side. The sweet sound of "Clair de Lune" floated on the air. The metallic strains caused a swelling in her chest. She could hardly breathe. *How very lovely.* She glanced at Gayle, who had her hands clasped together.

"It's so romantic." Gayle let out a loud sigh. She blinked rapidly, and her eyes were moist.

"Um, yes. Isn't it though?" The image of Frank's face sprang into her brain, shoving aside all rational thought. His face, as he had looked when she'd wanted to kiss him the day before. Even now, Reggie felt a flush spread through her chest, rising up her neck to paint her cheeks.

She pushed the stem in, thereby shutting off the tinkling strains of melody. The horses stopped spinning. The silence was crushing.

Clearing her throat, she straightened her shoulders. "Well, let's get back to work, shall we?"

Gayle sniffled and pushed out of the chair. "That was just the sweetest—" She left the room, shaking her head as though she couldn't understand why Reggie wasn't swooning.

Swooning on the inside. Reggie drew in a deep breath and exhaled. *Okay, so I have fallen under Frank's spell. I can't let him get to me. I have to remain cool. After all, I'm the editor. I must be professional.*

She scooted the music box to one side and moved the magazines closer. She had made notes of ideas for the Grady house, and she wanted to run them by Frank.

Reggie spent the next couple of hours pulling together the ideas she had come up with as appropriate to the Grady house. She snipped from the magazines and from her notebooks, made copious notes with her marker, drew arrows to illustrate what she had in mind.

There was a cork bulletin board on the opposite wall, and she used it to coordinate her images and notes. Securing her pages and snippets with pushpins, she stepped back to survey her progress. *Yes, this will make an amazing running story for the* Gazette. *Maybe I can even submit it to some decorator magazines.*

She was standing, entranced with her own imaginings, when Frank stepped through the open doorway. She didn't hear him until he was right beside her. His presence overwhelmed her, invaded her consciousness, gave her the insane desire to lean against him.

"Ms. Stafford," he breathed. "When you take on a project, you dive right in."

She turned her head, looking up at him with what she hoped was an appealing expression. He put a hand on her shoulder, and she almost stopped breathing.

"This is just…amazing." He gestured to the board. "You must have spent a lot of time in creating this display." He gazed down at her. The hunger in his eyes made her knees almost buckle.

Frank seemed to hesitate and then lowered his head to press his lips against hers. It was a tentative kiss, at first. And then another, more confident.

Reggie leaned into his arms and reached up to circle his neck. Frank's kisses set off a wildfire of emotion within her. She had never been kissed with such intensity, such passion. Her own passion simmered low in her belly.

"Oh!"

They drew apart as though scalded. Turning, Reggie saw Gayle and Milton standing in the doorway, both with mouths agape. Reggie felt her face turn red.

Frank adjusted his tie and heaved a deep sigh. "You caught us. I was just giving Reggie cause for a sexual harassment lawsuit."

"Good job." Milton advanced toward them, with Gayle trailing behind. She met Reggie's gaze with a conspiratorial smile.

Frank caught Reggie's eye and winked.

Milton averted his eyes and strode to Reggie's desk. He pointed to her computer. "I sent you the pictures I took yesterday at the Grady place. Thought maybe you already had a chance to look them over, but...it appears you were...busy."

Reggie scrambled to her desk and sat down to boot up her computer. She knew a blush stained her cheeks, and she was afraid to make eye contact with anyone.

Frank chuckled. "Let's have a look now."

Doesn't anything ever bother him? No, Mr. Cool as a Cucumber wasn't in the least affected by our kiss...or having been caught. Reggie swallowed and clicked on the email from Milton. She opened the attachment, and a seemingly endless train of images spread across the monitor.

"Those look great, Milt." Frank leaned on her desk and pointed at the screen. "You really do have a great gift for composition."

Reggie saw Milton stand a little taller. She made a mental note that Frank had a way of giving compliments to people and making them feel good about themselves. She supposed that was the sign of a great leader. Perhaps she should take a lesson from him.

She stole a surreptitious glance at Frank, and there was nothing to show he had been wrapped in a passionate lip-lock with her a few moments before. It probably didn't mean anything to him. *He must have women hanging off him all the time.*

That thought troubled her. Any man that hot and successful must have an armload of gorgeous women vying for his attention. So why was he hanging around Rambling? Why was he looking at her like she was the blue plate special at the local diner? How could he kiss her, sending electric impulses all the way down to her toes, and then act like nothing happened?

Suddenly, Reggie felt like a complete idiot. *I'm not the sophisticated woman he's used to. I'm just a small-town girl. Don't be such a dope. Frank is just here for the short term. He'll probably move on and have no further use for me.*

Plagued by doubt, she stared at the computer monitor as Milton and Frank talked about each image, but she didn't see anything. Her brain was replaying every nuance of Frank's kisses. She wanted more but figured she should get her act together and concentrate on being the best small-town newspaper editor she possibly could be so she could impress her staff and the community of Rambling.

Frank listened to Milton prattle on and tried to concentrate on the pictures. He was leaning forward, his hands braced on the desk. He hoped nobody had noticed the huge erection he had grown while pressing the beautiful Reggie against his body, while exploring her soft mouth with his tongue. He hoped he was carrying off his casual façade.

He was acutely aware of the woman on the other side of the

desk. He could still taste her kisses. Still feel her arms around his neck. If anything, kissing Reggie Lee Stafford had knocked him on his ass. He'd never thought she would kiss him with such passion. He was expecting less...way less. Now, it was all he could do to stand across from her and act like he wasn't shaken to the core.

"Great job, Milton. I'm sure Reggie will be able to use a lot of these photos." He tried to think of something to take his mind off the seriously sexy woman, but she seemed to be pulsing her own vibrations at him...and they all said "take me."

Milton glanced at Reggie, one eyebrow raised. "So Reggie's calling the shots on this one?"

Frank straightened suddenly. "Reggie is the editor. This is her story. Of course she calls the shots." Remembering his condition, he sank into one of the chairs in front of Reggie's desk and crossed one leg over the other. *Yeah, just be cool.*

"But I thought..." Milton's head ricocheted between Frank and Reggie.

Frank leaned forward and risked a glance at Reggie. She looked like a tiger ready to pounce. *Oh, down, boy. Do not look at her mouth. Or her eyes. Just don't.* He changed positions uncomfortably and crossed the other leg on top.

Reggie tented her fingers in front of her and gazed at him intently, as though his response was vital.

Frank cleared his throat. "I'm just the guy who owns the building, and I have a vested interest in supporting the *Gazette*. Yes, I want this to be a successful enterprise, but Reggie Lee is the one who makes all the decisions. I'm here to support her."

This announcement was followed by a tangible silence, so thick it was difficult to draw a breath.

"I see," Milton finally said. "Good to know how things stack up around here."

"No change, as far as I can see," Frank said. "Just make your editor happy and I'll be happy." He gave a wave of his hand.

"My purpose is to honor the memory of my Aunt Rose and share images of her home with the community she loved."

Milton gave him a two-fingered salute, did an about-face, and marched out of the room.

Gayle flashed a quick smile. "Is there anything else you need?"

Reggie shook her head, and the receptionist fled.

Frank and Reggie stared at each other for a matter of minutes. When she gnawed on her lower lip, Frank wanted to climb across the desk to nibble it for her.

"Are you okay?" he asked finally.

She heaved a sigh, keeping her gaze studiously fastened on her hands. "I'm not sure. That was certainly awkward."

He smiled. "I'll try to remember to close the door the next time I kiss you."

She looked up suddenly, meeting his gaze. A blush crept up her cheeks. *Not unattractive.* One side of her mouth lifted in a sort-of smile. "You think there's going to be a next time?"

He grinned. "I'm pretty sure. That was about the best kiss I've ever been a party to. It would be a shame if we didn't try to improve it."

She giggled. "Oh, Frank. I don't know. You make me feel so—"

"Yeah, me too. I better leave before the gossip mill has a field day." He stood up and gave her another long look before heading for the door.

"Wait!" She hurried from behind the desk to cut him off.

He stopped and turned, sending her a questioning gaze.

"I—I just wanted to thank you...for the music box. It's the sweetest, most thoughtful present I've ever received. I truly love it."

He ached to take her in his arms again. To tell her she could have anything of his she took a fancy to, but he stood gazing down at her, tongue-tied.

"And...thank you for supporting me. You know, with Milton."

She looked so engaging, her big brown eyes shining like a kid at Christmastime.

It suddenly dawned on him that she didn't really want him to leave. He reached out to softly stroke the side of her face. He leaned forward and kissed her cheek. "You are killing me here. I'd better go before I get us both in more trouble."

She nodded, and he turned to leave. As he strode past the *Gazette* employees, none met his eye. They all seemed to be extraordinarily busy.

Gayle was torn. She had wanted to share her story about the day care center, but when she had gone to Reggie's office to present her project, she had discovered the boss making out with the hot guy who owned the building.

Gayle sighed. Not the best time to be offering her story. She was proud of her first effort and wanted Reggie to be open to it, but judging from the expression on her face, she was definitely not focused on anything else but the hot guy noshing on her.

"Hi, Gayle."

She looked up to see Paul standing on the other side of the front counter. He grinned at her and waved.

Carefully stowing the printed copy in her desk drawer, she stood and crossed to greet him. "Hi, Paul. What can I do for you today?"

He grinned but blushed at the same time. "I—I just need to run another ad."

"Oh, you didn't get your dog back?"

"Um, no. Not yet."

"I'm so sorry. You must be devastated that Violet is missing."

He looked confused for a moment and then nodded. "Yes, Violet. I miss her so much."

"Aww... I hope we can help you find her." She thought he

looked cute today. Perhaps a little less stiff and a bit more relaxed. "Do you want to run the same ad again or change it up?"

"Um, if you have any ideas that would make it better…"

So they spent a few minutes changing the wording around. She noticed that he smelled good, like he had slapped on some after-shave before coming over to the *Gazette*. He would have had to go home after school to apply it, or maybe he carried it in his car. She inhaled. *Something spicy…*

When he was satisfied, he paid for the ad and departed.

"Hope you find her," Gayle called after him.

She returned to her desk and pulled the day care center story out again, wishing the meeting going on in Reggie's office would end so she could present her story…and hoping it was acceptable.

Reggie rocked a little on her feet as Frank left. It felt as though he had taken all the air with him. Swallowing hard, she rushed to the window to watch him climb into the BMW and roll out of the parking lot.

She smiled, bit her lip, and then pressed both together to keep from shouting with glee. *Frank Bell really likes me. Or at least he wants me.* That thought sobered her. She wasn't sure she could handle Frank's desire.

"Pardon me, Ms. Stafford."

Reggie whirled around to find Gayle standing in the doorway. She seemed to be hesitant to enter. "Please come in."

Gayle crossed the room to stand a few feet away. She ducked her head. "I'm sorry if I'm interrupting something important." Clearing her throat uncertainly, she thrust a sheet of paper toward Reggie. "I—I just wanted to show you this."

"What's this?" Reggie quickly scanned the document. "Oh, an obit."

Gayle nodded furiously. "My second one."

Reggie read it carefully. "This is lovely. Very sensitive." She handed it back to Gayle. "I'm certain the family will appreciate your kind words."

"Really?" Tears spangled Gayle's lashes.

"It's perfect."

"Sorry to be such a mush." She dabbed at her eyes. "It's just that I've always wanted to be a writer. Thanks for giving me a chance. I—I had so much fun at the day care center. I'm just putting the finishing touches on that article."

"I appreciate your enthusiasm. Maybe you can go out to cover some other news stories. Maybe the school events. I know you would fit right in."

"Oh, you think so? I would really be happy to do that. Thank you. Thank you so very much."

Reggie didn't know how to tell her that she was thrilled to have someone express some interest in the job. "You're welcome. I'll see about getting you a raise. Anything else you're particularly interested in?"

Gayle heaved a deep sigh. "I'm just a little frustrated at the moment. I've been doing a little research on housing here in Rambling, and I realized there are no apartment buildings. No place for young people starting out. No place for those who don't want to buy a house...or even rent one."

Reggie gnawed her lower lip thoughtfully. "Hmm... I hadn't known that. What made you think about looking into the housing market?"

"A young couple, with a child... They came here to try and find an apartment, but I couldn't help them. When I suggested the trailer park, the woman went into hysterics." Gayle shook her head sadly. "There are some really nice house trailers, but she was just horrified by the prospect."

"I'm sure they'll find something." Reggie gave Gayle an encouraging smile. "I just want you to know that I appreciate you for taking on the new challenges. Writing the obituaries takes a load off of me...and writing the feature story on the day care is a giant step forward. I know I can count on you to give it your best."

Gayle seemed to be floating when she left the office, clasping the obituary in both hands.

It felt great to be able to make someone happy. Maybe this would occur more often when she got more comfortable in her own job.

Reggie exhaled and turned back to her desk. She couldn't remember what she had been doing before Frank came in, but it must have been important. Her gaze lit on the images on the monitor. *Oh, yes.* The Grady house project. She checked out her bulletin board pinnings and decided they looked great. At least they'd looked great to Frank.

She sat down, still feeling flushed from her encounter with Frank. How could one man be so incredibly delicious?

Back to business. She scrolled back to the first of Milton's photos and felt her stomach catch. There on her monitor was the image of a shirtless Frank, intent upon swinging his hammer. Her mouth felt dry. *Oh, my!* Scrolling down she saw that there were three photos of her hunky boss, each more delectable than the last. Slowly, she remembered how to breathe and hit save. *Can't take a chance on misplacing these...some of Milton's finest work.*

Reggie let out a little chortle and then printed all three pictures. Eye candy for a rainy day. As she stared at each image, her chest filled with a sense of longing that was almost painful. She exhaled slowly and, gathering the images, slid them into her top desk drawer. *I should file them under Lost Causes.*

Reaching for the music box, she pulled out the stem and let the tinkling strains of "Clair de Lune" take her to a place where she could be in Frank's arms again.

Reggie Lee managed to focus her attention on her remodeling project, checking and rechecking her design and the colors she had chosen. She stepped back, feeling pleased with herself. She thought Miss Rosie Bell Grady would be pleased as well.

Seating herself at her desk, she glanced at her email. A little smile gathered on her lips. *There he is*.

A new message from Mr. Nice Guy had just arrived in her inbox. She opened it eagerly, anxious to learn about his success with his coworker.

Dear Irene,

I want to thank you for your great advice concerning my relationship with my coworker. You will be happy to know that I followed your advice and she was receptive. At least we're friends now. I don't know what to do next. How can I let her know that I love her? How do I show her how I feel about her?

Mr. Nice Guy

Reggie stared at the computer screen. *He loves her*. She felt the sting of tears. *He loves her*.

If only Frank felt that way about her. Well, at least she might be able to help Mr. Nice Guy.

Dear Mr. Nice Guy, she began.

It's good that your coworker was receptive to your initial overtures. If you want this relationship to go forward, I suggest you become sensitive to her needs. Listen carefully to learn what she really wants. What are her goals and dreams? Then you can decide if you have a place in her life.

Sincerely,

Irene

She read it over one more time, imagining a shy clerk or insurance salesman totally in love with a colleague. She printed it out to publish in this week's issue. *How sweet is this?* She hoped they would find true happiness…and they would owe it all to *Dear Irene*.

Chapter 9

WHEN FRANK ARRIVED BACK AT HIS HOME, HE SAT IN HIS BMW for a few minutes, gazing at the charming Victorian. He had taken it for granted, not realizing that it had value to anyone other than him. Of course, the property had value as real estate, but it also had historical value and a special value to the Rambling community as the home of a beloved citizen.

He was amazed that Reggie Lee had jumped on his proposed project with such enthusiasm. It was going to be costly, for sure... but if this brought him closer to Reggie, it would be worth it.

Frank climbed out of his vehicle and stretched his arms wide. He strolled up onto the front porch and settled in one of the wicker rocking chairs. "Well, what do you think, Aunt Rosie?" He set the other rocker in motion, imagining her amused smile over his conundrum. "I wish you were here to tell me what to do."

The day was pleasant, and he could see a platoon of small yellow butterflies flying around Aunt Rosie's pink hibiscus. He noted that the grass needed to be cut and wondered if there was a mower somewhere in the shed but then realized his great-aunt must have had a lawn service due to her advanced years.

But he recalled his boyhood, when mowing the lawn had been one of his tasks. How he had relished Aunt Rosie's words of praise when he was finished. She'd always made him feel loved...appreciated...like a better person in her eyes.

Everyone needs to feel important to someone.

He realized he had been happy here in the Texas Hill Country.

Really happy. He wondered how his life might have turned out had Aunt Rosie not insisted he go to college and then encouraged him to pursue his law degree. Could he have been the one to marry Reggie Lee and make babies with her?

"No, she hated me."

But now, he was here and had a second chance with her. *Just don't screw this up.*

"What does she need?" He stared off into space, picturing her lovely face as he had last seen it…a little flushed and a little turned on. *Yeah, that's the way I want to keep you.*

She needs…approval. She needs challenges. She needs love and passion in her life… She needs me.

Frank sat up straight. "She needs me." He smiled, suddenly aware of what he should do. Reaching in his pocket, he took out his cell to call Reggie at the *Gazette.* When he asked to speak to Reggie Lee Stafford, he could hear the smile in the receptionist's voice.

"Why, certainly, Mr. Bell. Just one moment."

Busted!

"Hello, Frank." Reggie sounded slightly out of breath.

He grinned, unable to contain it. "Hi, Reggie. I—um, I thought maybe we could have lunch together tomorrow."

"Lunch?"

"Yeah, to discuss the remodel. Can you pencil me in?"

She laughed at that. "Sure. I can squeeze you into my busy schedule."

"Great. I'll pick you up at noon." He disconnected before she could ask any questions.

Henry Stafford took a longneck out of his cooler and flipped the cap off as his friend Sheriff Vern Garland pulled up in his 1969 Camaro, a totally cherry automobile if ever one rolled off the assembly line. "Hey, Vern!"

"Hey yourself, Henry. Good to see ya." The sheriff walked to where Henry was seated in a folding chair under an oak tree at the park. Several of the other area owners of classic cars were gathering to discuss their upcoming parade and car show.

Henry gestured to the folding chair he had brought for his friend. "Sit yourself down, Vern, and help yourself to a beer."

Vern rooted around in the cooler and removed a longneck for himself. "Thanks, Henry. I needed this." He flipped off the cap and then gathered it up and tucked it in his pocket. "My daughter, Jill, is trying to save the world by recycling everything, so she's got me trained."

"Good job. We recycle too." Henry clinked his bottle against the sheriff's.

The sheriff gave out a hearty laugh. "I guess our girls are gonna save the world together." They admired each other's rides and commented on the other cars as they pulled up.

"How are things at home?" Vern asked. "Jill tells me that your little girl got a big job promotion."

Henry leaned back, his chest filling with pride. "That's right. My Reggie Lee is the brand new editor of the *Rambling Gazette*."

The sheriff's brows drew together. "I bet that came as a surprise."

"Big surprise," Henry admitted. "If the old editor hadn't been such a crook, it never would have happened." He took a long drink of the beer, enjoying the cold froth rolling down his throat. He had gathered an assortment of good-quality beer from his store just for this occasion.

"So I heard, but the building owner wouldn't press charges." The sheriff wagged his head in wonderment. "I could have sent that buzzard to jail. But the boy who inherited the building just wanted to let him off the hook." He heaved a big huff of air and shook his head. "He said he didn't want anything to mar the newspaper because it was his great-aunt's pet project. She had given the *Gazette* free rent to make sure there was a newspaper for this community."

Henry considered this information. "I have to admire that. Miss Rosie was a sweetheart."

"Yeah, but I really wanted to prosecute the guy." Vern's mouth turned down into a scowl. "We don't get a lot of white-collar crime here in Rambling."

"Not that I can recall," Henry agreed pleasantly. He figured most of the lawbreakers Vern and his men apprehended were motorists speeding through Rambling. Or a few drunk and disorderlies at the local bars and the occasional domestic dispute. Other than those misdeeds, Rambling was a pretty quiet place... and he liked it like that.

"What did you think of the guy who inherited from Miss Rosie? How did he impress you?"

Vern considered this. "He seemed okay, for a city boy. You know, fancy suit, handmade shoes." He shook his head. "Totally different set of values."

"But he was raised right here," Henry insisted. "Miss Rosie brought him up. You think he's changed?"

Vern shrugged. "Aw, I really didn't know him as a boy. Miss Rosie was very proud of him though. He must have been pretty smart because he graduated from some important law school."

Henry finished off his beer and placed the empty in a bag. "There's Richard. That old Chrysler looks better. He's working on it."

"Hot damn!" Vern said. "This car show is gonna be a pip!"

True to his word, Frank arrived promptly at noon the next day. He strode to Reggie's office and tapped on the frame of her open door.

Reggie had been watching for him out the window but had managed to sit down at her desk and grab a couple of papers to pretend she was hard at work. She glanced up, trying to appear casual, but when she saw his expression, her breath caught in her throat. "Frank," she croaked out. "Right on time. Let me get my purse." She gathered the folder containing her ideas for the house update and her handbag.

He gazed at her fondly, seeming to devour her with his eyes. He extended his hand.

She longed to run to him but sucked in a deep breath to control herself. Rising sedately, she tucked her purse under her arm and walked to the door. It didn't appear as though he would move aside, standing in the doorway until she was right in front of him. She lifted her gaze to meet his and, for a moment, thought he was going to kiss her, but he stepped aside, gesturing for her to pass.

Head high, she ignored the surreptitious glances that followed their passing. *I'm going to lunch with this hot guy to discuss updating his house. That's all.*

Once outside, she drew a breath of fresh air and pressed her shoulders down from where they had climbed up to her ears...or so it seemed.

He opened the door to his BMW and handed her in. She pulled in her legs, noting with pleasure that Frank's eyes followed her movement with an admiring expression. She sighed and sank down into the leather seat.

"Buckle up," he said as he slid into the driver's seat and started the car. "I want to keep you safe."

His words caused her insides to tumble. *Keep me safe?*

He drove a couple of blocks and turned into the park near Babes in the Woods, Shannon's preschool. He made a wide turn and pulled into a parking space. "I hope you're hungry."

She chortled. "Hungry enough to eat a cow but not graze on grass."

"Not to worry." He popped the trunk and climbed out. "I chose some delicacies for your dining pleasure. Follow me, mademoiselle." He gathered a large basket from the trunk and opened her door.

He looked so pleased with himself, she had to laugh. Placing her hand in his, she allowed him to pull her from the low-slung car. She tucked her hand in the crook of his arm and walked beside him to a picnic table. It felt oddly companionable, as though they had done this before, but at the same time exciting.

"Your table, mademoiselle." He made a grand gesture, complete with a bow from the waist.

She slid onto the concrete bench, eyeing the large basket expectantly. "That looks extravagant."

"I wanted to spoil you." He flipped the top off the basket, removing a linen tablecloth which he spread out in front of her. He then removed a bottle of champagne wrapped in a linen napkin from the basket.

"Champagne in the middle of the day?" She flushed when he cocked his head to one side and grinned. *He must think I'm such a hick.*

"I think you deserve it." He set about peeling off the foil and popped the cork. A froth of liquid trailed over his hand, spilling onto the napkin. He poured a small amount into a slender crystal flute. "Just taste it."

So this is not a plastic-cup-and-paper-plate kind of picnic. She accepted the flute and took a sip. "Oh, my. That's wonderful."

He nodded, then filled her flute and one for himself. Raising his glass, he gave her a wink. "To you, Reggie, my very dear and talented friend. You've done so much to—to make my life better." He clinked his flute against hers and then sipped, his gaze locked on hers.

A shiver that must have registered on the Richter scale rippled through her body. She swallowed hard. "Thanks." Lifting her flute, she let the champagne roll down her throat.

"Slow down... Take it easy." He took the empty flute from her fingers. "Let me serve you some food."

She nodded, feeling a bit numb. The champagne created a warming sensation in her chest and bubbled up her throat. To her embarrassment, she let out a loud belch. "Oh, sorry." She felt her face flood with warmth.

"No big deal." He continued to remove items from the basket and place them in front of her. Opening a packet of round crackers, he spread them on a plate before reaching for a small glass jar with a shiny lid. He spilled some of the contents onto the plate. "This is Sevruga caviar. I hope you like it."

Reggie stared at the plate. Thin white crackers and grainy-looking black stuff. Her throat convulsed. "I've never tasted caviar before."

His grin went wall-to-wall. "Then you're in for a treat." He picked up one of the crackers and spooned a generous dab of black stuff onto it. "Try this."

She stared at the glop-covered cracker he extended to her. "Isn't this very expensive?"

"Oh, no. This is the cheaper one. Beluga is the most expensive."

Reggie opened her mouth reluctantly as Frank held his offering closer. The cracker was flaky, and the caviar was delicious. "Mmm... Why didn't I know about this before?"

He chortled and loaded another cracker with caviar. "Well, now you do."

"Why are you doing all this?" She waved her hands to include the champagne and caviar.

"Because I just realized it's about time someone spoiled you." He lifted the cracker to her lips, and she opened her mouth like a baby bird as he gently placed the cracker on her tongue. "I decided that someone would be me."

Reggie's heart did a tumble and roll in her chest. She almost choked on the food in her mouth. The idea that Frank wanted to spoil her was both pleasing and terrifying. How could he so easily slide into the role of "spoiler"? And why did he feel she was worthy of his pampering? He seemed to be sincere, but some tiny kernel of doubt flickered in the back of her brain. Some leftover mistrust of Franklinstein.

"Ready for the main course?"

She nodded, wondering if he planned to hand-feed her the rest of the meal.

———————

Just before the end of the day, Gayle was surprised when Paul Harmon entered the building, smiling shyly. He greeted her with a timid wave.

Somehow this really appealed to her. "Hi, Paul." She couldn't help but smile.

He leaned his forearms on the countertop, grinning at her. The silence stretched on.

"Um, is there something I can do for you?"

"I wanted to thank you for your kindness." He gazed at her, his eyes like liquid chocolate.

She grinned. "No thanks necessary. This is my job."

"Oh, well, I brought you a little present." He pushed a small wrapped package across the counter to her.

"I'm not sure I'm allowed to accept presents." She eyed the clumsily decorated item.

He swallowed hard. "It's nothing really. Just a little token."

She opened the package and found a small gold charm. It was a filigree heart. "This is lovely, but I can't accept it. It's way too much."

He shook his head. "No, really. I just wanted to show my appreciation for all that you've done…"

"Well, thank you for thinking of me, but this is really not…"

"Oh, uh…well, I haven't found my dog yet."

"Your dog? You mean Valerie?" She gazed at him, expecting him to correct her, but no…

"Yes, my dog Valerie."

Hmm…something isn't right here… "I thought you said her name was Violet." She gazed at him steadily. "What's going on here?"

He turned red from his hairline to his neck. "Um...I have to go now." With that, he turned and almost ran out the door.

Gayle stood at the counter, holding the lovely gold charm, her mouth slightly agape, and a million questions racing through her head.

That evening, after she had put Shannon to bed, Reggie sank into the recliner and put her feet up. It had been truly an unusual day.

Henry looked at her over the top of his glasses. "You seem to be very satisfied with yourself. Anything you need to tell your dear old dad?"

"Mmmmm," she muttered.

He released a loud and dramatic sigh. "C'mon. You know you want to share." He set his book on the side table, carefully spreading it open to the place he'd stopped reading.

"Okay, Dad...but please don't judge me."

"Agreed."

"Franklin Bell fed me caviar, champagne, lobster, and asparagus tips in the park today."

Henry dropped the footrest of the adjacent recliner and sat up straight. "He did what?"

A grin split her face. "As a matter of fact, he hand-fed me the caviar on these tiny white crackers, and it was divine."

Henry frowned. "How could he—I mean, caviar? Here in Rambling?"

"I know. I expected barbecued ribs or something similar."

"Seriously? Lobster?"

A bubble of laughter gurgled up Reggie's throat. "I know. There must have been drones making deliveries. The champagne was perfectly chilled, and the lobster was freshly steamed."

Henry shoved his glasses back up on his nose. "Is that all you wanted to tell me?"

"Oh, yes. Lemon butter. There was lemon butter for the lobster and asparagus." She closed her eyes in remembrance and made an appreciative noise in her throat. "Heavenly."

"And then what?" Henry's voice dropped a whole octave. "Did he make advances?"

"And then he took me back to the *Gazette* and dropped me off." She failed to mention the kisses. *Kisses in the park. Kisses in the car. Kisses.*

Henry pushed back in the recliner and reached for his book. "Not sure what to think of that young man...but I don't hate him."

———

Gayle glanced at the big clock on the wall. The afternoon had been dragging by. She thought she would go home, strip off her work clothes, and put on her shorts and a T-shirt. She had checked out a new book from the library and thought an evening curled up on the sofa would be the perfect way to wind down.

Tomorrow would be another day with new challenges, but this workday was crawling to an end.

She was surprised when the little bell at the customer desk dinged three times. Gayle pushed back from her desk, where she had been working on her obituary skills with a practice run about a local politician she particularly disliked. *Take that!* She made sure the porky politician had been caught dead in a compromising situation.

Gayle was pretty sure she was still wearing a smug expression when she reached the front desk, only to find Paul Harmon smiling at her.

"Oh! Hi, Paul." She leaned on the counter, feeling comfortable that her workday was almost over. Just this one last customer. "What can I do for you? I hope you found Violet."

His smile disappeared. "Um, no. I'm still looking for her."

"Aw, sorry about that. Have you gone to the animal shelter?"

"Um, no... I guess I should do that."

"Yes, of course. Poor Violet may be moldering away in a crate, wondering why you haven't come to bail her out."

"Oh, um...well, I'll do that tomorrow."

She smiled at him. "You do that, Paul. I hope you find her."

He sucked in a deep breath and blew it out. "I was hoping you might be willing to have a cup of coffee with me... I mean, if you don't have other plans."

"Other plans?" Gayle felt a crushing sensation in her chest. On the one hand, she was tired and wanted nothing more than to sink into a tub of warm, fragrant bubbles...but on the other hand, Paul's hopeful expression tugged at her heart. "Well, not exactly plans."

His expression morphed from anticipation to despair. "Oh, I understand. I should have known that you would be busy..." He shrugged and turned toward the door. "Maybe some other time."

"No, wait. I don't have plans." She expelled a sigh. "It's just been a tough week, and I was aching to go home and relax." To her dismay, tears sprang to her eyes. "I'm sorry... I just..."

"No, don't worry about it. I didn't mean to upset you." Paul had returned to the counter and stood gazing at her.

She was surprised when his hand reached out to squeeze hers. It was just a quick bit of contact, but it caused a tingling sensation. They clasped each other for a moment and then both stepped back. "Oh, I'm so sorry."

"No, I didn't mean to impose." He swallowed hard. "I—I guess I'll see you at church on Sunday."

"Yes! I'll see you on Sunday." *Oh, what the heck.* "How about that coffee after church?"

A wide grin spread across his face. "How about lunch after church?"

"Oh—" She scrambled for words. "Yes. I would love to have lunch with you on Sunday...after church."

They stood grinning at each other, but just then Milton

Mayweather, the *Gazette*'s photographer, pushed out of the little swinging door that separated the office from those on the other side of the counter. *Them and us*.

Milton gave a jaunty wave as he strode to the front door. "See ya tomorrow, kid. I'm outta here."

"Oh, yes. It's quitting time. I guess I better go home."

Paul gave a little salute of sorts. "I'll let you go home and rest...and I'll see you Sunday." He backed toward the door, ran into it, and turned to escape.

Gayle stood for a moment, smiling and wondering what had happened. She seemed to have a lunch date with Paul Harmon on Sunday.

───※───

The next day everyone on the *Gazette* staff seemed to be rejoicing that it was Friday. There was a "let me outta here" vibe in the air.

Reggie's phone rang, and she answered it, hoping it was not anything that would require serious brain cells because she, too, wanted to go home and relax.

"Mr. Bell on the line for you," Gayle sang out.

Reggie could hear the smile in her voice. "Yes, put him through."

"Hey," he said, his deep voice wrapping around her like a caress.

"Hey," she responded, a little breathlessly.

"Is Monday okay for you?"

A rush of unreasonable joy flooded her chest. Whatever it was he wanted to do on Monday was fine with her. "Monday is good."

"I thought we could go to the city to check out the decorator marketplace. Anything you think will work in the house I can have set aside for us."

Reggie's heart fluttered against her ribs. "That sounds great."

"Can you block out a couple of days?"

"Um…" She thought she might pass out right there. What was he asking her?

"I'll book you a room at the Plaza. It's a short ride to the Design Center."

"Okay, I'll just make arrangements with my dad." She said goodbye and sat clutching the receiver in both hands. The dial tone interrupted her reverie, and she hung up, her hand shaking a bit. "Oh, my! What have I done?"

―――

Gayle drove herself to church on Sunday, feeling a little antsy about having lunch with Paul Harmon. He seemed to be a really nice man, and everyone she knew seemed to hold him in high regard. It was obvious that he liked her, but she wasn't sure she was interested in being liked.

At the moment, she was finally getting to take a step forward in her career. Okay, it had been a job up until the time when Reggie Lee Stafford had been elevated to the position of editor in chief of the *Rambling Gazette*…and when Reggie had allowed Gayle to take on some writing assignments. The obituaries had been a start, but now she wanted to cover real stories in the community. *Moving forward…*

She found a parking spot and climbed out, clutching her purse, her Bible, and an envelope for the collection plate. She joined others headed for the church, exchanging greetings with those she met.

When she sprinted up the steps, she found Paul waiting for her by the door.

"Hi, Gayle. You look lovely today." He was dressed in a dark suit with a tie, making him look different than in his usually casual gear.

"Oh, thanks, Paul. Um, you look nice too."

A blush appeared on his face.

Nice. Not an egotistical man. She liked that. "You didn't have to wait for me out here."

He cleared his throat. "I was anxious to see you. Shall we go inside?" He gestured to the entry doors that were propped open.

She stepped forward, and he fell into step beside her. They found a place to sit, and she was pleased that he was greeted warmly by other churchgoers. It felt a little uncomfortable that they gave her a knowing smile as though acknowledging that she and Paul were a couple. She felt like shouting, 'We're just having lunch.'

After the service, Paul took her hand to lead her down the aisle.

No! Gayle pushed that thought out of her head. *We are not walking down the aisle together...* but they were.

The pastor was standing by the door, shaking hands with people as they departed. "Gayle." A broad grin split his face. "And Paul." His expression changed a bit, but he managed to salvage a smile as he gave Paul a hearty handshake.

They made their way down the steps, and Paul gestured toward the parking lot across the street. "If you would like to wait here, I'll get my car, and we can go to lunch."

"Um. Well, I brought my car, so why don't I follow you?"

His face fell a bit, but he recovered quickly. "Uh, well, sure. That's fine. Would you like to go to the Grey Moss Inn? I, uh, I made reservations."

The Grey Moss Inn was the most expensive place in the county. Points to Paul. It made no sense for her to follow Paul all the way out there and then drive back to Rambling.

"I guess it would be better if we took the same vehicle." She shrugged. "Will you follow me to my house and I can leave the car there?"

He looked relieved. "Sure. That's great. Are you ready?" Paul walked her to her car and then went to get his own. In a matter of minutes, he was following her to her house.

She glanced in the rearview mirror. Yes, he was still behind her…and he was grinning. That caused her to grin too, and she had no idea why.

Gayle had realized some time ago that Paul liked her…but he was definitely not her type. She wasn't sure what her type was, but Paul wasn't it. She was focused on her career as a journalist. Okay, that was stretching it a bit, but that was what she was hoping to become. She didn't have time for a boyfriend, no matter how sweet he might be.

When she pulled into her driveway and climbed out of her car, Paul parked behind her. He jumped out to open the passenger-side door for her.

A gentleman. A sweet man and a gentleman.

She smiled and slid onto the leather seat.

"Buckle up, beautiful." He closed her door and rounded the car to take a seat behind the wheel.

Gayle realized it had been some time since someone had thought she was beautiful…or cared whether she was buckled up. "Thanks."

"I hope you're hungry," he said.

"I could eat." She laughed. In fact, she was ravenous.

When they arrived at the Grey Moss Inn, they were seated in a cozy corner. Although it was bright daylight outside, the interior of the inn was dim and candlelit. *Very romantic.*

"This is really a lovely place, Paul."

"Just wait until you taste the steak. The grill master is inspired."

The waiter came and took their orders. Gayle chose a bacon-wrapped filet instead of the larger cut Paul recommended. "I'm not used to huge portions."

"That must be how you stay so slim and trim." He saluted her with his iced tea glass.

Oh, yes. He says all the right things to make a girl feel good… but…I'm not sure I want a boyfriend. Gayle adjusted the napkin in her lap and then raised her eyes to regard the man sitting across the small table from her. *Not a bad man at all.*

After their meal, they took a short walk around the grounds of the inn. It was quite beautifully landscaped and well kept. As they stepped outside, Paul took her hand, and it felt good.

"Paul, this has been a very nice day. Thank you for making such nice plans."

"I've wanted to spend some time with you." He shrugged. "I'm glad you said yes."

"Me too."

He tilted his head to one side, looking extremely pleased and boyish. "I don't suppose you would consider giving me an encore next Sunday?"

Gayle sucked in a breath. This took her by surprise. She felt a blush creeping up her cheeks. "I suppose that would be a good thing... I mean, this has been such a nice...uh..." She was reluctant to call it a date, but now Paul looked confused.

She cleared her throat. "What I mean is, yes. I would be delighted to have lunch with you next Sunday."

When Monday rolled around, Reggie was all ready. She wasn't sure what to take, so she had packed for every possible scenario.

She had never been to the Design Center in Dallas, but she had read about it and was itching to prowl the multitude of upscale shops grouped together for the convenience of A-list designers to the Texas rich and famous. There were specialty stores vending literally everything from furniture for your penthouse to décor for your bunkhouse. A whole 'nother kind of life for Reggie, but not for Franklin Bell.

She was surprised her father was so complacent about her going out of town with a strange man, especially one with whom she had shared such a long-standing animosity. But her father had agreed without asking any questions. This in itself was remarkable. She wondered what he was thinking but didn't want to jinx it.

Frank had said he would pick her up at the house mid-morning on Monday. Her father had gone to his store and had taken Shannon to Miss Jill's on the way.

Now, Reggie was pacing. She kept glancing out the window, but when she saw Frank pull into the driveway, she was having grave misgivings. He jumped out and dashed up to the door, but she opened it before he had a chance to ring the bell.

He stepped inside, and for a moment, they grinned at each other without speaking. "Ready?" he asked and then looked around at her bags. "I don't think you're going to need all this."

She felt her color rise. "I—I didn't know what to pack."

He pointed to the small bag she had packed her toiletries and essentials in and picked it up. "This will be enough."

"What? But—"

"Relax," he said with a grin. "I plan to treat you to something new."

Reggie's mouth opened, but no words came out.

"Come on. This is going to be fun." He opened the front door and gestured for her to walk through.

"Um, okay." She forced a confident smile and followed his direction.

"I put the top up so you don't blow away." He opened the passenger door for her and then stowed her bag in the trunk.

The sound of the lid closing made Reggie Lee start. Her stomach was doing flip-flops. *I'm really doing this.* She fumbled with her seat belt as Frank climbed in and started the motor.

Once on the road, he headed out of town. He took the interstate toward Austin.

Reggie's heart sank. She had thought they were going to Dallas, to the big Design Center there.

Frank kept up a conversation, asking her opinion about various things. Nothing complicated, but enough to keep her entertained.

She was surprised when he turned off the highway and drove to a small airstrip outside Austin. "Uh, what are we doing here?"

"We're going to fly. You didn't think we would drive, did you?"

It was only a few hours' drive to Dallas. Half a day at the most. Reggie looked out the window at the small planes lined up in rows. "In one of those?" Her stomach did a flip-flop.

Frank snorted indelicately. "Of course not." He pulled up in front of a hanger and got out. He opened her door and held out a hand.

Reggie put her hand in his uncertainly but let him draw her from the vehicle.

A man rushed out of the hanger and greeted him. "Hello, Mr. Bell. We're all ready for you." He gestured to a plane sitting on the tarmac. It wasn't as small as the ones they had passed, but still...

"Good work, Earl."

Reggie sucked in a breath and let it out all at once. This was going to be an experience. She wasn't a seasoned traveler, only having flown a couple of times, and those trips had been in large commercial aircraft.

But Frank was chatting with the man and seemed to be taking things in his stride. Mr. Cool, Calm, and Collected went about making sure their luggage had been taken aboard. "Ready?" he asked.

Her stomach tightened. "Ready as I'll ever be."

"That's my girl!"

Am I? Am I really your girl?

He assisted her up the steps, and the ever-helpful Earl folded the steps up behind them.

Once in the cabin, she experienced a smothering sensation. She tried taking long, slow breaths, which was good since she didn't pass out.

"Now, where do you want to sit?" he asked.

"Wherever you're sitting." *Somewhere where I can cling to you and hide my eyes on your shoulder.*

"Really? Well, let's get settled then." He led the way to the cockpit and gestured her into the copilot's seat.

The contents of her last meal rose up in her throat. "You—you're driving?"

He chuckled. "Not exactly. I'm flying. Don't worry. I have a perfectly good pilot's license, and I promise to get you back here safe and sound."

"Mmmmpf." Cautiously, she edged into the seat, reconsidering her choice of seats. Did she really want to be sitting right up front with the wraparound window in her face?

Frank slipped into the pilot's seat and set about making arrangements to take off. He flipped switches and checked gauges.

She grudgingly admitted that he appeared to be capable and competent. He seemed to be at ease in anything he did. Surely he wouldn't take off without being adequately prepared.

"You've flown a lot?" she asked.

He turned to give her a reassuring smile. "Don't worry, Reggie. I've logged a lot of hours in the air."

"Okay. I'm just going to close my eyes until we get there." She squinched her eyes together.

Frank reached over and squeezed her hand. "You're going to be fine. Don't worry."

She opened her eyes, gazing at him earnestly. "I'm not worried. I'm way beyond that."

He lifted her hand to his lips and pressed a kiss against it. "I promise I will take care of you. I—" He broke off suddenly and placed her hand back on the armrest.

Reggie sucked in a breath and immediately curled her fingers around the armrests. She closed her eyes again. "Poke me when we get there."

~~~

Frank was stunned. He had almost blurted out the words "I love you," and he had never said those words before. He filled his lungs with air and let it out slowly. What was it about this woman? Why did she make him want to totally change who he was?

He shook his head and started the twin engines, taking satisfaction in the whine. This was something he could control. He taxied out onto the runway and prepared to take off.

What he could not control were his feelings for the woman beside him.

For some reason, when in her company, he became someone else. Someone who wanted to say the words "I love you." Who wanted to say the words "I'll be by your side forever."

In a few minutes, they were airborne. Reggie made a small mewl when they lifted off the tarmac and kept her eyes closed tight as they ascended, her fingers turning white where she gripped the armrests.

He wanted to comfort her, but he couldn't speak. He was too confused. Franklin Bell was a man of the world. He had beautiful girlfriends all over the globe. He was worth millions. He could buy and sell anything. He was a man who could make things happen.

He glanced at Reggie.

At the moment, all he wanted to do was figure out how to make her fall in love with him...*because I love you.*

Chapter 10

MONDAY AFTERNOON, HENRY STAFFORD WAS SITTING AT A concrete picnic table situated under a metal roof at Rambling Park. It was located near the dam and overlooking Rambling Lake. It was a beautiful day. The sun was shining, and several puffy white cumulus clouds dotted the sky. He had hired a competent young man to mind the store while he granted himself a little down time.

He sat with his legs outside the table and his back against the concrete tabletop. A fresh breeze kissed his skin. He took a deep breath, filling his lungs and holding it before blowing it out forcefully.

He had picked up his beloved granddaughter, Shannon, at Babes in the Woods Day Care, and she was sitting on the table with her feet firmly planted on the concrete plank her grandfather was seated upon. They were watching Vern Garland touching up his classic car, a red 1969 Camaro.

The sheriff was applying a coat of clear wax to his classic car. He opened the cover on the gas tank and lovingly wiped out that cavity until it was so clean and shiny you could eat off it. The chrome gleamed in the sunlight.

Henry grinned at his old pal. "Tell me how you decided that your car was a male."

"Are you kidding me? Just look at the balls on this thing." Vern snorted. "Have you heard him roar? When I start him up, ol' Brutus wakes up ready for battle."

Henry rolled his eyes. "You're killing me."

Vern turned to him, fisting his hands at his waist. "Well, how did Priscilla let you know she was a girl? I mean, she is sweet and dainty and all, but..."

"Aw, my Priscilla is a bad, bad girl. I had her up to 140 miles per hour, but don't tell that sheriff guy. He's such a pain in the ass."

"Hah! There better not be anyone speeding in my county. Bad girls or not."

"Well, it was a long time ago, but this pretty girl can still take off like a red-hot firecracker."

Vern returned to his task, shaking his head and laughing.

Henry had his arm around his granddaughter. "Shannon, did you know your uncle Vern was a bit daffy?"

"Nuh-uh." She shook her head, her blonde curls bouncing.

"That sure is one cute little girl," Vern said. "Now don't you go filling her head with a bunch of nonsense. She's gonna grow up knowing all about classic cars." He gave the passenger-side door a last swipe before going to sit at the picnic table with his friend. "What kind of fancy beer you got in your cooler, Henry?"

"You'll just have to dig around and find out for yourself." Henry always kept the big reach-in coolers at Stafford's Mercantile stocked with interesting and little-known brands of beer. The locals loved to prowl through his stock, and tourists were always surprised to find such a wide variety of pretty posh brands of beer in a small town.

Henry grinned as Vern knelt down to examine the contents of the ice-filled cooler.

The friends were the mainstay of the Rambling Cruisers Classic Car Club. They gathered every week at a spacious parking lot by the dam. The site was lovely, overlooking the lake surrounded by hills, many adorned with luxury houses. There were paths to hike through the oak and pine trees down to the lake. There was also a wide concrete walkway spanning the dam where many locals would take a walk, which was about a 2.4-mile round trip. With so many of the communities around the lake without sidewalks, the dam provided a safe place for people to take a healthy stroll.

Usually, it was Henry's daughter, Reggie Lee, who minded the store while Henry mingled with his tribe of classic car buffs. But now that she had assumed the duties of editor of the *Rambling Gazette*, he couldn't continue to depend on her when she had so much on her plate. He had hired two part-time employees to help him tend the store and allow him to also spend time with his granddaughter. She needed a good male role model, and Henry had stepped up to the plate.

Vern's gaze narrowed, and he gestured toward the wide parking area. "Now, what do you suppose that is?"

Henry was punching a hole in Shannon's juice pack with the tiny straw. His hands seemed to be way too big to accomplish this simple task. "Here you go, baby." He made sure she was able to suck the contents and turned to look at his friend. "What is it that you need my expertise for?"

"Right there in front of us. What is that little black number that just pulled into the parking area? Are you blind, man?" Vern seemed to have his gaze fastened on a car that was just rolling into a parking spot.

"Wow!" Henry stood and took a step forward before remembering that his granddaughter was sitting on concrete and stepping back to reach out a hand to keep her seated.

He stared at an iconic vehicle from the '70s. "See that curved windshield? That's a Super Beetle. I haven't seen it around here before. Wonder who owns it?"

"Dunno," Vern said. "Maybe he's gonna get out and be sociable."

The two men stared at the vehicle for a full five minutes, but it seemed that whoever was inside preferred to stay inside.

Vern shrugged and went back to polishing his Camaro, but Henry had to take his granddaughter to the bathroom.

"Come on, Vern. I need you to guard the door." Henry refused to take Shannon to the men's public restroom because it was generally extremely nasty but insisted his friend the sheriff stand guard outside the ladies' facilities.

Once inside, Henry meticulously placed two layers of seat covers on the toilet and lifted Shannon into place. While she was making her deposit, he mused that he would have never thought himself capable of providing this service for his only daughter's daughter.

When Reggie Lee had been growing up, she was fortunate enough to have a wonderful mother who did not work outside the home, so she had received a lot of individual attention. Now, he hoped his granddaughter would never recall her grandfather taking her to the women's restroom. He heaved a sigh and washed his and Shannon's hands.

When they exited the facility, he found his pal Vern chatting with two women. They looked him over very thoroughly.

"Here he is." Vern gestured to him. "I explained to these two lovely ladies that my best friend had finally found himself and was in the process of becoming the woman he had always wanted to be." Vern was grinning from ear to ear.

Henry heaved a huge sigh, glaring at Vern.

Vern was not the least bit affected. "Ladies, this is my friend Henry and his granddaughter, Shannon. I think he's secure enough in his masculinity to take his little angel to the potty."

Both ladies giggled. They were probably in their fifties and what Henry would consider high-dollar ladies. They both had immaculately manicured fingers, and their toes were painted in the same color. One of the ladies had improbably red hair, and the other's was jet-black. It appeared that both women wore fake eyelashes, and their makeup had been freshly applied.

"What a pretty little girl," the black-haired woman cooed. "What's your name, honey?"

Shannon stared at her, open-mouthed. She ducked her head and turned her face to her grandfather's leg.

There was an embarrassing silence.

Henry pulled her closer. "We don't encourage our kids to talk to strangers." He knew he was being somewhat rude, but he was not impressed by the women, who seemed to be mostly fake.

"Oh, well… I didn't mean anything by it." The black-haired woman blinked several times, having the effect of a butterfly flapping its wings.

"Lolly was just being pleasant," the one with red hair said. "We're from Houston, and we were interested in the classic car show."

Vern grinned. "Well, ain't that sweet? Henry, these lovely ladies are here for the car show." He turned to Henry and gave him a look that clearly said *Don't be a dick*.

Henry felt his back teeth grit together. "Yes, it's nice that you ladies are here."

The one named Lolly flashed a wide smile. "My friend Sandy drove us here in her Volkswagen. She's had it since 1971." She tilted her head to one side, gazing up at Henry in a manner she must have thought was appealing. "That makes it a classic, doesn't it?"

For his part, Henry was staring at the false eyelashes, trying to imagine how it must feel to have something that heavy on one's eyes. "Um, sure."

Vern was not so put off. "Well, of course it does. Tell me, Sandy, are you the original owner?"

Both men were horrified when Sandy burst into tears.

Lolly grabbed her in a comforting embrace and proceeded to give her thumps on the back, all the while assuring her that it was okay.

Vern looked concerned. "I'm sorry, ladies. Was it something I said?"

Sandy shook her head vehemently. "No-o-o-o! I shouldn't have come here." She dashed into the ladies' restroom, tears streaming down her cheeks.

Reggie was still in a daze. She couldn't believe she was actually in New York City. She had told her dad she was going to Dallas. That's what she had assumed. She could hear her dad's voice in her head telling her that's what she got for assuming.

She should have figured Frank would take her to his home turf...his center of power. *New York City... The Big Apple...*

Frank stowed her one bag in the trunk of the Lexus he'd rented. He kept up a running commentary on the way to the hotel. Once there, he got her registered and settled in.

Reggie crossed to the windows and gazed out at the tall buildings. "I never dreamed in a million years that I would ever be here." *And certainly not in a luxurious suite like this.*

"Well, you're here now." Frank had come to stand behind her. His voice was deep and seemed to embrace her, although he hadn't touched her since the kiss episode when he'd safely touched down at the airport.

She could feel heat radiating from him, or it could have been her imagination. Maybe it was that she wanted him to touch her... to kiss her again.

"I'll let you rest and get settled."

Reggie turned to face him. "What? You're leaving me here?"

He smiled. "My condo is nearby. I'll pick you up for dinner at seven. Wear something pretty." He gave her a wink.

She let out an exasperated gasp. "You made me leave my clothes in Texas. What am I supposed to wear?"

"There are several boutiques here in the hotel. Select whatever you like and charge it to the room...or you can check out any number of stores nearby." He held up a platinum card and then dropped it in her open hand. "Surprise me."

Reggie stared at the card and then glanced back up at Frank.

He was grinning broadly.

"Well, you better believe I'm going to spend you into the poorhouse, mister."

Frank laughed at that. "Just you go for it. I'll see you at seven." As he opened the door, a bellman stood outside with a rolling cart covered with white linen. "Room service for the lady." Frank handed the man some bills. "Take good care of her." He glanced back at Reggie and slipped past the bellman.

"Yes, sir," the bellman said enthusiastically as he pushed the cart into the room. He set up the covered dishes on a table and asked her if there was anything else, to which she shook her head. When he left, she locked the door behind him. Leaning against it, she heaved a huge sigh. *What was I thinking agreeing to all this? I'm in Frank's world.*

She straightened and crossed the room to inspect whatever was under the shiny silver dome. As though on cue, her stomach growled. "All right, I'm feeding you." She seated herself and reached for the napkin. Her feast consisted of a platter lined with lettuce on which shrimp salad, chicken salad, and a fresh fruit salad were artfully displayed. A basket held cloverleaf rolls nestled under a napkin. *Nice. Very nice.*

After her meal, she called her father to explain that she was not in Dallas.

"New York City!" Henry exploded. "What does that young fellow think he's doing, kidnapping you like that?"

"It was my fault, sort of. When he said the design center, I thought he was talking about Dallas, but he lives here in New York City, so of course this was what he was referring to."

Henry snorted. "Sounds like some hanky-panky going on."

"Nothing of the sort," Reggie explained. "He put me up at a very ritzy hotel, and he went to his condominium."

Her father grunted, making it sound as though his suspicions had not been allayed.

"How is Shannon doing? Does she miss me?" She envisioned her daughter being tearful.

"Aw, she's right here with me and Vern. We're at the park."

"Sounds like you're having a good time." Reggie sucked in a deep breath and let it out slowly. Everything was going well at home. She was a grown woman on a trip with a grown man...who had flown her to a posh hotel quite a few states away from Texas... and she was trying to be ready for whatever else he had in mind.

Reggie hung up after promising to be careful. *Yeah, right.* She picked up Frank's credit card and her handbag and headed out the door, determined to make him regret leaving her bags behind.

—∞—

Henry slipped his phone back in his pocket. The fact that his daughter had taken off with the grown-up boy who had made her miserable when they were in high school was a little worrisome, but his task was to care for Shannon and not interfere with his daughter's career. He was confident that she could handle the young man... Well, mostly confident.

He was horrified that one of the Houston ladies had burst into tears and run inside the women's restroom at the park.

Vern was trying to placate the remaining woman. "Sorry. I was just wondering about the car."

Lolly spread her hands and shrugged. "I'm sorry too. The Super Beetle was her husband's plaything. He was the original owner, but he passed a few months ago." She took a couple of steps to follow her friend. "Sandy's just been a wreck. I thought it would be good for her to get out a little." Her false eyelashes flapped as though she was in distress as well.

Maybe some sort of semaphore code, to Henry's way of thinking. Was she signaling an SOS?

Lolly flapped her hands and made a sound between a grunt and a squeal before entering the public ladies' restroom.

Henry and Vern gazed at each other in surprise bordering on shock.

"What do you suppose all that was about?" Vern asked.

"Beats me, but it's not our problem...unless you want to make it an official problem, Sheriff." Henry took a couple of steps away, intending to return to his cooler and bag of snacks. "C'mon, baby." He held out his hand to Shannon.

"Dat lady is cwying," she pointed out.

Henry hefted her back onto the concrete picnic table, her feet on one of the seats. "I guess she was feeling sad." He gave her a wink. "But we're not sad, are we? Not when we have PB and J sandwiches just waiting to be eaten. Are you ready for our picnic lunch?"

She nodded enthusiastically.

Henry took a hard plastic container out of the cooler and arranged a dishtowel on the table surface beside her. He laid out a paper plate and unwrapped a half sandwich for his granddaughter. He added some Goldfish crackers and ripped the lid off a small cup of applesauce. "Here you go, sweetheart. Eat up."

"I want Spwite," she insisted.

Henry gave her a half smile. "How about one of these yogurt drinks? I have strawberry, and I have orange. Which would you prefer?"

She looked a little pouty but nodded. "Stwawbaby."

"Coming right up." He opened the yogurt drink, congratulating himself for recalling that it worked better to give a child a choice than to argue them down about the thing they really wanted. He had learned this the hard way after spending many long hours arguing with a very stubborn young lady named Reggie Lee.

He looked up to see Vern chatting with the two women again. Apparently, they had finished whatever they were doing in the ladies' room, and the redhead was mopping at her eyes with a copious amount of toilet paper. It appeared she had cried off the false eyelashes.

Sandy wasn't a bad-looking woman. Other than the neon-red hair, she was quite attractive.

Vern was escorting both women toward the picnic table where Henry was supervising his granddaughter's lunch.

"Now we need to check out the Super Beetle and see if it has authentic Volkswagen parts."

Lolly nodded. "Yes, Sandy's husband babied this car like a firstborn child."

Sandy's lower lip trembled, and Henry thought she would dissolve into tears again. But she gave a little giggle and wiped her eyes some more.

"He sure did," Sandy said. "I think he spent as much time in the garage with Betty Lou as he did with me."

"Betty Lou?" Vern asked.

"That's what he named her. Betty Lou... Silly, I know."

The trio had arrived in front of Henry.

Shannon was alternately taking a bite of her sandwich and stuffing Goldfish into her mouth.

"I thought these lovely ladies might be deserving of a tour of your cooler, my friend." Vern looked at Henry expectantly.

"Of course," Henry said, gesturing to the cooler. "My cooler is your cooler. Help yourselves, ladies."

He watched as Vern made an extravagant bow and opened the cooler.

"Oh, my!" Lolly leaned over to pull a Stella Artois from the cooler. "I love this beer." She looked around. "Is there an opener?"

Vern laughed. "Real men don't need no stinkin' beer openers." He flipped the cap off with his fingers.

Lolly was delighted, giving him a wide grin. "Oh, Vern. That was so cool."

Sandy poked around in the cooler, finally selecting a Corona. "Mexican beer." She heaved a loud sigh. "George took me to Acapulco for our honeymoon, and we drank Mexican beer with lime." She handed it to Vern and asked him to open it for her.

Vern then seated the women on the opposite side of the concrete picnic table from Henry and Shannon, who was still systematically eating her sandwich and the Goldfish and drinking her yogurt drink.

Lolly smiled at Henry. "Are you into classic cars too?"

Henry took a slow and serious drink of his beer, letting the cold liquid roll down his throat. "Yes, ma'am. I am into my 1969 Pontiac GTO. If you cast your eyes right over there, you will see the badass Priscilla, my pride and joy after my daughter and granddaughter." He pointed to the blue-metal-flake vehicle gleaming in the sunshine.

Lolly tilted her head to one side. "She's a beauty." She took a sip of her beer. "I couldn't help but notice that you didn't mention a wife, Henry. Are you single?"

To his extreme embarrassment, Henry blushed. "I most certainly am not... My wife passed away some years ago. I was married for twenty years, and now I am a widower." He finished off his beer and went to fetch another from his cooler. He stood for a moment, gazing with pride at Priscilla, and then realized he had better get back in case Shannon decided to take a header off the picnic table.

"Hey, Mr. Stafford." Jill Garland greeted her best friend's father when he opened the door to his home. It had surprised her when he'd called and asked her to come over. He'd said it was an emergency.

There was a certain grim set to his jaw that caused her some alarm. She had expected him to ask her to stay with Shannon so he could work at the store, which she was willing to do.

When Reggie Lee had shared that she was leaving town with the notorious Frank Bell, she had been excited that her friend was taking a walk on the wild side...but Reggie had assured her it was just a business trip. She'd said she was going to help her hot boss refurbish the Grady place.

Jill hoped there was something more going on. Her friend needed a break.

Henry Stafford held the screen door open and motioned for Jill to step inside.

She sensed that he needed to unload something that had caused his jaw to be set that tight. She followed him as he went back to the kitchen. "You and my dad were playing with your cars at the park, weren't you? Was Shannon a good girl for you today?"

"Perfect." He snorted and set a cooler on the floor in the kitchen. "My granddaughter is always perfect."

"Okay." She saw that Shannon was following him like a puppy. "Then did my dad get under your skin bragging about his car?"

"No!" He huffed out a sigh and began unloading bottles of beer into the bottom of the refrigerator. "Why do you ask me something like that?"

Yes, he was frowning.

"Well, you're all swelled up like a toad, and you're snapping at me." She managed a frown of her own. "What's going on?"

"Sorry. I'm really sorry." He made a sort of growling sound. "I swear...when Vern runs for reelection, I will vote for his opponent...no matter who it is."

"Now, Mr. Stafford. My daddy is your best friend. You two have been best buds since boyhood. What could possibly have ticked you off at Vern?"

Henry's face had taken on a quite florid tone. "My friend Vern—" He stopped abruptly and heaved a huge sigh. A muscle in his cheek twitched. "There were these two women in the park. They came from Houston..."

Jill noted that he appeared about ready to explode. "Breathe, Mr. Stafford. I don't want to have to call 911. And Reggie won't understand if I let you stroke out."

"That might get me out of this fiasco tonight."

"Tonight?"

"Those two women... Vern offered to take them to the VFW tonight...and he volunteered me!"

Jill's brows drew together. "So, you're saying you have a double date with my dad and two women from Houston...and you're taking them to the VFW?"

"That's what I said, isn't it?"

Jill had to chuckle at his apparent discomfort. "What's the problem, Mr. Stafford? I'm here to sit with Shannon. Auntie Jill will make sure she has a good time. You spring for a burger at the VFW and maybe dance a little. It will be good for you. You need to get out a little more."

Henry snorted. "I get out plenty."

"Yes, but it's all about you and my dad and the classic cars. It won't hurt you to spend some time with nice ladies... Wait! These are nice ladies, aren't they?"

"Oh, I guess they're nice. Just kind of fluffy... Not my kind of women."

Jill leaned back against the counter and crossed her arms over her chest. "Please tell me what is your kind of woman."

"You know... Natural. Not with all that stuff on 'em."

"Stuff?"

"These two looked like everything was fake. Fake eyelashes. Fake fingernails. Fake hair color. It made me wonder what they were trying to hide."

"Aww, Mr. Stafford. They probably just wanted to feel pretty for you."

Henry leaned back against the opposite counter and echoed her stance, crossing his beefy arms over his broad chest. He exhaled heavily. "Well...you know...Reggie Lee's mother was just so beautiful without a speck of makeup... And she never colored her hair, even when she got some white threaded in among the blonde."

"She was a wonderful person. She had a snack ready for Reggie and me every day after school. She was like a second mom to me."

He looked so sad that Jill had to cross the room to hug him.

"Aw, Mr. Stafford. I know how much you loved your wife... but she's gone... She's been gone for some time now."

He hugged her fiercely. "I know...and I miss her every day." His voice went to a higher octave, and he sniffled against her shoulder. She held him tight as they both lost themselves in memories of the woman neither could forget.

―∾∾∾―

Frank rode up in the hotel elevator a few minutes before seven. He had checked the mail at his condo and generally kicked back. He didn't want to crowd Reggie Lee. He sensed she was nervous and somewhat overwhelmed. Catching sight of himself in a big gilded mirror above a table near the elevator, he straightened his tie. Surprised that he was nervous, he raked his fingers through his hair before striding to the designated room.

He knocked on the door, and Reggie answered it immediately.

She was attired in a short black sleeveless sheath with a layer of lace over the top. The black lace against her fair skin made him want to throw her on the bed, or at least reach out and touch her...a lot.

"Don't you look gorgeous!" He stepped into the room. "I mean, you always look gorgeous, but tonight you look even better."

She dimpled at him, her big brown eyes shining. Then she did a pirouette, allowing him to get a good look. "What do you think? Did I spend your money well?" She had twisted her hair up with little tendrils curling down around her face and neck.

Frank grinned. "I would say you made a very wise investment. You've never looked lovelier than you do at this moment."

Reggie flashed her trademark dimpled grin. "I'm glad you approve." She reached for a small black bag that couldn't have held more than a lipstick and the room access card.

"Are you hungry?" he asked.

"Not famished. That room tray you had sent up was most satisfying."

Without thinking, he reached out to touch the side of her face. He felt himself drawn into her gaze. Entrapped in the depths of her warm brown eyes. He leaned down to brush his lips across hers.

She closed her eyes and leaned toward him, her lips soft and yielding.

His gentle kiss led to another, not so gentle, and another after that. Pulling away, he gazed down at her. "You seem to be my drug of choice. I can't get enough of you."

Reggie looked really happy. In fact, her face was glowing with happiness. Frank imagined this was the way he looked too because he couldn't remember feeling this elated. He cleared his throat. "We'd better go. I have reservations at the Carillon."

Reggie nodded, and a slight tremor shook her body.

"Are you cold?" he asked.

She shook her head. "Just excited. I know this is everyday stuff for you, but this is all a big deal to me."

If only you knew. "Let's go, then." He took her arm and gestured to the door.

Downstairs, he helped her into a waiting taxi.

"I thought you had a rental car," she said, settling into the seat.

He slid in beside her. "I do, but it's easier to use a cab to get around the city. No parking to deal with." He pressed a kiss against her temple. "This way I can look at you instead of traffic."

She smiled up at him. "That was sweet, Frank. You're showing me a whole different side of you."

"I'm the same guy. Maybe I just grew up in the years I was away." He slipped an arm around her, marveling at how content he felt.

Complete.

He felt as though he had become a part of a very important whole. Something that had been missing in his loner life.

The cab wove through and around traffic. Reggie was acutely aware of the man beside her. The handsome, urbane man with his arm snugged around her shoulders.

She tried to keep from grinning...couldn't.

Her insides were light as a feather. She had almost forgotten how to feel this carefree...to let someone else take charge.

Just for tonight, she wasn't responsible for anything or anyone.

The taxi stopped, and Frank handed the driver some cash. He stepped out and leaned in to offer his hand to Reggie.

As she got out, her already-short dress slid up to reveal more of her thighs.

Frank's gaze fixed on her thigh-high hosiery, and she had the distinct impression he was trying hard to appear unaffected.

She stood and smoothed her skirt down, meeting Frank's gaze without flinching. *Deal with it!*

He grinned openly. "You're killing me here."

Inside the very upscale restaurant, the hostess showed them to an intimate table. No booths or plastic seating. Each chair was upholstered in a rich wine-colored fabric. A candle was lit and offered a very close and private feeling.

Reggie was aware that she turned a few heads as she passed. Maybe the little black dress was working its magic. She recalled the smoldering look on Frank's face when it slipped up to reveal even more thigh.

Maybe they're staring at Frank. He looks unbearably hot tonight.

When they were seated, a waiter came to greet them. "Good evening, Mr. Bell." He nodded at Reggie and handed Frank a wine list, hovering nearby until Frank had made his selection.

Reggie let Frank order for her, and they started off with a selection of seafood appetizers. He explained the difference between oysters Rockefeller and oysters Lafitte. Both were delicious, but she liked the tiny crab cakes best.

Their main course was a perfectly seared steak with all the trimmings. Frank ordered different wine to go with each course. She marveled that he had gained such worldly acumen.

"Hello, Frank."

Reggie was startled to see an incredibly beautiful redhead standing by the table. She wore a low-cut dress with a skirt so short Reggie hoped she didn't bend over. The woman was glaring at Frank through narrowed eyes.

"Hello, Gina." Frank stood, his expression grim.

"I didn't know you were in town," Gina said, accusation rife in her tone.

"We just arrived today." He gestured to Reggie.

Gina's lips tightened as she swept Reggie with a venomous glance. "Oh, I see." She half turned and then rocked back on one hip. "Call me." She stalked away, her long legs carrying her across the restaurant.

Frank reclaimed his seat. "Well, that was awkward."

Determined to appear calm, Reggie shrugged. "I'm sorry if I caused a problem with your girlfriend." Her hand shook when she reached for the wine glass.

"Not my girlfriend. Just a girl I've dated in the past."

She met his gaze, not sure what to make of that statement. *The past? What was past? Last week?*

They ate in silence for a while until Frank cleared his throat. "I don't want you to think I'm a player, Reggie."

She leaned forward, smiling. "Frank, you have every right to be a player. You're a very attractive single man and successful, so, as my dad would say, you're free to sow your wild oats."

A muscle twitched in the side of his face. "I think I'm over that. I'm not sure what I'm looking for now, but..." He eyed her tentatively. "I think I'm closing in on it."

It was all she could do to hold his gaze. She wanted to ask him to spell it out but couldn't quite form the words. Instead, she took a sip of wine and set the glass down carefully. "I wish you good luck in finding whatever it is you want, Frank."

He leaned a little closer, the candlelight setting sparks glinting in his green eyes. "Tell me what you want, Reggie. What is your ultimate goal?"

Straightening her shoulders, she exhaled. "I'm not that complicated. I just want to be able to provide for my daughter. I guess the thing I would like most of all would be to have a home of our own." She shrugged. "I love my father, and I appreciate that I could take Shannon and crawl back home after Kenny split...but I would really love to have my own place. It doesn't have to be anything fancy. Just a home for us, where I can change the paint anytime the mood hits. I want to draw castles and dragons on Shannon's walls. Really make it special for her." She stopped, her color rising. She hadn't meant to reveal anything so personal. But she had. "That's my goal," she whispered.

Frank reached for her hand and lifted it to his lips. "Here's hoping both our dreams will come true very soon."

After the meal, Frank escorted her from the restaurant, and she found he had hired a horse-drawn carriage for the night.

"Oh, this is just so—so—" Her voice trailed off. *Romantic. It's very romantic.*

Frank handed her up into the carriage and climbed in beside her.

She felt as if she were on display, sitting in the open carriage surrounded by all the lights of the city. Of course, this was nothing new to all the sophisticated New Yorkers, but she was a first-timer, visiting an alien planet. *Frank's planet.*

He pointed out places of interest, including the building where he leased a condominium.

It struck her as odd that he didn't refer to it as "home," but considering he was a world traveler, she wasn't quite sure where he considered home.

The driver turned the carriage into a tree-lined park. The lighting wasn't as bright here, but she still felt exposed. The traffic noises abated, and the rhythmic clop-clop of horse's hooves lulled her, giving her a sense of tranquility.

"Ooh, this is beautiful."

"Central Park. You can't visit New York City without a drive through the park."

A gust of cool air whispered over her skin, causing her to shiver. She rubbed her palms over her bare arms.

Frank removed his jacket, slipped it around her shoulders, and then pulled her into an embrace. "I don't want you to take a chill." His deep voice seemed to resonate through her, melding her body with his, becoming one, at least for the moment.

Reggie snuggled in his jacket, still warm with his body heat. This was feeling very comfortable. She turned to gaze up at him. "What are we doing, Frank?"

"Me? I'm just relaxing while holding the most beautiful woman I've ever known in my arms. I hope you're enjoying it as much as I am."

She pursed her lips, teasing him with a little pout. "There seems to be a plethora of beautiful women in your fan club."

"Plethora," he repeated. "You're the only person I know who could pull off using that word in conversation without sounding pretentious." He kissed her temple and drew her back into his arms. "Just chill out and enjoy the ride."

She giggled. "Yes, Franklinstein."

"About that…"

She twisted so she could see his face.

"Could we just be Reggie and Frank from Rambling? A couple of star-crossed lovers who finally found their way back to each other?" There was a wistful yearning in his voice.

Star-crossed lovers…"Okay, I can do that." Reggie snuggled back against his chest as his arms closed around her. She couldn't recall feeling so content, just leaning back, wrapped in Frank's jacket and in his arms.

―᠅―

Vern had volunteered to pick up Lolly and Sandy at their motel room, so all Henry had to do was show up. He was clean and smelled good, but he sat in his GTO, gripping the wheel. He watched people going into the VFW, some couples, some small groups, and some singly. It was that kind of place. The veterans made sure everyone had a good time. There was a group within the group that prided themselves on grilling the best and fattest hamburgers in the county. They were big, thick, hand-built ground beef patties, seasoned and grilled to perfection by men who put their hearts into it. There was a lot of pride in those burgers. And the wives of these gentlemen, as well as the female veterans, were enthusiastic about promoting the various projects, such as selling tickets and coordinating events to include those frail veterans who resided in the local nursing home. All in all, this was a good group, and Henry was proud to be a member, having served in the Army when he was a much younger man.

He had seen Vern's Camaro, so he knew Vern was inside with

the two colorful women. They had probably glued their fake eyelashes back on.

Henry heaved a sigh, gutting up to face his fate. He was a strong man, and he could spend an evening entertaining empty-headed women who thought they had to paint themselves with bright colors to be attractive. He got out of his car, having parked far enough away to avoid getting dings from other drivers, and strode across the unpaved parking lot to the VFW post.

"Hello, Henry." Fay Wilks, former Air Force nurse, was manning the door. She held out her hand to collect his money and stamped his hand with an expertise born of having performed this task for many years.

"Hey, Fay. You're looking mighty fine tonight." He smiled, noting her lack of makeup…well, maybe a little blush on her cheeks.

She winked, waved him inside, and turned to accept money from the next person in line.

Henry passed into the large open space. It was used for many functions, from bingo nights to town meetings to wedding receptions.

He hung out near the entrance, trying to be inconspicuous, as he scanned the gathering crowd. It didn't take long for him to locate the sheriff, Vernon Garland. He was standing on the other side of the large room amid a small group of cronies.

Henry spied the two Houston women seated at a table nearby. They were chatting, when suddenly the one named Lolly spotted him and nudged the other woman. Together they waved and apparently said something that caused Vern and his cadre to turn.

Henry arranged a passably warm smile and crossed the room to greet them.

"Henry," Vern called. "We were wondering if you had wimped out."

"Funny," Henry snarled. He nodded at the two women seated at the table. "So, what is your plan here?"

Vern reached out to grab Henry by the shoulder and turned him toward the grill located on the opposite end of the building. "I was on my way to get these ladies a bite to eat when these guys ambushed me. Let's get a pitcher of beer."

"Hmph! I'm gonna need it." Henry trudged along beside Vern, who was keeping up a line of chatter. When they finally made it to the front of the line, Vern ordered for the ladies, who apparently didn't care for onions and preferred mayonnaise to mustard. Henry ordered a cheeseburger basket "all the way" with a side of fries and a pitcher of beer.

The two men trekked back to the table.

Henry had been wondering which of the ladies Vern had assigned to him, but when they reached the table, Vern placed his tray across from Lolly instead of beside either one. He doled out the ladies' burgers with a large order of fries while Henry poured beer into plastic cups.

Henry took a seat across from Sandy. He noticed that she had left the false lashes behind and actually had quite nice eyes.

"Henry, I didn't realize you were a cowboy," Lolly commented. She gazed at him intently. This woman definitely had not forgotten her fake eyelashes.

"Cowboy?" Henry squinted at her, his brows puckered. "I own a store. Stafford's Mercantile."

Vern chuckled. "My friend here usually dresses like a cowboy. We always wear western shirts and boots. It's a Texas thing, y'know?"

"We live in Texas," Lolly protested.

"You live in a city in Texas." Vern shrugged. "Here in the country, we dress this way. From the time I was a little bitty boy, I was clomping around in my cowboy boots."

Henry nodded. "Me too. If you ladies were expecting suits and ties, you need to go back to the city." He flashed a grin. "But while you're here, we're gonna make sure you get to know the real Rambling, Texas."

Sandy laughed. "Is this the real Rambling, Texas?"

Henry spread his hands, indicating the people around them. "This is about as Rambling as it gets."

Sandy took a big bite of her burger and chewed while making appreciative sounds. "This is delicious."

Lolly agreed. "This meat is so juicy."

Vern was chomping away on his cheeseburger.

"These burgers are formed by hand. Lovingly... Not mashed by a machine. And those same hands then grill them to perfection." Henry kissed his fingers.

Lolly and Sandy giggled.

Henry bit into his cheeseburger. He figured this evening might not be so bad after all.

Sandy eyed her hamburger. "So, you're saying this meat has been mashed by human hands and that makes it better?"

"You betcha." He winked at her and continued eating.

"I just have one question, Henry." Sandy carefully placed her burger back in the basket and wiped her fingers on a paper napkin. "Can you dance?"

Henry had a coughing fit as he choked on his burger. "Um... Um, of course I can dance. Can you?"

"Why, Henry...I thought you would never ask." She smiled prettily. "Why don't we finish our hamburgers and I'll let you give me a whirl on the dance floor?" She picked up her burger again and took a big bite.

Henry managed to swallow and took a long drink of his beer. He exhaled and gazed at the woman across the table from him. "I think that's a good idea." He saluted her with his red plastic Solo cup and drank more. He thought he would need it.

—⁓—

Frank wasn't sure what was going on, but he was extremely happy at that moment. This was a new feeling for him. He was used to being on the move, always reaching for the next goal. Always hungry. His climb was endless.

But at that very moment in time, he was experiencing something his life had been short on. *Contentment*.

Yes, it was all about being with Reggie Lee. About holding her in his arms. About how she seemed to be comfortable in their new relationship. *Just Frank and Reggie from Rambling*.

As they circled Central Park, he pointed out the various sights to see. She sat up when he told her about Belvedere Castle.

"Ooh, a castle. How lovely."

"We can come see it in the daytime, if you'd like."

She flashed him a grin and settled back into his arms. Somehow, just holding her made his pulse race. He buried his lips in her hair. The fragrance was something floral with vanilla overtones.

When their ride ended at her hotel, he climbed down and held out his arms. Having her reach for him was like a dream come true. He wondered how their relationship would have progressed if they had been high school sweethearts instead of enemies.

He walked with her to the elevator and rode up to her floor holding her hand. He had no idea where this evening was going, but he didn't want it to end. He couldn't seem to get enough of Reggie.

At the door, she fumbled with the key card, and he took it from her, effortlessly sliding it into the slot. The door swung open and started to close.

Reggie stepped inside, casting a look at him that squeezed his heart.

He took a step toward her and leaned forward. She placed her palms on his chest and slid them up to clasp his neck. *Kiss the girl*.

Just as he wanted, she stretched up to offer her soft lips. The first kiss led to another and another after that. He lifted her against him, and the door closed behind him. Reluctantly, he wrenched his mouth from hers. "You're so beautiful," he whispered. "You take my breath away."

Reggie smiled. "You make me feel beautiful."

He held her off the carpeting, held her as though she were the most precious thing in his world. It suddenly occurred to him that she was.

"I guess I'd better go," he said, but made no move to put her down.

Her embrace tightened. "You don't have to leave, Frank."

That totally rocked him. "Are you sure?"

"I want you to stay," she whispered against his lips, placing kisses on his mouth and then touching her tongue to his lips.

"Then I will." The next kiss took place against the wall. He cupped her butt with one hand, and the sexy, short dress slid up as her legs encircled his waist. The thigh-high stockings had a lacy edge at the top. He wanted to bite them off her. Instead he stroked her thigh as he carried her toward the bed and reluctantly set her on her feet.

Reggie slipped out of his jacket and tossed it across a chair. Now she was loosening his tie, but he stripped it off and threw it with the jacket.

Passion flared in her eyes, and he realized she wanted him as much as he wanted her. *Impossible.*

Reggie's fingers quickly unbuttoned his shirt. She stroked his chest, her short nails softly abrading his skin. He let the shirt drop to the floor.

"My turn." Frank unzipped the black dress, the sound setting his senses on high alert. The straps slid down her arms, revealing a lacy black bra and matching panties. "Whoa!"

She grinned, stepping out of the dress as it slid down her thighs and landed in a puddle at her feet. "You like?"

His throat tightened up, but he managed to swallow. When he could speak, his voice came out all raspy. "Understatement." He drew her close and nuzzled her neck.

She emitted a little mewl of pleasure. "Good. You paid a lot for them."

"Worth every penny." He sank onto the bed and reached out to her.

Reggie slid into his arms, her smooth skin setting fire to his libido and his emotions. He rolled her onto her back, caressing her breasts and then trailing kisses over her stomach. He stroked her thighs and drew the stockings down her legs, one at a time, allowing his fingers to linger on her warm flesh.

"One of us is wearing entirely too many clothes." Her voice was soft and husky.

He hoped she was choked by passion. He certainly was. "I'd better fix that right away." He rose from the bed and quickly divested himself of the rest of his clothing. Reaching in his pocket before he tossed his pants over the chair, he found one of the condoms he'd had the foresight to bring with him. He'd thought he was being entirely too optimistic when he had done so, but now he was glad he did.

"You must work out a lot," she commented, looking him over critically.

"Not really." He slid onto the bed beside her and reached to unsnap the black lace bra. "I do practice martial arts. That keeps me in pretty good shape." His fingers trailed from her collarbone down to softly stroke her breast. He circled her nipple with his thumb, smiling when it tautened at his touch. "Just beautiful," he whispered, before tracing the same route with his tongue.

Reggie lay back against the pillow, gazing up at him with her large luminous eyes.

He had never thought to see that expression on her face. Why had he called her the Ice Princess? It was because she had been cold as ice. Well, she'd thawed out for him now. *Just don't blow this. It's your one chance to be the man she wants you to be.*

Frank slipped his hand in the lacy black panties. Gently, he slid them off, his fingers trailing over her silky skin.

Fighting the urgency building in his groin, he wanted to make certain their first time together was memorable for Reggie. He trailed kisses from her neck over her shoulder and took his time to pay special attention to her breasts.

Reggie arched toward him, offering herself up as a delectable treat.

He let out a shaky breath. "Your skin feels like warm silk. I can't stop touching you."

She opened her eyes, looking pleased. "I like your hands on me. I like—" She gasped as his fingers found their target. "Ooh," she moaned. "That feels...good."

He traced a path down her ribs with his tongue, taking a detour to investigate her navel. Her soft giggles and moans intrigued him, so he trailed his mouth lower to taste the sweetness of her mound.

Reggie sucked in an audible gasp as his tongue teased her innermost core. He varied the intensity as his tongue manipulated the tiny button.

"Oh, please, now... I need you inside me...now."

He quickly applied the condom and eased inside, thrilled as she wrapped her thighs around him and pulled him closer. He settled on top of her, bearing his weight on his forearms.

Her face, flushed with pleasure, made him determined to ensure that this, their first time together, would be something to remember.

She arched up, writhing against him. Her nipples grazed his chest, setting his insides ablaze.

He was torn between raging passion and melting into the sweetness of the moment.

Reggie moved beneath him, setting a rhythm for him to match, and he picked it up, stroking deep inside her. The sound of her breath coming in sweet little gasps was interspersed with words of encouragement. "Oh, yes."

Suddenly, her body stiffened, and she clung to him for a few moments before collapsing back onto the pillow, her breathing ragged. "That was—just amazing."

"Oh, no," he crooned close to her ear. "I'm not done with you."

She opened her eyes wide. "You're not?"

"Just relax and leave the driving to me."

Reggie laughed as he brushed her hair away from her damp forehead. "And just where are you taking me, Mr. Bell?"

He delivered a passionate kiss. "All the way to heaven, Ms. Stafford. All the way…"

He proceeded to bring her to orgasm twice more before he joined her. They lay together, wet and breathing hard.

"I—I—" He stopped himself before he blurted out the words *I love you.*

Flushed with passion, she opened her eyes. "Did you say something?"

He swallowed hard. "I—uh… I need some water." He reached for a bottle of water on the bedside table. "Are you thirsty?"

She laughed. "Not thirsty."

He unscrewed the cap and sucked down several gulps. *Lame… totally lame.*

Reggie giggled. "Wouldn't want you to be dehydrated. You've got work to do."

He swallowed the water the wrong way and had a coughing fit.

—⁂—

Reggie's heart pounded against her ribs. She tried not to sound like an overheated dog panting, consciously breathing through her nose and drawing long, slow breaths. In her limited sexual history, she had never experienced anything approaching the intensity of Frank's passionate lovemaking. By the time their bodies finally joined, he had invested a significant amount of time in foreplay to ensure that every molecule of her being was screaming for relief. And relieve her he did…four times. *Talk about stamina.*

Now, he held her tenderly, her head cradled against his shoulder. He kissed her forehead gently and stroked her hair. Resting against his hard body was the ultimate luxury after such an eternity of solitude.

Grinning in the dark, Reggie felt completely satisfied. In fact, the term *sensory overload* came to mind. She'd just experienced the most thorough workout she could imagine. Words tumbled through her brain as she tried to think of something to say…something clever that didn't sound like she was desperate or needy…couldn't.

"Are you okay?" Frank's deep voice resonated through his chest, vibrated through her bones and flesh, annexing her as an extension of him.

"More than okay," she breathed.

He chuckled, pressing kisses against the side of her face. "I—I feel the same way."

"Really?" She was pretty sure that wasn't what he had intended to say, but he'd checked himself. *Well, if he's feeling the same way, he's floating in the stratosphere.*

"Yeah, really." His arms tightened around her. "Tell me something. Do you want me to leave or stay?"

"What?" She twisted to look into his eyes.

Frank heaved a sigh. "I just mean, are you comfortable with me staying here all night?" He kissed her temple again. "I love holding you in my arms, but if you're not feeling the same way, I can go to my condo and pick you up in the morning."

"Oh." Not being a sophisticated woman with many affairs under her belt, she wasn't sure what her reply should be. She wondered what he would say if she confessed that he was only the second man she had slept with…not that much sleeping had taken place this time around. "Um, I'm comfortable if you are." She cringed. That didn't sound at all romantic.

Frank snuggled closer. "I'm very comfortable," he whispered close to her ear.

A light shiver caressed her skin. *Comfortable, indeed.*

Chapter 11

FRANK LAY GRINNING IN THE DARK. HE WAS ELATED. IN THE PAST, THIS was the way he'd felt when he had achieved something monumental.

Like when he had closed a big deal or sold a piece of property at a huge profit... *No, it isn't the least bit like that. This is different. This is personal.*

And yet it wasn't like any previous physical relationship he had ever experienced.

Reggie Lee settled against him. He felt her relax...inhaled her soft fragrance...listened to her gentle breath sounds...

He felt content. Content and elated all at the same time. Willing himself to unwind, he tried to analyze his feelings. *Surely, I'm not ready to say the L word.* Yet he'd almost said it. Almost declared his love right out loud, something he had never done before.

In fact, Frank was an expert at *not* saying it. He could *not* say it in several languages.

He consciously tried to decode his feelings. What was it about saying the words "I love you" that he found so objectionable?

Declaring one's love implied commitment. As long as he never said those particular words, he was still free to pick up and leave... to go on his merry way. As long as he didn't say it, his various girlfriends knew that their relationship was transient. Something easy between them. Something that didn't tie either one down.

Frowning, Frank buried his lips in Reggie's hair. *Tied down. What the hell does that mean, anyway?*

At the moment, he didn't feel tied down, but rather...

He groped for the right words, thinking it was important to define his new state.

He was feeling a part of something. *What?*

A relationship. *Yeah, sure...but what kind of relationship?*

Swallowing the tangle of emotions at the back of his throat, he realized he was thinking the other word he had relentlessly avoided... *Forever.*

Jill Garland heaved a big yawn and raked her fingers through her hair. She had fallen asleep on Henry Stafford's sofa, and apparently he had covered her with a blanket when he got home.

Now, she heard movement and smelled bacon, that tantalizing aroma that could have brought her out of a coma. She straightened her clothes and followed her nose to the kitchen, where she found Henry bustling around, obviously at home in his duties as chef, and Shannon sitting at the table in a booster chair with a sippy cup of juice.

Henry saluted her with a spatula. "Good morning, Jill. I hope you don't mind that I let you sleep. You looked so cozy, and I hated to think of you driving home when you were tired."

She stifled another yawn. "Thanks. I slept like a dead thing."

He chuckled. "Well, I have just the thing to fix you right up, young lady. A good hearty meal to start the day off right."

"It smells incredible."

Henry had started cooking breakfast. The bacon was draining on paper towels, and he had a pan of biscuits baking in the oven.

She took a seat at the table beside Shannon. "So, how was your date last night, Mr. Stafford?"

"Over easy or scrambled?"

Jill's smile faded. "That bad, huh?"

Henry's brow furrowed. "I wouldn't say that."

Jill tried not to overreact. "No? Well, how would you describe it?"

Henry broke two eggs into the skillet. They both heard the

hiss and watched the clear part turn white. He slipped the spatula under each egg and turned them over long enough to cook that side and then slid them onto a plate. He handed it to Jill.

"Thanks, Mr. Stafford. This looks great."

"I remember what you liked when you used to have sleepovers with Reggie and the other girls." He made another set of over-easy eggs and finally scrambled two for Shannon. "You go ahead and help yourself to bacon, and I'll get the biscuits out of the oven."

"You sure did go to a lot of trouble." Jill saw a bib on the table and tied it around Shannon's neck.

"I wanna biscuit." Shannon pointed to the pan Henry had just removed from the oven. Her big blue eyes gazed at the biscuits with longing.

"Well, let Grandpa get them out of the pan first. You show me how you eat your eggs, young lady." Henry gestured with the spatula, and Shannon immediately scooped a bite of scrambled egg into her mouth.

Jill took a sip of orange juice. Why was he stalling about his evening out with her dad? Vern Garland could be a bit of a jokester, but had he gone too far? Had the date been that bad…or that good?

Henry placed the biscuits in a napkin-lined bowl on the table and seated himself beside Shannon. "That's my good girl. Let me butter a biscuit for you."

Jill reached for a biscuit and proceeded to use it to sop up her egg yolk. She closed her eyes and made an appreciative sound, which brought a smile to Henry's lips. "Thanks for making breakfast, Mr. Stafford. I wouldn't have done near as well."

"Nothing's too good for my granddaughter and the world's best babysitter."

"But you're going to stall me about your date last night?" She took another sip of juice.

"It wasn't a date…exactly." Henry looked thoughtful. "It was more of a get-together…among friends."

Jill grinned triumphantly. "So you and this lady are…friends?"

Henry nodded. "Well, maybe we are now. I had a good time, and I hope the others did too."

She sat up straight, examining him carefully. "I thought you were sort of ticked off at my dad for getting you involved. What turned you around?"

He shook his head slowly. "I guess it was Sandy... She is a widow from Houston." He wiped Shannon's mouth with her bib.

Jill tried to get hold of her emotions. She was rather appalled that her own father was interested in a woman other than his deceased wife...and that he had gotten his best friend to get similarly involved. She took a deep breath and exhaled slowly. There would be a face-to-face with her dear old dad. "I'm glad you found someone interesting."

He made a waving gesture. "It was just an evening with friends. Vern was right. It was fun to hang out with a couple of nice women. I actually danced with Sandy. I hadn't danced in so long." His face took on a very sad expression.

Jill blotted her mouth with her napkin. "I am so very glad you had a nice evening. I'm sure Reggie Lee wouldn't want you to be alone."

He smiled. It was a smile that almost looked happy. "I'm not alone. I have my two girls. Reggie Lee and Shannon are my whole world."

Jill swallowed hard and managed not to break down in tears. "You have a great family, but it's good to have friends too." She stood and took a few steps toward the refrigerator to hide her expression from her best friend's dad.

He regarded her stonily. "I have friends."

She reached over to squeeze his hand. "I know you do. I'm just letting you know that..." She swallowed hard. "That it's okay for you and my dad to have female friends. I don't want you to think that I would be judging you if you find someone nice...to be with...you know?" Jill spread her hands and leaned back against the refrigerator, while Henry stood gazing at her uncertainly.

Henry snorted out a little huff of air. "I appreciate your

permission, Your Majesty." His brow was furrowed as he glared at her. "But I don't need your permission to have friends...to have a friend of the female persuasion."

"Aw, I know you don't. I just wanted you to know that I'm okay if you and my dad are ready to start dating. My mom's been gone a while, and I know she wouldn't want him to be lonely."

Henry's face was unnaturally red, so Jill turned to the refrigerator. She opened the door and looked inside with no idea why she had chosen to do so. Finally, she reached for a carton of orange juice and refilled her glass. She glanced at Henry again and poured a glass for him as well. "Here you go. I think we both need some vitamin C...so drink up."

Wordlessly, Henry reached for the glass and sucked it down in record time. Then he rinsed his glass and placed it in the top rack of the dishwasher. Henry was done talking.

———— ᴧᴧ ————

In the morning, it was rather confusing. Reggie Lee woke up tangled in the sheets and Frank's limbs. For a moment, she had forgotten where she was...and what she had done the night before.

Her neck was resting on Frank's cushy bicep, and he was still asleep.

Watching him, she noted his peaceful expression. Dark-brown lashes rested on his cheeks, hiding those green eyes that seemed to reach all the way to her soul.

The fact that Frank's arms were still curled around her was very comforting, especially considering her wanton behavior the night before. No, she couldn't blame this escapade on him. He had given her plenty of chances to shy away, but...her needs screamed for release.

A little smile played around her lips. *Just this once, it was all about me.*

She gazed at him again. Glad she had given in to her desires. Glad Frank had been the one to fill them. Sad that he was not the kind of man to settle down.

Still, she didn't regret losing her heart to him. Whatever the consequences, she would have this good memory of their time together.

She refused to become embittered, like the redhead in the restaurant the night before. The image of the beautiful woman's angry and jealous face popped into her mind...but the woman hadn't wanted to cut ties with Frank. "Call me," she'd said.

Reggie Lee swallowed. *No! I won't become some bitter, left-behind woman. I'm going to wallow in whatever attentions Frank gives me, and then when he moves on, I will never let him know how much I ache for him. Never...*

When she glanced at Frank again, the green eyes were regarding her with great interest. "Good morning, beautiful." His voice sounded even deeper than usual.

She smiled. "Good morning."

"Did you sleep well?"

Reggie let out a snort of laughter. "Yeah, sure."

"Me too."

They made love with less urgency than the night before. This could best be described as languorous. Frank seemed driven to find each and every erogenous molecule of Reggie's flesh. When he was done with her, she collapsed against him, gasping for breath.

"Oh, Frank...that was just...just..."

A wry grin spread across his face. "Exactly." He kissed her temple and snuggled her close for a few minutes. "I—I think we should get out of bed and explore this beautiful city."

"Mmm...does that have something to do with breakfast?" she said. "Because I've used up a lot of calories and I'm feeling a bit peckish."

"Peckish?" He roared with laughter. "Really?"

A flush crept up from her neck. "I...uh, I read it in a book once."

Frank kissed her again. "I'm feeling peckish too. Head for the shower and I'll join you in a minute." He opened a drawer in the bedside table and removed a menu. "I'll order breakfast."

Reggie slipped off the bed, intensely aware of her lack of clothing. When she glanced at Frank, he was studying her.

"Work of art. You...are a work of art, Reggie."

She drew a sharp breath but smiled as she walked to the bathroom. Maybe there was a little swagger in her step.

"Stafford's," Henry answered the landline in his store. It was a slow day, and there was only one customer inside.

"Henry? That you?"

Henry rolled his eyes. "Of course it's me, Vern. Who did you think it was?"

Vern chuckled. "Just making sure."

"It must be a slow day for crime in Rambling, Texas." Henry leaned against the counter.

"Ha! That's about right. I just sent three deputies to direct traffic at the schools. Not that there's much traffic, but it will keep them boys busy for a while."

Henry heaved a loud sigh. "I suppose there was a purpose for this call, although it seems to have eluded you. Were you just feeling lonesome?"

Vern let out a loud guffaw. "Aw, I was just lonesome for the sound of your voice, you old heartbreaker, you."

Henry held the phone away from his ear as his friend's raucous laughter continued. "Glad I could amuse you. Maybe you should get back to work. Isn't that what we taxpayers are paying you for?"

"Sure thing," Vern said. "I just thought you might like to know how your date with Miss Sandy went."

"Oh, brother! I know how it went. I was there." Henry put the phone down on the counter while he rang up his customer and counted out change. "You come back to see us," he called out as the customer left the store, setting off the metal bell clanking against the glass of the front door.

"Hank? You there?"

Henry picked up the phone again. "What are you yapping about, Vern?"

"Well, I was going to share some news with you. My friend Lolly called me from Houston to tell me what a good time she had at the VFW."

"That's really nice, Vern. I'm glad you showed Lolly a good time. Is there anything else? I need to unload some cases that were delivered earlier."

"Aw, you're no fun." Vern let out a derisive snort. "I suppose you don't have time to hear what your date thought of you...so I'll just be hanging up now."

"Wait!" Henry realized he was being tooled around by an expert. "Okay, spill it." He drummed his fingers on the counter.

"Well, it seems that Miss Sandy had a great time. Lolly told me that she hadn't seen her best friend so relaxed and happy since her husband passed away."

"That's great. Glad she enjoyed herself."

"Aw, Hank. Don't be such a jerk. It's a big deal." Vern huffed out a sigh. "It's a good thing that you did. You know, being nice to your fellow man, but she's a woman."

Henry leaned against the counter. "Listen, Vern, my good friend. It was nice to go out, and I did have a good time, but this lady lives four hours away. There is no point in trying to make a big deal of it. It is what it is. We're here. The ladies are there." Henry raked his fingers through his hair. "I'm not interested in a long-distance relationship. If I wanted to have a girlfriend, there are plenty of local ladies available. Every Sunday, I take my daughter and granddaughter to church, and the ladies outnumber the men, like, five to one...at least the ones in our age group." He made a growling sound. "Trust me, if I wanted to date someone, I would choose a nice lady who lived right here in Rambling. You know, a local girl...someone I have something in common with."

"Aw, Hank. Don't get your feathers ruffled. I'm not suggesting that you marry the woman, but it's okay to have a good time once in a while. I was thinking they could come here now and then... and maybe we could go to Houston. You know, for fun. You do remember fun, don't you?"

Henry heaved a sigh. "You may remember that I own a store and it's open seven days a week. I do not have time for fun. My idea of fun is playing with my granddaughter and keeping my beautiful 1969 Pontiac GTO Priscilla in mint condition."

"Aw, you're no fun at all."

"I'll see you at church, Vern." Henry hung up and nodded at a longtime customer who always came in to get his weekly scratch-offs.

—◊◊◊—

"She's much bigger in person." Reggie gazed up at the Statue of Liberty as the ferry cruised by. "But she's gorgeous...and green."

"You're gorgeous and not even green." He slid his arm around her shoulders and was gratified when she leaned against him.

The day was overcast. He was afraid it might rain, and he hadn't brought an umbrella. Reggie wasn't dressed for the weather, but he thought they would stop and buy her more suitable outerwear.

His throat tightened when he realized he felt very protective of Reggie. *What else?* Protective and possessive. Squeezing her shoulder was comforting to both of them. It also alerted other males that this woman belonged to him. *Back off, buzzards.*

After the harbor tour, Frank took her to lunch in Chinatown. She seemed to be delighted with every aspect of New York City... his city. And every time she expressed her delight, his chest swelled with pleasure.

"Thanks for the coat." She stroked her hand over the cashmere sleeve. "It's beautiful."

"Nah. It's a coat. You're beautiful."

She dimpled, a flush staining her cheeks. She started to protest, but he held up his hand.

"No argument. You're beautiful. That's a stone-cold fact." He toasted her with his tea.

Glancing down, she straightened the napkin in her lap. "Um... How do you eat with these things, anyway?" She picked up her chopsticks and waved them in the air.

"You pretend they're tongs." He demonstrated the action, picking up a snow pea and offering it to her. When she leaned forward and opened her luscious lips, he fed her as though she were a baby bird.

"Very tasty, but can't I just have a fork?"

He gestured to the waiter. "Please bring the lady a fork."

She smiled her gratitude. "Thanks," she whispered. When she was fully armed with the utensil, she scooped up a bite of moo shu pork and chewed thoughtfully. "Yummy. Why don't we have Chinese food in our little corner of the world?"

"Because someone would undoubtedly chicken-fry it and pour gravy over it."

"You're probably right, but I'm going to miss this."

That made him smile. "Good. I'll have to bring you back to the city for your next fix."

"I'm in. What is this stuff?" She gestured to another bowl on the table.

"Stir-fried rice with shrimp. One of my favorites."

"Oh, gimme some of that one."

He obliged, scooping a generous serving onto her plate. He was pleased that Reggie was open to new experiences. Glad she was on his turf for a change. He took a deep breath and released it slowly, glad he was on his own turf and feeling less like he had to prove himself every day.

"What are we doing this afternoon?" she asked.

"I thought it was time we buckled down to business. We're going to the Design Center. I'm looking forward to having you redecorate my house."

Reggie rubbed her palms together. "Not as much as I am. I love your house. When I was younger, I used to pretend it was my home."

"Seriously?"

She nodded, stuffing another shrimp into her mouth and chewing thoughtfully. "When Miss Rosie would invite me to visit, I would soak up every molecule of my surroundings. I loved the beveled glass and lace curtains. I coveted the damask Queen Anne chairs and doilies." She glanced up at him. "I suppose that sounds crazy."

"Not at all. I'm trusting you not to let me screw this up." He tried to look needy. "You know I have absolutely zero talent for this sort of thing."

Her lips curved into a wide grin. "Oh, yes. You can trust me. I wouldn't do anything to wreck the Grady house. It's my dream house."

"And you know all about Victorian house decor... Right?"

"Right. I've studied all about Victorian architecture and interiors. That's my favorite style." She reached across the table to grasp his hand. "Please believe me. I can do this."

He placed his other hand on top of hers. "Believe me when I say I trust you implicitly. My house and I are completely at your mercy."

––––––––

After their lunch, Frank hailed a taxi and loaded Reggie inside. The odors of the many people who had preceded her worked on her gag reflex. *Ugh!*

She couldn't recall ever having ridden in a taxi prior to her foray into New York City. She accepted that this form of transportation might be quite useful in big cities, especially those with huge populations crammed into a relatively small footprint.

Houston or Dallas had large populations, but area-wise, both cities took up quite a bit of real estate. They were so spread out, she couldn't imagine how ordinary citizens could afford taxi fare across either city. Perhaps this was why there were so many cars and trucks in Texas...and freeways.

Frank slid in beside her and spoke to the driver. "Two hundred Lex."

"Lex? What are lexes, and why do we need so many?"

He grinned. "Lexington Boulevard. The Design Center. That's the address. It's famous."

Reggie felt a blush creep up her neck. *He must think I'm a complete redneck hick.* She resolved to try and keep her dumb questions to a minimum.

Frank reached for her hand and cradled it in both of his. It felt good. It felt normal. Just Frank and Reggie Lee...normal people.

She realized she was holding her breath and made an effort to take in air without gasping. *Slow and easy. Normal.*

"Here we are," he crooned as the taxi slowed. He tossed a bill toward the driver, opened the door, and extended his hand. "Time to shine."

Reggie placed her hand in his and climbed out of the taxi. Tilting her head back, she regarded the Design Center towering above her. "Oh, my. That is one tall building. Is it all part of the Design Center?"

Frank tucked her hand in the crook of his arm and gestured to the gleaming structure. "You bet. There are sixteen stories and over five hundred thousand square feet. This building houses almost one hundred different showrooms."

"And you just happen to have those facts memorized?"

He opened one of the doors for her. "Nope. I wanted to impress you, so I looked it up."

They spent the next few hours meandering from showroom to showroom. Frank had made a list of those specializing in Victorian classics and historically accurate furnishings and decorations. He seemed to have thought of everything.

Reggie was overwhelmed at first. The profusion of colors, fabrics, and patterns swirled around in her brain. "Oh, I'm confused. Where did we see that drapery fabric I liked so much?"

"Victorian R Us," Frank supplied. "You have a sample in your bag."

"Oh, that's right. They gave me a swatch and stapled their card to it. And I liked the breakfront they had."

He nodded. "Uh-huh. Whatever you say."

"No, seriously," she said. "There is just too much stuff here."

A one-sided grin twerked his face. "That's why it's called shopping. Take all the samples and brochures and photos you want. We'll simply take them home and you get to decide what works best. It's all up to you, but there's no deadline."

Reggie released a pent-up breath. "Right. We're shopping."

"And we're good at it." He gave her a wink.

———

"Henry?" It was a woman's voice.

"Yes, this is Henry Stafford." He didn't recognize the voice right off, but it sounded vaguely familiar.

"It's Sandy." Her voice was soft and sounded insecure.

"Yeah, Sandy. What can I do for you?"

There was a long silence. "I—I don't know, exactly. I guess I was just having a real case of the blues." She took in a deep breath and exhaled. "It's such a big and empty house, and I..."

"Aw...I understand. I know what it means to be lonely."

"I—I hope it's not too late for me to be calling."

Henry was in bed. He had gone to sleep early after putting his granddaughter to bed with a bedtime story. "No...not at all."

She made a noise that wasn't quite like crying, and yet it was quite pitiful.

Henry sat up and turned on the bedside light. He reached for the digital clock on the table beside his bed. Eleven p.m.

"Um…how are you and Lolly doing? You ladies having a good time in the big ol' city of Houston?"

"Oh, we're all right. Just hanging around the house…but some days there just doesn't seem to be any reason to get out of bed in the morning."

Henry put his bare feet on the cool polished-wood floor. This brought him fully awake. "You really sound sad. I'm sorry, Sandy."

"Weren't you sad and lonely after your wife passed away?"

Henry considered this question. He had been miserably lonely…still was. He swallowed hard. "Sure. I was lonely. I missed her every moment of the day, and nights were even worse."

She was definitely crying softly now. "How did you get through it?"

The major difference between Henry's situation as a widower and what Sandy was facing at the moment was that he had a daughter…and his daughter had married a worthless asshole. In the aftermath of his wife's passing, his daughter had given birth and been abandoned, so he had been busy. His grief was interwoven with rage against the man who had hurt his beloved daughter.

"Well…I had my daughter and granddaughter to think of, so I spent a lot of my time with them. We pulled together to get through it."

In truth, he wondered if he would ever get through the pain of losing his life partner. "But I still miss her and think about her. It's sad that she isn't here to spoil our granddaughter. Everything that Shannon does, each and every new phase brings me great joy, but there is a core of sadness that my wife is not here to appreciate the great job our daughter is doing in raising her."

"You're so fortunate to have a family."

Henry considered the sad woman on the other end of the line. "I'm sorry you don't have the support of family, but there are lots of things you could do."

"Oh?"

Henry sensed that his next words would be important. He cleared his throat. "I'm not suggesting that you're being selfish... but you might want to look around and see if there is someone else who needs you. You know, volunteer. Houston is a big city, but even here in this little town we have an old folks home, and those people really love to get a visit. There's an animal shelter, and I have a friend who just goes to play with the dogs. He says it makes them more adoptable if they are used to playing."

"I guess..."

"And another friend of mine goes to the veterans' hospital in San Antonio and reads to some of the patients who may have lost their sight." He paused, but there was only silence on the other end of the line. "I know it's a lot to consider."

Sandy squeaked out a sob. "It is. I—I really wouldn't know how to begin finding something like that."

"How about your church? We never talked about religion, but if you go to services, I'll bet your minister could give you some great suggestions." He made his way to the kitchen and poured himself a glass of water.

"I suppose so."

"Sandy, honey. It's all about being needed."

She sobbed quietly for a while, and he was silent. "Sorry. I'm just feeling sorry for myself."

"You have a right. Where is Lolly? How about you two girls get into some trouble?"

There was a deep sigh. "Lolly has gone to visit her daughter and her family in Galveston. It's the older grandchild's birthday, and Lolly wanted to spend some time with her precious ones... I don't blame her."

Henry shook his head. "No, family has to come first." He cringed for saying that when he knew Sandy was childless. "I mean...I can understand why she wants to spend time with them. I feel that way about my little granddaughter. It seems like I blink and she's growing up on me."

"I'm sure you're right."

"What are your hobbies, Sandy? Surely there's something you enjoy doing."

She heaved another sigh. "Art. I used to do a little painting... and photography."

"What else?"

"Travel. My husband and I loved to travel."

"Now that sounds like fun. Why don't you and Lolly visit a travel agent and maybe take one of those cruises? Aren't there some cruise ships just for single people?"

"Yes. Good idea." Her voice sounded brighter. "I'll bet Lolly would go with me."

Henry had checked on Shannon and then wandered back to his bedroom. "There you go. You'll have a great time."

"Thank you, Henry. I was so down in the dumps. I appreciate you for lifting my spirits."

"Not a problem, Sandy. That's what friends are for." He sat down on the edge of his bed.

"Is it all right if I call you again sometime?"

"Sandy, honey, you can call me anytime the mood strikes you...and you are coming to our classic car show, aren't you?"

She laughed. The sound was a huge departure from the sad person he'd first spoken to. "You bet we'll be there. Lolly and me."

"Glad to hear it. You be good and look into some of your former activities. Maybe you can take an art class..."

"Yes, sir. I'll look into them first thing in the morning. 'Night, Henry." She disconnected, leaving Henry feeling as though he had made a real difference in someone's life. He was right. It was all about being needed.

———— ∿ ————

Back at the hotel, Frank watched Reggie as she spread her hoard of swatches and booklets on the bed.

"Oh, I feel so rich." She clapped her hands and turned to face him. "Thank you so much for trusting me with this project."

"Trust you?" He made a scoffing sound in the back of his throat. "You're doing me a favor." He gave her a kiss on the forehead. "And you knew Aunt Rosie. You're helping to preserve the Grady house, and you know it was close to her heart. So you're honoring my great-aunt as well."

She gave a little squeal of delight. "I am. That's exactly what I'm trying to do. I want to think Miss Rosie would approve."

Her expression tugged at his heart. He swallowed hard, and his voice was husky. "Aunt Rosie would be proud of you."

That evening, he took her to dinner in yet another new dress. This one was a deep chocolate-brown that complemented her creamy skin tone and luminous brown eyes.

He had to fight the urge to peel her out of the dress and order room service. But he took a deep breath and complimented her instead.

"You really like the dress?" She turned around in a circle.

"Yes, I do." *And I love what's in it.*

That thought caused him to take a step back. *I love her. It's true. I love her.*

"Where are we going?"

"I'm taking you to one of my favorite restaurants, and then I thought we might go to a little club and dance."

"Oh, that sounds wonderful. I haven't been dancing since high school. I'm not sure I remember how."

He stroked the side of her face. "I'll bet it will come back to you."

She blinked, glancing down. "I—I hope so. I wouldn't want to embarrass you."

Frank's chest tightened. He pulled her to him, pressing her against his chest. "You couldn't embarrass me if you tried. I'll always be proud to be with you."

His declaration seemed to fluster her, but she looked pleased.

He had arranged for a limo to transport them. There was a line at the restaurant, but they were instantly shown to one of the best tables. The wine steward had just left when he heard a shriek.

"Frank Bell! Honey, it's Frank Bell."

He turned to see a woman who had bought a restaurant from him. He stood to greet her. "Mrs. Harwell. It's so good to see you again."

A fiftyish woman leaned in for a hug. "We're celebrating our thirty-fifth anniversary and decided on a night out. You remember my husband, Gerald, don't you?" She gestured to the balding man behind her, who raised his hand in a friendly wave.

"Of course. How are you, Mr. Harwell?" He shook the man's hand.

Mrs. Harwell's eyes lit on Reggie. "And who is this lovely creature?"

Frank grinned. "This is Reggie Lee Stafford, my—" He paused. *My what?*

But Mrs. Harwell rushed to give Reggie a hug and was babbling at her. "We thought we were ready to retire, but Frank let us buy his sweet little restaurant upstate. We're having so much fun with it."

"Won't you join us?" Frank offered, but she waved him off.

"Oh, we've already eaten. We're going to see a musical on Broadway."

"That sounds wonderful," Reggie said.

He realized he should have gotten tickets to a Broadway play... something light and uplifting...a musical perhaps. Reggie would have enjoyed that. *Next time...*

The Harwells left the restaurant, and Frank took his seat.

"They were nice." Reggie leaned toward him. "You sold them a restaurant?"

He nodded. "I bought a small eatery from a widow who was anxious to unload it. I fixed it up a little. Updated the interior and exterior. Then I changed the menu. It was fun."

Reggie's brows lifted. "But you didn't keep it?"

He shook his head. "I never intended to keep it. The challenge was in taking a run-down restaurant and turning it into a first-class eatery. Fortunately, the Harwells took it off my hands."

She was strangely silent, her lips tightening a bit. She released a sigh and straightened the napkin in her lap, seemingly reluctant to meet his eye.

Puzzled, he'd thought she would have considered his venture a brilliant investment and praised him for his clever business acumen.

The wine steward returned, bearing a bottle of wine wrapped in a linen napkin. He removed the cork and poured a bit into Frank's flute before taking a step back. He gazed at Frank expectantly.

Frank took a sip and gestured for him to fill Reggie's flute and then top off his own. When the steward had gone, Frank raised his flute. "To the most beautiful woman in the room. I'm so glad you're here with me."

She blushed but touched the rim of her flute to his. "Thank you, Frank."

They dined on crab, haricots verts, and rice pilaf. She seemed to like the cuisine but declined the offer of dessert.

"None for me, thanks. I'm stuffed. I've probably put on five pounds."

"Then we'd better dance it off."

He escorted her to the waiting limo, and in a very short time they arrived at a club in Soho.

The bouncers at the door greeted him. "Mr. Bell. Good to see you, sir."

Frank nodded at them and led Reggie inside.

The club was noisy. A band was ripping out deafening music onstage, while the dance floor was crammed with gyrating dancers. Others were seated at tiny tables dispersed around the room, talking loudly to be heard, while bartenders and waitresses clinked glassware.

"Hey, Frank!"

He was hailed from the dance floor, where a few people he knew casually raised a hand to acknowledge him. He nodded and lifted a hand in return.

"They know you here." Reggie turned to him uncertainly.

"Yeah, I've been here a few times." He felt uncomfortable for a moment, but she smiled.

"Nice."

"Let's grab that table and then we can dance."

"Frank." She took his hand. "Thanks for making this trip so special for me. I'm having a great time."

He lifted her chin and kissed her. "My pleasure. I'm having a great time too."

"Then let's dance. This is my last night in the city, and then it's back to real life."

Real life... Yeah, there's that. He plastered on a smile and nodded, leading her through the crushing crowd and into the dancing mob. He arranged himself where he could give her some protection from the overzealous flailing of arms and legs.

She was grinning and moving to the music, timidly at first and then with more confidence. Her natural grace took over, and she closed her eyes, letting the rhythm transport her.

Frank saw her in a new light, not as the mother of a rambunctious preschooler or the abandoned wife of a small-town bully and not even as the editor of the *Rambling Gazette*. Tonight, Reggie Lee Stafford had been transformed into a beautiful, carefree creature. And she was dancing for him.

—∿—

Gayle had been working on a new series. She hoped that her boss would approve when she returned from her trip.

She had been to visit the local animal shelter to search for Violet, Paul's lost dog. Although he didn't seem to be as concerned about the dog as she was.

Her idea was to feature a different animal's picture each week with a little story about the dog or cat to encourage people to adopt.

"Adorable Animals." She spoke aloud, letting the words settle in her brain. "Animal Pals." No, that didn't sound right.

She had snapped a few pictures with her phone and scrolled through the ones she'd selected. "Really cute. Nice. Ooh, this one is adorable...really adorable."

There was a fluffy orange-and-white kitten...and a part-terrier puppy. She scrolled back and forth between the two. *So difficult to choose.*

She continued to scroll and stopped, gazing into the eyes of an older dog. One with some white hairs in her black muzzle. Her big brown eyes were soulful. The dog was seven years old and had been abandoned when her owners had moved to a city apartment.

Gayle swallowed hard. How could someone abandon their longtime pet? Especially one with such beautiful brown eyes. Her name was Heidi. Heidi needed a home.

"Hello, Heidi. I'll help you find a home. Someone who will give you a forever home and love you a lot."

Gayle spent the rest of the afternoon writing a very poignant story about Heidi and her need to find a permanent and loving home.

She felt enormously satisfied with herself, as though her journalism had just won her a Pulitzer Prize.

"Oh, what the heck."

She picked up her phone and scrolled through the animals again, selecting two more poor unfortunate creatures. "Don't worry, Bubba. I'll save you." Bubba was a large shepherd mix. He had been neutered, and his owner was now living in a nursing home. Bubba had been loved and cared for until the elderly owner could no longer manage it. That was sad too.

Gayle sighed. If she had her way, she would bring all the dogs and cats to her little house. At least she felt passionately about this project and hoped she could sell it to Reggie Lee.

One more. Three was a good number. She should have three stories to present to Reggie Lee. Three was better than two. This would show Reggie that she was seriously dedicated to the project.

This time a feline. She scrolled through her pics and decided the orange-and-white kitten would be a sure winner. Rusty was two months old and had been found in someone's garage. But that person brought him to the animal shelter. Rusty needed a loving home. She wrote a cute little story about Rusty and ended with his adoptable status.

"Adorable... Adorable Adoptables. That should do it."

She printed all three stories accompanied by the photos and closed her laptop. She didn't see how Reggie Lee could possibly say no to this project. Much more exciting than the local high school sports events, and lots of column inches were devoted to memorializing those young athletes, not to mention 4-H projects and church bulletins.

Gayle put the pages in a folder, planning on handing it to Reggie Lee, or perhaps she would just leave it in her mailbox at the *Gazette*. That would be easier. Gayle wouldn't have to have a nervous breakdown while trying to gather the courage to approach her boss.

She scrolled through the pictures again, smiling when she realized she was perhaps their best chance of getting adopted.

Chapter 12

ON THE RETURN FLIGHT, REGGIE TRIED TO KEEP UP A BRAVE front, even though she was on an emotional roller coaster. On the one hand, she was still glowing with the combination of new love and lust from their passionate and romantic rendezvous. While on the other hand, she was devastated to be returning to the real world after living out several days in a romantic fantasyland.

A thousand questions were feeding her insecurity. Did Frank really care for her, or was she just another conquest in a long line of women he would forget? What would happen once they returned to Rambling? What would her father say? Would he know at once that his daughter had indulged in such wanton behavior? And what about the *Gazette* staff? Would the gossipmongers go into a feeding frenzy? Could she slip back into her old skin: Henry's daughter? Shannon's mother? *Gazette* editor?

Frank reached for her hand and drew it to his lips. "What's on your mind? You look worried."

Reggie pasted on a smile. "Who, me? I'm not worried."

He gazed at her sadly. "Liar," he whispered. "Tell me what's on your mind."

"It's just—"

In the silence that followed, he examined her face. "Don't be afraid. We can make it through whatever is weighing on your mind."

She drew a deep breath and released it slowly. *I hope so.* She relaxed into her seat and tried to let go of her doubts.

Thankfully, she was less terrified on the flight back to Rambling. There was little turbulence, and she was able to appreciate the view.

When they landed, Frank drove her back to her father's home. The original luggage she had packed for the weekend remained inside the house. But now she had the addition of a new bag of treasures. The clothes Frank had insisted she purchase on his credit card were neatly folded into a brand-new suitcase he had selected for her. It was much finer than anything she had owned previously, making her old bag appear shabby.

He rolled the new bag up to the door while Reggie carried her tote with personal items in it. Glancing around, she hoped none of the neighbors happened to be peering out their windows. She was certain that her return with baggage and a handsome man driving a BMW would be enough to set tongues to wagging. But when he clasped her in a swoon-worthy embrace and kissed her so that her toes tingled, she knew she would be the topic of gossip for months.

"I had a lovely time, Frank." Her voice came out all breathy as she smiled up at him.

"I did too." He didn't release her from his grip. "Thanks for helping me choose everything for the remodel."

"It was great fun."

He kissed her again, releasing her finally when he was done. "I just can't seem to get enough of you." Taking a step down from the porch, he was at her eye level. "I'll see you tomorrow at the *Gazette*."

Reggie nodded. "See you." She watched him return to the car and drive away, suddenly swamped by an immense sense of loss. Swallowing hard, she heaved a deep sigh before dragging her bags inside.

The house seemed disconcertingly quiet when she entered. She stowed all the luggage in her room, taking care to place her new finery on hangers, wondering if she would ever have the occasion to wear them again.

She emerged thinking she would pick Shannon up early from day care and take her to the Dairy Queen for an ice cream treat.

Reggie Lee sorted through the mail her father had left on the credenza for her. She found a letter addressed to her in a handwriting that was eerily familiar. Her mouth went dry and her stomach flip-flopped as her shaky hand reached for the envelope.

Not now. Not when my life is just beginning to come together.

She ripped the envelope open and shook out the contents. A single sheet of paper slid out. She grabbed it, unfolding it to stare at the scrawled handwriting.

Oh, no!

Her ex-husband, the devious and untrustworthy Kenny Landers, had written, and she was terrified. What could he want? Their divorce was final. He'd had no recent contact with their daughter. In fact, he hadn't bothered to check in on her since he had left town. Shannon didn't even remember him.

Reggie read the first line, and the twisting sensation in her gut felt as though she had been run through a meat grinder.

Hello Gorgeous!

I sure have missed you. I will be in Rambling next week, and I plan on stopping to see you and my little daughter. Will be with you on Tuesday.

Love you, girl
Kenny

The letter fluttered to the floor as Reggie Lee ran to the bathroom to throw up. She was shaking all over as she splashed cool water on her face. "Oh, nooo. You can't do this to me now, Kenny Landers. Just when things were going well."

Patting her face dry with a hand towel, Reggie gazed at her reflection in the mirror. *What can Kenny possibly want now? "My little daughter"? Did he forget he signed away all rights to her in return for not having to pay child support?*

She paced back and forth across the bathroom. *No way! I don't want to see him. I can't let him see Shannon.*

Her first thought was to call Frank. *No. This is my problem. I can't drag him into it.*

Pacing from the living room through the dining room and into the kitchen, she gazed out the back door without seeing anything. She gnawed her lip and then turned to trace her steps back to her starting point. *I cannot allow Kenny into my life again…or Shannon's.*

She swallowed hard, realizing that she had no control over whatever Kenny had planned. She would have to figure it out and go into full combat mode whenever he arrived.

Reggie grabbed her purse and strode out the door, intending to follow through with her plan to take Shannon for ice cream. At least that was something she could control.

Frank returned to the Victorian, marveling when he realized he was walking around with a grin plastered on his face. He raked his fingers through his hair. When did he get to be this happy? He let out a loud snort.

He knew exactly when that had happened. About the same time things started to heat up between him and Reggie Lee Stafford, that's when.

Shoving his hands deep in his pockets, he wandered around the house, reliving the past few days he had spent in her company. A lifting sensation filled his chest when he visualized her face. He could lose himself in her gorgeous dark eyes, bask in the warmth of her smile, and thrive in the luxury of her embrace.

Frank grabbed a bottle of water from the fridge and headed out the back door. Twisting the cap off, he took a long drink. He leaned his forearms on the porch railing.

He had dropped Reggie off at her father's house a short time ago, but he already missed her. How could he suddenly feel so empty? Like someone had lopped off a part of him...an essential part. Sucking in a deep breath, he blew it all out. *Not a problem.* He would see her again soon. Maybe he could give her a call to find out if she wanted to go to dinner with him. Maybe he could invite her to dinner with Shannon. He would show her how great he was with kids, and then—

He brought himself up short. *Whoa!*

His reverie slipped away. *What was I thinking? This is not me.*

Paralysis held him in place. He blinked and sucked in a breath. He felt as though he was being ripped apart. On the one hand, being with Reggie was the best thing he had experienced in a long time...maybe ever.

But on the other hand, he knew who he was. Frank Bell was the consummate bachelor. He didn't have time for relationships. He had always thought that if he were to form a long-standing relationship with someone, she would be a sophisticated woman of the world. Someone with no ties, who could be ready to go at a moment's notice.

Not a woman with deep roots embedded in this small town. Definitely not a woman with a small child. Frank shook his head, envisioning Reggie Lee and her daughter.

He let out a long breath. Shannon was a perfect child. Any man would be proud to be her father...or, for that matter, her stepfather. His chest felt tight.

He wasn't sure what he was feeling, but he was scared. Yeah, the big, strong, powerful man was terrified...of a beautiful woman and her precious child.

Frank raked his fingers through his hair. He was just coming off a wonderful trip with the woman he had crushed on since high school. The fruition of all his teenage fantasies, but better than he could have imagined. He should be feeling completely satisfied, but his euphoria was short-lived. Now all he felt was panic.

He gazed out at the property he now possessed. Owning so much property was a commitment.

Massaging the tightness at the back of his neck, he rationalized that he owed it to Aunt Rosie to take care of the property she loved. But there were managers in place. He knew Evan would make sure the vineyard continued to thrive. And the other businesses had managers. The Dairy Queen. The coffee shop. The *Gazette* building would still be there.

He huffed out a sigh. Reggie would manage the *Gazette*, but she would never forgive him if he distanced himself from her. Not after their long weekend together. Not after making love so passionately. Not after he had finally gained her trust.

Frank finished drinking the water and crushed the plastic bottle. He returned to the kitchen and pulled out the recycle bin. This had been one of Reggie's additions. Miss Save the World, one plastic bottle at a time. He smiled and lobbed the bottle into the bin.

Straightening his spine, he reached for his phone and scrolled for his calendar. Yes, he could afford to take off for a few days. He needed to sort out his feelings. He was confused, and Franklin Bell was never confused.

Reggie Lee was more than a little disturbed. She was afraid. Afraid that her ex, Kenny Landers, might actually get his hands on Shannon. That was unthinkable. Would a judge award joint custody to a worthless man like Kenny?

She couldn't afford to take a chance. Not with someone as

cherished as her own daughter. Kenny was so irresponsible she couldn't imagine that he would put Shannon's well-being ahead of his own self-centered interests.

She gripped her hands together, trying to stop them from shaking. She took several deep breaths and let them out slowly to help clear her brain.

Maybe I'm wrong. Maybe Kenny has grown up… Maybe the tooth fairy is real.

She paced around for a while, but nothing brilliant came to mind. She was always a woman with a plan, but tonight she was just a woman with a problem.

Every fiber of her being wanted to reach out to Frank, but something stopped her. This wasn't his problem. Although he claimed to be fond of Shannon, he wasn't her father. He wasn't anyone's father. Franklin Bell had no idea how to be a father. There was only one man for this job, and Reggie called him Daddy.

While Shannon was still in day care, Reggie drove straight to Stafford's Mercantile and parked in front. She practically ran through the door, clanking the metal bell against the glass. "Daddy, I need you."

Henry Stafford had been stocking the shelves with canned goods, but he turned at the sound of her voice. "Hello, sweetheart. How was your trip?" His wide smile faded when he caught sight of her face. "What's the matter, baby? What did that bastard do to you?"

Her face crumpled. "Oh, Daddy. I'm so miserable."

"I'll kill him." He shook his fist menacingly. "Frank Bell is a dead man."

"No, not Frank. He's been wonderful." Her voice trailed off into a whine. "It's Kenny. He's going to be here. He wants to see Shannon." Tears rolled down her cheeks, unnoticed. "I can't let that happen."

"Then I'll kill Kenny." Henry crossed his arms over his broad chest and planted his feet. "The weasel who broke my little girl's heart has no place in your life now and no place in Shannon's. I'll be damned if I allow him to just waltz back in here, thinking he can pick up where he left off."

"I know, Daddy."

"Don't you worry. I'll talk to the sheriff. I'll talk to the judge."

Both the sheriff and judge were fellow members of the VFW as well as classic car buffs. That should have been enough to quell her fears.

But she nodded, not sure these measures would deter someone as stubborn as Kenny Landers. She hated to admit it, but he did tend to bully people. He never considered the other person's point of view. Everything was always about him.

"That bastard walked out on you and Shannon," her dad raged. "He has no business just showing up here again."

A rush of gratitude flooded her chest. "I know. I appreciate you for paying for the divorce." A tear rolled down her cheek. "And I appreciate you for giving us a home. I don't know what I would have done if—if…" Her voice trailed off as she contemplated what might have been had her father not stepped up.

He made a noise in the back of his throat that sounded like something between a growl and a snort. "I was glad to get you out of his clutches. He was way beneath you, Reggie Lee."

"I used to think he was wonderful. All the girls were crazy about him."

"Bah! Big football hero." Henry smacked his fist into his open palm. "Big jerk is what he is."

"Daddy, I didn't want to upset you. I just wanted you to know that Kenny wrote me that he's going to be in town and wants to see Shannon."

"Not gonna happen." The expression on her father's face sent a shiver coiling down Reggie's spine.

—--m—--

Gayle had taken it upon herself to make sure everything was running as it should at the *Gazette*. She was surprised when the rest of the staff seemed to accept her inquisitiveness as being some sort of supervision. They all shared what they were doing and made sure to keep her in the loop.

She felt a little guilty for letting them assume she had been given some kind of assignment from Reggie Lee to keep an eye on things. Gayle had been very positive, making sure to compliment each of her coworkers on their particular area of expertise.

"Milton, the pics you took of the high school basketball game were spectacular. I can't believe you got that jump shot in stop action. Brilliant!"

She watched as the older gentleman grinned, his ears turning somewhat pink to display his pleasure.

"Aw, I been doin' this a long time," he said. "And I was in the right place at the right time to get that shot."

"You're awesome, Milton. The *Gazette* wouldn't be the same without you." She shoved her hands in her pockets and strolled away, grinning to herself.

She had also taken it upon herself to write up an announcement for a baby shower and an engagement party. Maybe Reggie Lee would appreciate her efforts when she returned. Maybe her boss would slap her down for overstepping her job description. So far, Gayle's job description was still receptionist.

Yes, indeed. She had overstepped her position.

"Hey, Gayle."

She turned to find Paul leaning on the front counter. He looked cute and boyish. "Hi, Paul. Is school out already?"

"The bell just rang, and I came right over here." He stood grinning at her as though she could read his mind.

"Um, are you still looking for Violet?"

His grin faded. "Uh, yes. Sure. I need to run another ad for

Violet." His brow furrowed, which was an abrupt change from his previous expression.

"Did you go to the animal shelter to look for her? I was hoping they might have her there waiting for you."

He gnawed his lower lip. "Uh, yes. She wasn't there." He heaved a sigh. "I'll just keep looking for her."

She had been there, of course, and hadn't seen any dog that looked as Paul had described her. *Brown and white and black. Hmm...*

He shrugged. "I'm still hopeful."

"Aw, that's so sweet. I'm glad you're still looking for her." Gayle leaned forward and lowered her voice. "Had you thought about going over to the radio station and asking them to make some announcements? They're very nice, and I'm sure they would be happy to help you."

"Yes—yes, I'll try that... By the way, I just wanted to remind you about our lunch together after church on Sunday."

"I didn't forget."

That seemed to reassure him. He flashed the boyish smile again. "Well, I'll see you at church on Sunday." He raised a hand and waved, then backed out the door.

Well, that was interesting. She returned to her desk, read over her story on the engagement party, and gave it a couple of tweaks before printing it out and putting it in Reggie Lee's mailbox. She hoped Reggie would find the article acceptable.

Now, all she had to do was keep smiling until Reggie returned... and until Sunday after church.

Frank made his way to the kitchen and took another bottle of water from the fridge. Twisting off the lid, he held it to his lips. As he swallowed, he did not feel refreshed.

When he turned around, Aunt Rosie's kitchen seemed to close

in on him. He felt suddenly bereft. After spending time alone with Reggie, the loneliness wrapped around him like a shroud.

He had always valued his privacy, but this was something different. He missed her already. He ached to be with her, but he figured Reggie had had enough of him for a while. She had a child… and her father probably wanted to spend time with her too. But that didn't lessen the pain.

He sat down at the kitchen table, recalling her sweet face when they had parted. She was happy. He had given her a great adventure in the big city.

A smile spread across his face. And Reggie Lee had given him even more. She'd opened herself up to him. They had been lovers, but it was so much more than the physical pleasure. He couldn't recall ever being so enamored of a woman. She tantalized him.

How could he keep from throwing himself over the edge of that deep abyss called love? He swallowed hard. What if Reggie was really the one love of his life? Did he believe in the concept of soul mates? How could he be sure?

He didn't want to ruin his relationship with Reggie. This startled him.

"Relationship." He pronounced each syllable separately and then wondered if he was in one.

Chapter 13

THE NEXT MORNING, REGGIE LEE WALKED INTO THE *GAZETTE* AND froze in her tracks. Everyone in the office turned to stare at her at the same time. Her throat constricted as she felt her cheeks redden.

"Hello, Ms. Stafford." Gayle stood, smiling at her. She held a sheaf of papers in her hands. "I have your mail and some things you need to sign off on."

Reggie accepted the paperwork, gave a terse nod, and headed for her office. The other employees stared at her as she made her way to her office. They were grinning.

She closed the door and collapsed back against it. *They know!* Reggie sucked in a deep breath and let it out slowly. *Damn! They know...*

Crossing to her desk, she tossed the stack of mail, messages, and other papers needing her attention onto it.

Well, if the entire staff of the *Rambling Gazette* knew that she, the editor, had spent a few days being romanced by an incredibly hot and outrageously rich hunk, that was just too bad. Yes, he now owned the building, but it wasn't as though she had slept her way to the top. Reggie had earned the job of editor by excelling at her job for years, and that was why Phil had named her to the position...and that was before Frank had ever asked her out. And who would have ever thought that her high school nemesis, the notorious Franklinstein, could be so charming?

She took a moment to see how that felt and realized there was nothing she could do about it. Heaving a loud sigh, she decided her reputation couldn't be repaired. Everyone knew she was a fallen woman. *Might as well hold my head up and just go on with business as usual. Whatever that means.*

Checking through the papers before her, she separated them into three piles: her mail, her phone messages, and the miscellaneous papers that needed her signature.

She slit open the envelopes and unfolded the first of the enclosures. It was disturbing when she realized she had been staring at the page for a couple of minutes without seeing it.

There was a tap at the door.

"Come in," Reggie said absently.

Gayle peeked inside. "I found another message. Sorry I misplaced it."

"Not a problem." Reggie heard the bite in her voice. She heaved a sigh and raked her fingers through her hair. "Sorry. I didn't mean to snap at you."

Gayle smiled her sweet smile. "Don't worry about it."

"Tell me the truth. Why is everyone smiling at me? They look so smug."

Gayle looked down. "You're our boss. Don't we always smile at you?"

"Not like that." She stood up abruptly, sending her chair rolling back to hit the console behind her.

"Well, you looked so happy when you first came in. We're just happy for you." Gayle met her gaze and shrugged.

"So does everyone know that I went away with Frank...Mr. Bell?"

Gayle flinched. "Um, well—I guess so. It wasn't a secret, was it?"

Reggie felt a squeezing sensation in her chest. "Nooooo," she groaned.

"Don't worry, Ms. Stafford. Nobody's judging you."

"I'm pretty sure they are." Reggie sat down again and shuffled through the pile of messages. "I guess I'm embarrassed. This is a small town. I don't want anyone to think badly of me." She reshuffled the messages without seeing them. "I mean, I have a daughter to think of."

Gayle dropped into the chair on the other side of the desk. "You don't need to feel embarrassed. You and Mr. Bell make such an attractive couple." She clasped her hands together. "It's so romantic."

Romantic? Yes, it was that. Mr. Franklin Bell sure did know how to wine and dine a girl. But it was probably over. A wave of sadness clenched her insides.

Reggie Lee Stafford, hometown girl, had zero in common with Franklin Bell, sophisticated world traveler. How could she even think she could hold his interest? She recalled the gorgeous redhead from the restaurant. If a woman that hot couldn't hold on to him, how could a simple mother of a young child hope to compete?

She cleared her throat. "You shouldn't make too much of it. Mr. Bell is my friend, and I'm helping him remodel his house. It's a historical treasure."

Gayle was clearly disappointed. "Sorry if I jumped to conclusions."

"We're going to do a feature story about the house renovation. People around here who loved Miss Rosie Bell Grady will enjoy seeing the house restored."

"That's a great idea," Gayle said. "I can see why Phil made you the editor. You have a natural knack for getting to the heart of a story."

"Thanks, Gayle. I guess I'm just a little anxious. I haven't been in this position long enough to take things in stride."

Gayle shrugged. "It's only natural, but the *Gazette* has picked up quite a few new subscribers since you took the helm." She stood and headed for the door. "While you were gone, I found a couple of things to write about. I put them in your mailbox whenever you have time."

"Well, let me see them. I need to get back in the right frame of mind."

Gayle's face lit up. "I'll grab them. Be right back."

Reggie was glad she could at least make one member of her staff so happy. She realized that it was Gayle who made her job easier. She took out her memo pad and made a note for the book-keeper. She wasn't sure what positions were open, but if there wasn't something appropriate available, she would create the right position.

Gayle rushed back into Reggie's office, clutching two fold-ers. She was grinning and plopped down on one of the chairs in front of Reggie's desk. "I'm so excited. I hope you like them." She passed the first to Reggie and seemed to be holding her breath.

Reggie scanned the local articles Gayle had written. "Oh, wow! You really nailed these. I'm so impressed that you took it upon yourself to cover these stories while I was gone." She glanced up at Gayle. "I hope you will keep it up."

"Oh, I will. No problem. Thank you." Gayle was practically bouncing in her seat.

"What else?" Reggie gestured to the other folder Gayle was still clutching.

Gayle swallowed. "A friend of mine... He lost his dog. So I went to the shelter to see if it was there." She stopped, blush-ing. "Oh, Reggie. There were so many animals there, and they all looked so lonely. I took some pictures, and then later, when I was thinking what I could do to help them, I started writing..."

Reggie smiled at her. "Writing about the animals?"

"Yes. Some of them had been lost, and some had been surren-dered by their owners. Just sad. I was hoping you would allow me to write a little about a different orphan animal each week, and publish it along with their picture in hopes someone would adopt them." Gayle finally released the folder and slid it across the desk to Reggie.

She saw an adorable orange-and-white kitten and read about Rusty. "Gayle, this is awesome. I'm sure we can find room for this weekly feature."

Gayle let out a little shriek of joy. "I sure do appreciate it. I know most people don't know that these animals are available. I mean, they know, but if they aren't reminded, they might never check them out."

"I think that's a great idea. Very creative." Reggie scanned the next picture, gazing into big brown doggy eyes. "I'll make sure there is a format change so this can be a weekly feature. Good job."

"Oh, thank you...thank you so much."

Reggie heaved a sigh. "I can't tell you how much I appreciate you for holding down the fort while I was gone. And you can expect to see an increase in your paycheck."

Gayle's grin went wall-to-wall. "Oh, thank you so much. I haven't had any kind of raise until now. I'm so glad you took over the editor's desk."

"It's what you deserve, Gayle. And I appreciate you for making sure everything was running smoothly while I was gone."

"I—I, uh..." She paused and sucked in a deep breath. "Do you recall when I told you about the young couple that came in looking for an apartment?"

Reggie nodded.

"Well, I may have a solution and a way to provide housing for people who don't want to own a house." She gazed earnestly at Reggie. "I mean, a lot of people don't want to bother with the upkeep of a house or deal with yard work."

"That makes sense."

Gayle pressed her lips together and then popped up from

her seat. "Could you just come with me? It won't take long, I promise."

"Sure." Reggie pushed out of her chair and followed Gayle, surprised when she made her way to the back of the building. They went past the seldom-used employee break room and a storeroom all the way to where a stairway was affixed to the back wall. It ran up to a little landing turnaround and then rose to the second floor. Gayle was on the stairs going up to the next floor.

Reggie climbed up after her, noting that the handrail was a bit loose and needed to be sanded and repainted. She was more than curious about what Gayle might have discovered while she was in New York City.

When they arrived at the second-floor landing, Reggie was a little out of breath. "Wow! Kind of gloomy up here."

Gayle was grinning though. "Just look at this. It's got this long central hallway and offices on both sides." She approached one of the doors and twisted the knob. "Of course, no one has been in here in years, but just look at the space." She threw the door open and displayed a dust-covered room filled with out-of-date printing equipment and a broken desk.

Reggie was stunned. "Are you proposing that these offices be turned into apartments?"

Gayle gave a little squeal of delight. "Yes! I'm so glad you can see it too. I figure that there can be four spacious apartments on each floor. I'm sure they will be filled with renters right away."

"But—but who would want to walk up to the fourth floor? That's quite a climb." Reggie turned around in a full circle, looking at the high ceilings and grime-covered windows.

"Oh, no. There is an elevator, but I wasn't sure how safe it is, so I thought we could just take the stairs and look around."

Gayle's excitement was contagious, and Reggie could see the possibilities. "You're right. This could be a really cute place. Lots of daylight and plenty of space."

Gayle let out a whoop. "I knew you would be on board. I just couldn't let that sweet couple and their dear little baby down."

"Hold on," Reggie said. "Frank owns the building, and I'm not sure how he feels about being a landlord. The *Gazette* pays no rent. It was his great-aunt's charity project because she believed this community needed a newspaper." She huffed out a sigh. "I'm just not sure if he would want to make the investment."

Gayle's face crumpled in disappointment.

"I mean, he would have to add plumbing for bathrooms and create a kitchen for each unit. That would be a huge amount of money."

Gayle nodded. "Well, maybe you could mention it to him and see if he would be interested. I know there would be lots of interest."

"I'm sure you're right." Reggie gestured toward the stairs. "I'll be sure to get his opinion, and perhaps you can show him what you've researched."

They made their way back down the stairs and emerged into the front offices.

"I want you to know how proud I am of you for taking this initiative. Very creative problem-solving."

Gayle blushed. "My pleasure. I'll get back to work."

Reggie paused and held up one hand. "Wait! Gayle, would you do me a favor?"

Gayle turned expectantly. "Of course."

Reggie sucked in a deep breath and expelled it. "Would it be too much trouble to—I mean, could you possibly—"

"Whatever I can do..." Gayle frowned uncertainly.

"If anyone asks about Frank—I mean, Mr. Bell—and me..." Reggie gnawed on her lower lip. "Could you explain that we're just working on his house...and the story?"

Gayle brightened immediately. "Certainly. I'll tell them that it's just business...if anyone asks."

Reggie flashed a wide smile. "Fine. That will be fine...if anyone asks."

When Gayle had departed, Reggie collapsed into her chair. *What have I done?*

Heaving a sigh, she attacked the pile of papers. She read through the messages, noting the calls she would need to return.

She finished with signing off on certain items and affixing her name to a few checks. That being done, she booted up her computer and scrolled through her emails, finally opening the file with the *Dear Irene* inbox.

Well, well, well... There was another letter from Mr. Nice Guy. Staring at it for a few moments before opening the missive, she realized she was smiling. She actually looked forward to this one.

Dear Irene,

I'm so confused. I think I love my coworker, but I'm not sure that I'm the right guy for her. In truth, we have very little in common. When we're together I'm really happy, and I'm sure she is too. But in the long run, I don't think we have the same goals. I'm not sure this will work out over the long haul. What do you advise?

Mr. Nice Guy

Reggie stared at the screen, the words seeming to dance before her eyes. What was going on with Mr. Nice Guy? He had been so crazy about his coworker, and now he was getting cold feet. Was he one of those men who enjoy the chase much more than the catch?

She huffed out a sigh. *Well, just let me tell him what a jerk he is.* She dashed off a biting reply, but before she hit send, she paused, her finger hovering above the button. She read over her words before deleting them and beginning again.

Dear Mr. Nice Guy,

You seem to be confused as to your feelings for your coworker. True love is a wonderful and enduring state. In the best scenario, this leads to a committed lifelong union. But sometimes people get caught up in the excitement and mistakenly think they are in love when in truth they do not have the basis for a genuine relationship. Being in love is the best thing ever. If you're lucky enough to find the right person, don't ever let them go. Perhaps you should step back and consider the depth of your emotional attachment. It might be kinder to end the relationship before anyone gets seriously hurt.

Irene

Reggie read over her response, heaving a sigh before printing it out and placing it in the *Dear Irene* folder. *It's done. Right or wrong, the letter has been answered.*

She had thought it sweet when she read Mr. Nice Guy's first letter, but now she felt a bit disappointed that he'd turned out to be such a wimp. His coworker was probably better off without him. *Poor girl.* Maybe it hadn't gone too far. Better to know early on that he wasn't a keeper.

A keeper. What do I know about keepers?

Reggie reflected on her notoriously bad taste in men. First, Kenny...a prime example of a man who couldn't commit. A man who ran away at the first sign of trouble...such as the arrival of a baby girl.

And now she was desperately in love with Frank Bell. A handsome urbane man of the world who couldn't possibly be interested in more than a fling with a naive small-town woman...a mother with a trainload of baggage.

Reggie gnawed her lower lip. *Yes, better for Mr. Nice Guy to ease off his relationship and not even pretend he is interested in anything serious.* Huffing out a sigh, she pushed back from her desk, thinking she shouldn't hole up in her office. That would give her staff the idea she was hiding, ashamed of her affair with her boss...which she had been...but not anymore.

Frank opened the latest copy of the *Rambling Gazette*. He turned the pages until he found the feature he had been anxious about. The *Dear Irene* column. A wide grin spread across his face when he recognized the sender, Mr. Nice Guy.

Hello, Dear Irene. That was fast.

His smile faded when he read Reggie's response to his letter from Mr. Nice Guy. He swallowed hard and read it again.

Confused about my feelings? *I'm not confused. I—I—*

Frank sat down on one of his great-aunt's delicate-looking Queen Anne chairs. One with lacy things pinned to the arms and the headrest. He stared at the screen until the words blurred before his eyes... *Perhaps you should step back and consider the depth of your emotional attachment. It might be kinder to end the relationship before anyone gets seriously hurt.*

Frowning, he let the paper fall to the floor. He felt much as he had in high school. Rejected.

Frank huffed out a breath. That was ridiculous. Reggie had no idea it was he who had sent the letter. She wasn't rejecting him. Not personally. She was rejecting Mr. Nice Guy.

But that's me.

He sat for some time, staring into space as he reviewed everything that had occurred between the two of them since he had returned to Rambling, Texas. He relived his ardent courtship and the ultimate thawing of the girl he had crushed on since they were both teens. His pursuit had culminated in a long, passionate weekend with Reggie in his bed.

A tightness gathered in his chest as he recalled waking up with her in his arms. It had felt so right. But now he was torn by inde-cision. He knew he couldn't just keep treading water with Reggie. Most of all, he didn't want to hurt her. He would have to either move the relationship forward or step back.

Now, she was telling him to step back.

Reggie counted out the cash for the till, arranging all the bills face up before tucking them in the correct slots. Opening the store on a Saturday morning to give her dad a break had been a frequent activity when she had been a mere reporter for the *Rambling Gazette*. Now that she had been appointed to the position of editor, she hadn't had time to tend the customers of Stafford's Mercantile. But since he had done double duty taking care of Shannon while she was in New York with Frank, she felt she owed him a little time off.

Huffing out a sigh, she considered her situation. More like an oncoming disaster. How could she prevent Kenny from inject-ing himself back into her life? It had taken so long to get over him. When she had realized he wasn't coming back, she had been crushed. It was inconceivable that a man could walk out on his wife and beautiful baby girl. Thankfully, her dad had been there to pick up the pieces.

She closed the cash register drawer with a satisfying metallic clang. She doubted that giving her dad a Saturday off now and then could ever repay him, but at least it was a small way to let him know she appreciated his support.

The metal cowbell over the door clanked against the glass. First customer of the day. "Good morning," Reggie sang out as she turned, a bright smile on her face.

"Ain't you the pretty one?" It was Kenny Landers. He stood grinning at her. His broad-shouldered, six-foot-five-inch frame took up all of the doorway.

The smile froze on her lips. A tightness gathered in her chest, forming a constricting band that kept her from drawing a full breath. She blinked several times, considered what she would say to him, but finally heaved an uncomfortable sigh. "It's you."

Kenny winked at her, a smirk spreading across his face as he approached her. "That's right, baby girl. I'm here." He stood on the other side of the counter, staring down at her with that same fond expression in his eyes that she had first fallen in love with. He reached across to cup her cheek in one hand. His palm was rough, but the gesture was tender. "Damn! You're just as beautiful as ever."

Reggie swallowed hard, stepping away from his touch. "What are you doing here, Kenny?"

He appeared to be hurt by her words. "I just wanted to see you. I've missed you something fierce."

"Really?" She tried to keep the sarcastic edge out of her voice.

"Yeah, really. I just want to talk to you."

"I thought we had said everything we needed to say a couple of years ago."

He raised his hands in a gesture of surrender. "Aww, baby. Don't be like that. I came back to Rambling because we belong together. You know I can't get you out of my head."

Keeping a tight rein on her emotions, she tried to regard him dispassionately. "You left two years ago...left me with a baby, and you never looked back. What kind of man does that?"

He shrugged. "So I made a mistake. I came home to make things right."

"Home? You don't live here anymore." She felt her lower lip tremble. *No! I won't let him see me cry.* Straightening her spine ever so slightly, she sucked in a deep breath.

Kenny surveyed her thoughtfully. "I thought we had a thing going on. I thought you loved me." He laid his great ham of a hand on his chest where his heart should have been.

"I did, but I was young and very naive. I'm over you now."

A smile twerked the corner of his mouth. "Are you?"

She eyed him speculatively. "Yes, I really am." For the first time, she realized it was true. "Now, if you want to buy something, that's great. Otherwise, you need to go on your way. There is nothing between us anymore."

His face turned an ugly dark red as his gaze narrowed. A muscle in his jaw tensed, then relaxed.

A tingle of fear spiraled around Reggie's spine. She suddenly realized how totally alone she was with a man who had a reputation for brutality. She managed to control her expression, suppressing her fright and presenting a facade of pure confidence.

With seemingly great effort, he managed to rein in his anger and back away. "We'll just have to see about that." He turned and stomped out of the store, setting the cowbell clanking so hard against the glass she was afraid it would shatter.

She stared after him as he climbed into an old beater of a truck and revved the engine. He backed out of the parking lot without looking and raced off.

It surprised her to realize she was clinging to the edge of the counter, unable to draw a breath. A wave of fear washed over her. She had heard rumors of how mean Kenny had been in high school, but that was years ago. She had thought it was just because he was so aggressive on the football field, but now—seeing all that rage directed at her left her trembling all over.

She needed to call Frank. She needed his arms around her. She needed to hear his soothing voice tell her things would be all right.

Slowly, she released her grip on the edge of the counter and forced herself to draw a deep breath. *No, this is my problem.*

She thought surely she could deal with her ex without dragging Frank into it. They were divorced. She had the papers to prove it.

Frank took a last look around the house. He made sure everything was turned off and locked up tight.

Standing on the front porch, he surveyed his domain...or at least this cozy little part of it. He heaved a sigh, realizing this lovely setting just was not the real Franklin Bell, international playboy...man of the hour...power player.

A lineup of images ran through his brain, the faces of the many beautiful women he had dated. Emphasis on *dated* and not *married*. No, he was the complete bachelor package. *Love 'em and leave 'em*. Yeah, that was his style. He never made any promises. He always made it clear he wasn't the marrying type.

Resolutely stepping off the porch, he strode to his BMW, tossed his bag in the back seat, and slid behind the wheel. The retinue of his past flings receded, only to be replaced with images of Reggie's beautiful face. The large, dark eyes accused him. *Are you running out on me?*

"No," he muttered aloud. "I'm just—" He shrugged. "Trying to do what you wanted...giving you some space." *Stepping back...*

Heaving a deep sigh, he turned the key in the ignition, enjoying the roar of the powerful motor coming alive. He turned around in the driveway and headed down the lane leading from the house. As he paused to turn onto the highway, he glanced in the rearview mirror. The tree-lined drive with the lovely old Victorian was an image that would live on in his heart. A picture of things that might have been, if only he had been a different man.

—◌◌◌—

Frank hadn't called her on Saturday, and on Sunday she was feeling itchy. She carried the phone around, jammed in a pocket, just so she could get to it easily without having to grope for it. She didn't even turn it off when she went to church, but it was on vibrate, and she would have grabbed it immediately if it had even twitched.

Not a problem. She figured he was too busy to call and was sure they would be in contact come Monday morning. The image of his face, with its lazy and very sexy grin, swam through her brain.

Oh, no! I'm lusting in church. Surely I'm going to hell.

Hurriedly, she smoothed out the wrinkles in the church bulletin she had grasped in her hand. The pastor droned on about something she wasn't processing. The tone of his voice had lulled the man in the pew directly in front of her to a sound sleep with his chin on his chest and rhythmic heavy breathing.

The pastor announced another hymn, so she stuffed the bulletin in her pocket and reached for the hymnal. Flipping through the pages, she found the correct page. As the choir stood, she hummed along and managed to make it through the chorus.

When the service was over, she went to the nursery to retrieve her daughter before joining her father at the front of the church.

"There are my girls." Henry greeted her with a wave and a smile. He reached for Shannon and hefted her into his arms.

Reggie nodded and shook the pastor's hand before trailing her father to the car. She watched him secure Shannon in her car seat before she climbed in on the passenger side.

"What's wrong?" Henry glanced at Reggie.

She shook her head. "What makes you think something is wrong?"

He snorted. "Many years living in close proximity with my daughter." He turned to gaze at her critically. "Come on and tell your dear old dad what's going on. Has your new boyfriend done something to upset you?"

"N—no. Nothing like that." She shrugged. "He's been wonderful." *Just a little invisible lately.*

"Then what is it?"

"Could we just go home? I'm really tired."

Henry reached across to ruffle her hair, just as he had done when she was a little girl. It was a strangely comforting gesture.

"Sure. Let's get to the house." He started the engine and pulled out into the stream of cars leaving the church parking lot. "But I'm not going to let up until you tell me what's upsetting you."

"It's Kenny. He came to the store yesterday."

"Oh, Lord!" Henry struck the steering wheel with the heel of his hand. "What does that waste of skin want with you?"

Reggie bit her lower lip. "I—I don't know. He acted as though we weren't divorced. He was talking crazy."

Henry made an animal-like sound. "I would tell you what I really think of your worthless ex if there wasn't an impressionable child in the back seat."

In spite of her angst, Reggie had to smile at that. "Hold it in, Dad."

"I expect a full report when we get to the house."

She sat a little straighter, accepting that her father would be her confidant, like it or not. Maybe it would be better to share... Maybe it would be better to leave her concerns about Frank out of the equation.

Chapter 14

FRANK TRIED TO RELAX. HE STOOD AT THE HUGE WINDOW INSIDE his condo staring down at Central Park. He had a first-class ticket to Monte Carlo but somehow dreaded climbing on the plane the next morning.

He was alone and lonely. Two different emotions swirled through his chest. He missed Reggie, but he knew she wanted him to step back from their sometimes-unsettling relationship. He realized he had been pushing her hard, and it was difficult to back off. He had been unable to blurt out his true feelings, but in truth, Reggie had never even said she liked him, let alone made any declarations of love. Maybe she'd just needed a fling?

With every fiber of his being, he wanted to be with her, but she had to want him too. She had to be willing to stand with him, no matter what.

He shook his head and turned away from the magnificent view he'd not been seeing. *Too bad*. Reggie was the first woman he'd thought he could be with on a long-term basis. Even worse, he had fallen for her child as well. Without Reggie and Shannon, his life felt hollow.

Maybe it was karma smacking him on the head. He had walked away from quite a few beautiful women. Perhaps it was only fair that the one he really wanted had just kicked him to the curb.

He raked his fingers through his longish hair. *No, it wasn't fair*. He was in love with Reggie. He couldn't recall a time when he hadn't been in love with her. Maybe she had bewitched him when he'd first smacked into her back in school? *Maybe?*

"There is no such thing as love at first sight." His voice sounded too loud in the condo, echoing back at him off all the hard surfaces. His words sounded false, even to his own ears.

Throwing himself down on the leather sectional, he considered his alternatives. In truth, he was in a foul mood. He was certainly not up to Monte Carlo. And even if his phone was jammed with contact information for dozens of beautiful women on both continents, the prospect of spending time with any of them was not enticing.

He thought about checking out the action at some of New York City's hottest clubs but rejected that idea. Instead, he canceled his flight to Monte Carlo, deciding to stay in his leased condo filled with leased furniture and leased artwork. He could lick his wounds until he felt he could face the world again.

Frank opened the sparkling mirrored doors set into the wall. Hidden inside was his very well-stocked liquor cabinet. He selected a cut-crystal glass and poured a prodigious amount of good Irish whiskey into it, reasoning that he would either feel better or feel nothing. Either one was preferable to his current state of misery.

--- ∾ ---

Reggie sat in her mother's recliner, Shannon asleep in her arms. She was staring at the television, but not seeing the images on the screen nor hearing the voices.

Her dad was engrossed in the game, but images of Kenny's smirking face played nonstop through her brain. She felt paralyzed with fear. The return of her ex-husband was the last thing she had ever considered. She had no illusions that he was still in love with her...if he had ever been in love with her. Sadly, she was pretty sure he had no particular feelings for his daughter.

It occurred to her that Kenny had first started drawing away from her when she had accidentally become pregnant.

Reggie placed a soft kiss in Shannon's hair. "Well, he just doesn't know what he's missing."

"What's that?" Henry asked.

"Nothing, Dad. I'm going to put Shannon in her bed." Struggling to her feet, she cradled her precious cargo in her arms. She tiptoed down the hallway to her daughter's room and silently turned the knob. Miraculously, she was able to jostle Shannon onto her bed without waking her. She snuggled the quilt around the child.

"Oh, baby," she whispered. "Don't you worry. I'm going to protect you, no matter what it takes."

She left the door ajar and changed into her gown and robe in her bedroom across the hall. Taking the time to cleanse her face and brush her teeth, she knew she was putting off the inevitable heart-to-heart talk her father was anticipating.

When she returned to the living room, her dad was watching the news. He raised an eyebrow and turned off the television with the remote.

Reggie plopped into the recliner and folded her hands in her lap. "Let's get this over with, okay?"

Henry exhaled a deep breath. "I don't know what you mean."

She made a scoffing sound. "Oh, come on, Dad. You're going to lecture me about marrying Kenny in the first place. I know you weren't thrilled when you walked me down the aisle, but I thought I was in love."

"I know." He shook his head. "We can't rewrite history. Let's just figure out where we're going from here. Why do you suppose Kenny happened to show up at this particular time?"

"I don't know."

"I mean, he hasn't exactly been a model father. No child support. No visits."

"I know, Dad. You don't have to remind me." She lolled her head back on the headrest.

"Sorry. I just want to know why he's back now."

She sucked in a deep breath and let it all out at once. "I have no idea, but whatever it is, I'm sure he's got an agenda of his own."

Henry's brows drew together. "That's what I'm afraid of. I think I'll have to call Sheriff Vern Garland tomorrow. See what he has to say."

—⁓—

The next day, when Reggie was in her office going over the ad sales with Elvis, she congratulated him on signing up two new advertisers.

"I'm so proud of you, Elvis. You're really doing a great job."

Elvis grinned sheepishly as a red stain crept up his neck. "Thanks, Miss Reggie. I'm trying to do a good job for you."

A soft tap on the door interrupted their meeting. Gayle opened it and peeked inside. "Sorry to disturb you, but there's a...a gentleman here to see you."

Reggie glanced at her calendar. "Hmm...I'm not expecting anyone."

"He said his name is Kenny Landers and he was sure you would make time for him." Gayle looked uncertain.

Reggie's stomach knotted up in fear. Her breath seemed to have been squeezed from her lungs. She pressed her lips together. "Fine. I'll see him."

Elvis gathered his pages and slipped out of the room just before Gayle returned, escorting a smug Kenny into the office.

"Hey, babe. I thought I would drop in to see how you're doing." Uninvited, he plopped into the chair Elvis had vacated.

"I see." She closed the ledger she had been working on.

He craned his neck, looking all around her office. "Looks like you hit the big time, girl. You're the big boss now." He shook his head. "Who woulda thunk it? My sweet little wifey made it to the top of the heap."

"I'm really busy right now."

"Too busy to spend some time with the man who loves you?"

Reggie snorted indelicately. "No, you don't get to play that card, Kenny. If you had loved me, you would never have left."

He looked injured. "Aw, babe. I was confused. I didn't know what I wanted." He put his boots on the edge of her desk, seemingly completely at ease. "Seems like you've done pretty well for yourself. You must be making some serious bucks now."

She struggled to maintain a disinterested expression. "I really do have work to do."

Kenny sat up straight, dropping his feet heavily to the floor. "Are you throwing me out?"

"I'm busy. What can't you understand about that?"

He glowered at her. "I understand, all right. You're brushing me off."

"Well, I didn't know you were coming. Most people call for an appointment."

Pushing himself out of the chair with both hands on the armrests, he towered over her. "An appointment?" He leaned over her desk, pointing a finger at her. "You don't tell me what to do." His face reddened, and a vein stood out on his forehead. "You're my wife, and you don't talk to me like that." He slammed his fist on her desk.

Her heart pulsed in her ears, but she lifted her chin, determined not to be bullied. "I am not your wife," she said softly. "I haven't been your wife for some time."

"Excuse me, Ms. Stafford." Gayle stood in the doorway. "I took the liberty of calling the sheriff's office. They just pulled up outside."

The tightness in Reggie's chest loosened a bit as she managed to aim a smile in Gayle's direction. "Thank you, Gayle. Please show Mr. Landers out. He was just leaving."

Kenny snarled at Reggie before stomping out of her office.

Gayle stepped aside just in time to avoid a collision. "Oh, my!"

Reggie slowly covered her eyes with both hands. "Thanks."

"Who was that man?" Gayle stepped into the office.

"My ex...my very ex-husband."

———

Gayle's heart was beating so fast she thought it might flutter out of her chest. The man named Kenny Landers had been a football player at the high school, but he had been a couple of years ahead of her. The rough-looking man who had just departed gave the impression that he had been living under a bridge. He needed a haircut, and the scruff on his face looked more like neglect than an attempt to look sexy.

Her boss appeared to be quite shaken. Whatever the reason for their encounter, it had not been a good one. Reggie had dropped her face into her hands. Although she was not weeping, she was close to tears, and her voice had risen a whole octave.

The Landers guy had been enraged when he left. As he'd passed her in the doorway, his jaw was clenched so tight a vein had popped out at his temple.

"Um, he's gone now," she said. "There's a deputy outside in his cruiser. Do you want to talk to him?"

Reggie gnawed her lower lip. "Yes... No... I don't know."

"Well, why don't you just have a chat with him? It couldn't hurt." Gayle looked at Reggie, hoping to encourage her.

Reggie swallowed hard. "Yes... Ask him to step in."

Gayle left the office door open and made her way quickly to the front of the building. Yes, the deputy was still parked in front. She stepped out and knocked on the driver's side window.

The deputy lowered the window. "What can I do for you, young lady?"

She had to smile at that. "Could you please come inside to speak to the editor? Ms. Stafford is pretty shaken up."

The deputy climbed out and gave her a salute of sorts, with two fingers touching the brim of his hat. He left the lights flashing as he sauntered up the steps and into the *Gazette* office.

Gayle heaved a sigh, glad that her life was not as complicated as Reggie Lee's.

"Are you okay?"

She turned around to find Paul Harmon gazing at her. She nodded absently. "I'm fine."

"I was driving by and saw the flashing lights and thought I should make sure you were all right." Concern was written all over his face. "I was afraid something might have happened here. You know, there are crazy people out there."

Gayle felt like hugging him. "That is so sweet, Paul. I'm fine, but my boss...not so much."

His brow furrowed. "Oh? What's going on?" He reached out to her, and without thinking she reached back. Now they were holding hands in the newspaper parking lot.

"It was personal. Her ex came for an unannounced visit, and I had to call the sheriff's office. The ex left when the patrol car arrived."

"I can't imagine," he said. "Of course I cannot imagine having an ex. When I marry, I hope my wife will keep me around forever." He raised her hand to his lips and brushed a kiss against it.

This small gesture caused a squeezing sensation in Gayle's chest. She couldn't control the wide grin that spread across her face, and when she leaned into his embrace, she lingered, soaking up the feeling of being surrounded by someone who truly cared for her.

Frank read the *New York Times* online and sipped his coffee. He worked the daily crossword and the Sudoku, then deleted them. Bored, he turned on the wide-screen television and flipped through the channels. *Nothing.*

Maybe he would go out for a walk. *Maybe not.*

For some reason he couldn't fathom, the joy seemed to have faded from his life. He scrambled to find something to occupy his time...anything to take the place of the beautiful face resonating in his brain.

He had dreamed about Reggie Lee and how sweet she looked with Shannon and how peaceful she appeared when she slept in his arms. He awoke with a smile on his face, imagining he could smell the soft fragrance of her hair, longing to touch her skin. An ache rolled through him, causing physical pain from his gut through his chest. *How can one guy be so messed up?* Surely he could step away, if that was what she truly wanted.

In school, she had always been the smartest person in every class they'd shared. Now, it seemed she was smart enough to realize their differences and decide she didn't want to prolong the agony.

He sucked in a breath, telling himself she hadn't rejected him. She had merely replied to Mr. Nice Guy's email.

"But I'm Mr. Nice Guy."

Somehow, it just didn't seem fair.

He rolled out of the leather recliner and stomped around the condo. Perhaps he could change. If he had to make a choice between Reggie Lee and everything else in the world, could he turn his back on the life he had created and settle in a small Texas Hill Country town where everyone thought the same way, attended one of the five churches, and voted the same ticket?

He wound up in the sparkling-clean kitchen, where he never cooked. Opening the refrigerator, he stared at the meager contents. He should just put on his jacket and go shopping. Surely laying in some basic supplies would lift his spirits. There was a deli and market a block away. He would browse the items and fill up the empty space in the fridge—and maybe the dead space in his heart.

Frank rode the elevator down all by himself. It seemed the other condo owners were either at work or locked inside their own ivory towers.

The doorman snapped to attention. "Good afternoon, Mr. Bell, sir. Enjoy your outing."

Frank nodded at him, unable to recall his name.

Once outside, the air was brisk and smelled…well, like city air. He inhaled exhaust fumes mingled with odors from food vendors. He picked up his pace, passing the food cart where the vendor was serving up a sauerkraut-topped hot dog.

Yes, he reasoned. The city was where he belonged. He couldn't imagine Reggie plodding along these streets, hanging onto Shannon's hand.

Frank shook his head. That wasn't right. He would carry Shannon if they were walking somewhere. Or he would hail a cab or hire a car. He swallowed hard, thinking they could make it work…if she was willing to make it work.

He waited for the light to change and then crossed to enter the corner market. Selecting a basket, he set out to find food, a basic instinct. He followed his nose to the bakery section and chose a fresh loaf of pumpernickel and one of whole wheat. Feeling foolish for his impulse purchases, he knew the bread would turn green before he could eat it, but he couldn't make himself put one back.

At the deli counter he ordered a half pound each of smoked turkey and pastrami plus a variety of cheeses. He moved down the line toward the cashier.

"You wan' some sides or a pickle?" The tiny lady behind the counter gazed at him dispassionately, her hair hidden under a white cap and her hands in oversize plastic gloves.

He nodded. "Sure. Give me a pickle and some potato salad."

"How about a side of slaw?" She gestured to a cabbage mélange.

"Um, okay." When she had served him, he moved to the line waiting to pay the cashier.

"Hello, Frank." A low-pitched female voice spoke close to his ear.

He turned. "Uh, hello." The sultry-looking brunette looked familiar, but he couldn't recall her name.

"Why didn't you call me to let me know you were in the city?" She threw her head back, tossing her mane of hair and puffing out her breasts.

"Well, I wasn't sure when I would be back." He gazed at her uncertainly.

Her eyes narrowed. "I can't believe it! You don't even remember me." She punched his arm. "Dammit! We had a great time."

Frank expelled a deep breath. "I'm sure we did, it's just—"

The brunette tapped her stiletto impatiently. "Just what?" she snapped.

"I think I'm in love with someone...someone wonderful." He flashed a brief smile, hoping for understanding. "I can't seem to even think about anyone else."

"Well! I've never been treated like this." She tossed her hair again. "Trust me, Franklin Bell. Your reputation will be trashed by the time I get through with you. You'll never get another date in this town." She huffed out a breath and spun on her very high heels, taking long strides to the exit.

"Next," the cashier sang out.

Frank felt as though he was in a daze. Suddenly it all made sense. He handed his Visa card to the man behind the cash register. A grin split his face. At last, he knew what he had to do.

———

The next afternoon, Gayle stopped by the animal shelter. She planned to make sure the orange kitten was still available for adoption in case she needed to swap out another deserving animal. The volunteers greeted her enthusiastically, delighted that she was going to feature some of their furry friends in the *Gazette*.

She went back to see Rusty the kitten, feeling both happy and sad that he was still occupying a cage with another kitten.

He came to the bar and reached a little white paw out to her.

Gayle scratched him on the head. "Don't you worry, little fellow. I'm going to show the citizens of Rambling how adorable you are. I'm sure the perfect person will fall in love with you and rush in to pay your bail."

She took a couple of pictures of other felines and then went to the canine side of the shelter. The dogs were excited and perked up immediately, greeting her with yips and arfs. "Hi, guys." She was sad to see that Bubba was still in his cage but was told that Heidi, the smaller dog, had been adopted.

"Well, good for you, Heidi." She made herself a promise that she would beef up Bubba's story so that the right person would come in to rescue him.

She took a couple more pictures of dogs and then came to an abrupt stop, staring at a small, fluffy dog. It was white with black and brown spots on it.

Gayle could hardly breathe. Could this be Violet? "This dog!"

The volunteer came over and opened the cage. "Isn't she cute? Such a little puff ball. Look at her little plume of a tail." She turned the dog around to show off her fluffy little tail.

"Does she have a collar?" Gayle asked, reaching out to sink her fingers into the luxurious fur.

"No collar, and she isn't chipped." The volunteer offered her to Gayle. "Just hold her. You'll fall in love."

Gayle snuggled the dog against her chest, delighted when the dog licked her cheek. "Oh, I want this dog."

"Awesome. There are a bunch of papers to fill out." The volunteer grinned. "We can't let just anyone adopt one of our little fur kids."

Gayle stroked the dog's head, locking her gaze to the bright and shiny shoe-button eyes. "I'll do whatever it takes...but I'm taking Violet home with me today."

The woman's eyes opened wide. "Violet? That's a perfect name. She looks like a lovely little Violet."

Gayle followed the volunteer to the front office where she filled out a massive amount of paperwork, describing her home and fenced yard as well as her willingness to provide ongoing veterinarian care. She then forked over a plastic card to pay for the adoption fee.

If this was truly Violet, then she was sure Paul would be thrilled to have her back...but if he had manufactured an imaginary Violet to get her attention, she would keep Violet for herself. This was a win-win situation all around. The truth would come out, and Violet would have a home.

Chapter 15

"WHERE ARE YOU GOING?" HENRY STOOD WITH HIS HANDS fisted at his waist.

Reggie pulled the knitted cap down to cover Shannon's ears. "I thought I would take Shannon to the park. We can't stay cooped up here forever."

"Yes, you can." He nodded to the window. "Is that your ex sitting a couple of doors down in that ratty old truck?"

A sinking feeling enveloped her as she rushed to the window. "Oh, no! I mean, yes. It's him." She closed the drapes and peeked out. "What is he doing out there?"

Henry reached for the phone. "I'll take care of this." He punched in some numbers and made a guttural sound deep in his throat. "Hey, Vern. You remember that louse, Kenny Landers?" A short pause. "Yeah, my daughter's ex-husband. Well, he's stalking her. Sitting right outside the house. And he made a scene at her office yesterday."

Reggie sat on the floor, clutching Shannon close. "It's going to be okay, baby. Don't be scared."

Shannon gazed at her with big eyes and a solemn expression.

Henry covered the receiver with his hand. "She's not scared. Don't you be scared."

She nodded furiously. "I'm not, Daddy."

He rolled his eyes and returned the receiver to his ear. "That's right, Vern." He hung up and huffed out a sigh. "Why don't you take Shannon to the kitchen for some ice cream?"

"Ice cream? Daddy, it's a little cool for ice cream."

"Just take her out of here, okay?"

"Ice cweam!" Shannon squealed.

Reggie gathered her daughter and headed to the back of the house. She glanced at her dad, who peered through the glass panel high on the front door, glaring fiercely.

Shannon tugged on her hand. "Ice cweam."

Reggie allowed herself to be drawn to the kitchen, where she seated her daughter at the table. She opened the freezer, staring at two gallon tubs of ice cream. "Too bad. It looks like we're all out of ice cream. How about a couple of cookies?"

Shannon's lips formed a pout, which quickly disappeared when Reggie reached for the cookie jar. "Let's see what we have. Oh, there are some peanut butter cookies in here and some chocolate chip. Would you like one of each?"

Shannon nodded vigorously.

The sound of a siren blurted one short blast just outside their house. Reggie quickly arranged the cookies on a paper napkin and hurried to join her father.

"Daddy, what have you done?"

He was grinning. "I just called my good friend, Vern Garland. We're both members of the Elks, y'know?" He raked his fingers through his hair. "And the Veterans of Foreign Wars...and we are the founders of the Rambling Cruisers Classic Car Club." He nodded as though this should impress her with the solidarity of their friendship.

"Are you talking about Sheriff Vernon Garland, my friend Jill's dad?"

"Damn right." Henry's grin was so wide it appeared his face might break.

Reggie pulled the drapes aside to see a patrol car pulled up behind Kenny's truck. Two uniformed deputies climbed out, weapons drawn. Her heart fluttered in her chest. "Are they going to shoot him?"

"I hope so."

"Not funny, Daddy."

The deputies ordered Kenny out of the truck. He threw the door open and came out yelling and red-faced. Waving his hands, he approached the officers. One officer grabbed him by the arm, spun him around and slammed him against the truck's fender while the other stood by, his weapon pointed at Kenny.

"Hah! Way to go, gentlemen."

"Daddy!"

"Well, I never could stand that guy."

She raised her brows as high as possible. "Oh, really? Name one male I ever dated who you did like."

Henry rubbed his chin thoughtfully. "Well, there was that one guy…"

Reggie noted that Kenny had been handcuffed and was being loaded into the back of the deputy's vehicle. "Daddy, you have to know that I'm in love with Frank Bell. Don't worry. I don't think he cares that much for me." She shrugged. "It's not like we have anything in common." She turned to find her father frowning at her. "What?"

"All this 'things in common' stuff is a lot of hooey. Your mother and I didn't have that much in common. We got married, and guess what?"

"What?"

"We got things in common. We had a budget. We had bills. We had the store. We had a kid." He waved his hand in her direction. "But we loved each other, so we worked it out. Just find someone you can love as much as your mom and I loved each other. That's all it takes." He flapped his hand at her as though she was being totally frivolous.

She frowned. "What are you saying?"

Henry opened the drape and waved. "There goes Kenny. Hope they lock him up for a hundred years." He turned to face Reggie. "Here's what I'm saying. I don't hate Franklin Bell."

"You don't hate—"

"No, I don't. He seems to be a responsible young man."

Reggie was stunned. She couldn't recall her father ever approving of anyone she had been involved with. Of course, that amounted to a couple of nerdy high school boys before Kenny... and now Frank. "Well—well, I'm glad you like him because I'm crazy about him." *I just haven't heard from him.*

Henry nodded. "Good to know."

The next day brought a ton of work. Seeing Kenny being hauled away in handcuffs had brought her a sense of relief, at least for the evening. She had slept well and awoke feeling rested.

But as the day progressed, so did her anxiety. She wasn't naive enough to think spending the night in jail would deter Kenny from whatever he intended to do. She hoped he wasn't serious about wanting to spend time with Shannon. Surely he didn't intend to do the dad thing. It just wasn't in his nature.

"Here's the last of them." Gayle slid another folder onto her desk.

"More invoices?"

"Yep. You can put them off until tomorrow, if you like. It's getting dark outside."

Reggie glanced out the window and noted that, indeed, night had fallen and it was black outside. Thankfully, there was a full moon to brighten the sky. "Why don't you go on home, Gayle? I'll just sign off on these and put the folder on your desk."

Gayle glanced toward the door. "Okay, if you don't mind. I need to run by the grocery store on my way home." She stood and headed out.

"I'll be right behind you."

"See you tomorrow." Gayle gave her a little wave as she left the office.

Reggie moved the picture of Shannon atop her desk, smiling

as she did so. She sighed and picked up her pen again. Going over every invoice was important. She had found several errors in the billing and refused to authorize any invoice for payment unless she had examined it personally and signed off on each one.

When she finally pushed her chair back, she stretched her cramped limbs before standing up. She took her purse out of the bottom drawer and picked up the folder, dropping it on top of Gayle's desk. Taking a last look around the deserted office, she flipped off the lights and stepped outside. It only took a few moments for her to find her keys and match one with the front lock. She turned to see her solitary car parked nearby, gleaming in the bright moonlight.

Her footsteps crunched in the gravel as she crossed to her vehicle. She clicked the remote and heard the comforting chirp. She had just reached for the door handle when she was jerked backward.

"Surprise." Kenny's voice was rough, close to her ear, and he reeked of alcohol. "You think you can screw me over and I'll just walk away?" He maintained his grip on her arm, making it impossible to move.

"Stop. Let me go."

Kenny huffed out a single laugh. "You don't tell me what to do." He slammed her against the car, knocking the breath out of her.

"P-please stop. You're hurting me."

"You think you're so high and mighty now." He pulled her back against his chest, his breath hot against her cheek. "With your fancy office and all those people kissing your ass."

Reggie tried to control her fear, but her voice came out all thready. "I'm not like that, Kenny. What do you want?" She braced herself for his response.

"What do I want?" His grip tightened. "I want what's due me. If you want to stay in your little ivory tower with our kid, you need to pay me for that privilege."

An epic shiver convulsed her body. "P-pay you?"

"Yeah. You wouldn't have none of that without me. And I'll do what it takes to get the kid if you don't play ball."

"Kenny, I don't think—"

"Shut up. You just don't know when to shut up." He raised his free hand as though to strike her.

"No, don't," she screamed.

Heart thudding against her ribs, Reggie tried to twist out of his grasp, but he held her in a punishing grip.

Headlights washed the parking lot as a car pulled in and came to an abrupt stop, the tires spewing gravel.

"Get your hands off her." It was Frank. He was out of his BMW and coming on fast.

Kenny made a growling sound. "Well, if it ain't the pretty boy from school. Didn't I whip your ass enough back then?" He spat out a derisive laugh.

Frank snorted. "Apparently not. Let Reggie go."

Kenny released her and swung around, his fists raised. "I'm gonna kill you."

"Reggie, move away." Frank dodged a roundhouse punch, but Kenny managed to grasp Frank's shirt, popping off the buttons as it ripped down the front. Frank shrugged out of it and danced away from Kenny's powerful punches.

Reggie shrank away, rubbing her bruised wrist as she ran toward the fence. Gasping for breath, she turned to see Frank take a running leap, landing one foot in Kenny's midsection. Kenny let out a grunt and fell backward with a thud, landing hard against her car.

He cursed and rebounded, his fist raised, but as he attempted to punch Frank, he was caught off-balance. Frank grabbed his wrist and spun him around, flipping him face-first down onto the gravel. "Call the sheriff's office."

Reggie glanced around for her purse, finally locating it near her front tire. She fumbled with the clasp and drew out her phone.

"Oh, be careful, Frank." She punched in 911 and spoke hurriedly to the operator.

"Not a problem."

Kenny threw Frank off and scrambled to his feet. Blood dripped from his lip. He wiped it away and ran at Frank again.

Reggie watched in horror, cringing as Frank stood calmly in the path of the rushing behemoth. He appeared as a statue, both hands fisted in a pose to protect his core, his expression composed but watchful.

Kenny, on the other hand, appeared to be rabid. His face looked like raw liver, and his lips were drawn back in a grimace.

Reggie wondered why she had ever found him attractive.

As Kenny made a grab for him, Frank struck out, popping his foe in the nose.

It happened so fast, Reggie wasn't certain what she had seen.

A spurt of blood streamed down Kenny's face. He stood as though dazed, shaking his head as Frank circled around him. He let out a scream of rage that sounded more like a bleat.

Kenny flexed his muscles, turning to face Frank.

"You need to stop," Frank said. "Just stop being such an ass, Kenny."

"You broke my nose," he shouted. "I'm gonna rip you apart."

Frank didn't appear to be fazed by this pronouncement. "Bring it," he bit out and waggled his fingers in a "come on" motion.

Reggie couldn't seem to move. She was mesmerized by Frank's confidence and the rhythmic way he moved. He was almost dancing as he circled and fended off Kenny's attack.

A squad car rolled into the parking lot. The siren whooped once before a spotlight scanned the area. Both doors flew open, and two deputies sprang out the moment the vehicle drew to a stop. Weapons in hand and yelling orders, they approached the combatants cautiously.

Frank stepped back, his hands raised, but Kenny lurched toward him.

Reggie screamed, causing Frank to turn suddenly. That was when Kenny's fist connected with Frank's jaw, knocking him off his feet. He did something like a sideways somersault, landing on his feet in a crouch.

"Nooooo," she moaned.

One deputy tased Kenny, who fell face-first to the gravel, twitching. The other deputy squatted above him. Ignoring the spasms, he fastened handcuffs around his wrists.

Reggie rushed to Frank, kneeling beside him. "Oh, Frank. Are you all right?"

Grinning, he rubbed his chin. "I'm okay. How about you?"

She burst into tears, nodding. Throwing her arms around Frank's neck, she rained kisses on his face. "I don't know what would have happened to me if you hadn't shown up."

Frank cast a menacing glare at Kenny. "I hate that he even touched you."

She nodded. "Thank you, Frank."

As one of the deputies was loading Kenny in the back of their vehicle, he seemed to recover. "That's my wife," he shouted.

Both deputies looked at Reggie.

"No, we've been divorced for years. He attacked me when I came out of my office." Her voice faltered.

"He assaulted her." Frank spoke calmly, but there was a deadly undertone.

"Is that right, miss?"

Reggie nodded. "Mr. Bell saved me. I—I don't know how this would have ended if Frank hadn't shown up."

Kenny cursed and struggled but settled down when the deputy pointed the taser at him again. They shoved him in the back of the squad car and slammed the door.

One of the deputies took out a notebook and wrote down the

details of the incident, advising Reggie and Frank to go to the sheriff's office to make a formal complaint in the morning.

The deputies drove away, leaving Reggie clinging to Frank like a lifeline.

He held her tight, kissed her hair, and didn't appear to be in the least bit interested in letting go.

"How did you learn to do whatever it was you did?" She gazed up at him.

Frank shrugged. "I've owned six different bars over the past years, and sometimes the patrons got rowdy. Somebody had to handle it."

A nervous giggle escaped her throat. "And that somebody was you?"

"After quite a few intense lessons in various martial arts, it was me."

The weight that had settled between her shoulder blades lifted. She felt a sense of lightness and security. "I'm glad."

He kissed the tip of her nose. "I'm glad I could be here for you."

"Speaking of that, where—"

"Let's get out of here." He lost no time in helping her gather her things and loading her into the passenger seat of the BMW. He tossed his ruined shirt under the seat.

"Where are we going?" she asked when he inserted the key in the ignition.

"Does it matter?" He sent her a scorching look. "I just need to be with you." He backed out into the street and took off with a squeal of tires. "We have some important things to discuss."

Her stomach caught. He sounded so serious. Was he about to break up with her? Had he already done so?

He drove to the park and got out, slamming the door. The park was bathed in light from the full moon, reducing everything to black, white, or shades of gray.

Reggie jumped out before he could open her door. She

swallowed hard when she glimpsed his face in the moonlight. *Grim* could best describe his expression.

He paced away from her, pivoted, and returned to stand before her, his face a study in distress. "Reggie, I—"

"I—I missed you," she stammered.

"I missed you too." He tilted her chin up and kissed her lips. "I missed you so much I thought I was going to die from it."

She pulled away, exasperated. "If you missed me so much, where the heck have you been?"

"I—uh—I…"

"You didn't come by, and you didn't call." She heard the accusation in her voice.

He took her hand and led her to the concrete table and benches they had used for their picnic. With ease, he lifted her to sit on the table. "I was confused. Everything was happening so fast. One day I was a free and easy bachelor with no responsibilities and no ties at all, and the next—"

"And the next?"

He rubbed the back of his neck. "And the next I'm in love with you."

His pronouncement caused a swirling sensation in her chest. "I'm not some disease you caught like measles or the plague."

Frank drew a deep breath and exhaled. "Not a disease. More like being blown off course by a storm…Hurricane Reggie." He shrugged. "Everything in my life changed when I looked into your big brown eyes. I was knocked for a loop. And then there's Shannon. For the first time in my life, I thought how great it would be to become her father. To watch her grow and maybe…maybe give her a brother or sister."

Reggie's stomach did a tumble and roll. "So what are you saying?"

He threw his hands up in the air. "I got scared. I was afraid I couldn't live up to the whole 'forever' thing." His voice dropped in timbre. "So I left. Just took off."

"You could have called me. You could have let me know." She crossed her arms over her chest, a protective gesture.

He raked his fingers through his hair. "I wanted to... I just didn't know what to say."

"Anything would have been better than not knowing... I thought maybe you had called your New York girlfriend."

"No way." He held her by her shoulders, gazing deeply into her eyes. "You didn't call me either. After our getaway in New York, I thought maybe you were having second thoughts."

"Second thoughts? How could you think that?"

"I'm Mr. Nice Guy." He stared down at her.

Confused, she blinked. *Mr. Nice Guy?* Her stomach clenched as though a giant fist squeezed it. "You—you're Mr. Nice Guy?" A flicker of anger spiraled through her. "How could you lie to me? How could you—?"

"Easy, baby. You made no secret of the fact that you hated me...but I needed you to tell me how to bridge the gap."

"Bridge the gap? You made a fool of me... You preyed on my sympathies..."

Frank gathered her in his arms and stopped her tirade with a kiss, a kiss so deep and passionate she could barely breathe and certainly couldn't recall why she had been angry a moment before.

He pulled away slightly but spoke against her lips. "I have been in love with you since I first laid eyes on you...but we didn't sync when we were teens. And when I returned to Rambling, I realized I was still crazy about you. But you were so cold and distant. I had no idea how to get through your shell...how to let you know that I wasn't the boy you hated...that I had grown to be a man you could trust." He nuzzled her cheek and ear, sending tingling sensations down her spine.

Reggie made a sound somewhere between a whimper and a moan.

"As Mr. Nice Guy, I confessed how I felt about you, but you told me to step away. I know we're miles apart on some things, but I hoped…" Heaving a deep sigh, he sat on the table beside her, feet on the concrete bench, elbows planted on his knees. He looked dejected. "When you told Mr. Nice Guy to get lost, I thought that might be the only fair thing to do. I don't have any experience in a real relationship. I've never been in love before." He shrugged, looking as helpless as a hot guy could look. The muscles in his bare shoulders flexed with the movement. "I was afraid I couldn't live up to your expectations. My parents shoved me off on Aunt Rosie when I was a kid. No matter how much I want it, I don't know if I'm a good enough person to take on the role of parent."

Kenny's angry face flashed through Reggie's brain. "Yeah, I can see how you might have come to that conclusion. I guess not everyone is cut out to be a parent." She reached out to stroke the side of his face. "But I think you will make a great dad…whenever…"

A wide grin lit his face. "Do you really think so?"

He looked like a hopeful little boy…well, as much as an incredibly hot guy with a ripped naked torso could look like a little boy.

"I do think so. Frank, you're the guy who can do anything he sets out to do. You've proven that time after time."

He spread his arms, and she leaned into his embrace. "Even if we don't have a lot in common?"

In spite of herself, she let out a nervous giggle. "Yeah, my dad has a theory about that."

"Your dad's a great guy."

"My dad? How do you know what kind of man my dad is?"

"I went by your father's house looking for you." He flashed a grin. "It gave us a chance to talk. He's really nice."

Reggie wondered at that. Was her father mellowing in his old age? "What did you talk about?"

"Things…you and me."

"You didn't!" she squeaked out.

He lifted her chin and gave her a slow, toe-curling kiss. "I asked him how he felt about marriage...yours and mine in particular."

She sucked in a breath, making a whimpering sound. "Marriage?"

"Yeah. I figured your dad was a pretty old-fashioned kind of guy, so I officially asked for your hand in marriage."

Reggie held her breath. For a moment there was no sound except that of her heart pumping in her ears.

"He was okay with it...especially when Shannon ran over to hug my neck and call me 'Fwank.'" He released her and fumbled in his pocket, drawing out a small blue box. "Reggie Lee Stafford, I am crazy in love with you. Will you make me the happiest man on the planet by becoming my bride? Will you marry me?"

"I—uh... Oh, Frank, of course I'll marry you." She was grinning, but tears filled her eyes. She recognized the blue box as coming from Tiffany's. "Oh, my goodness. I've never seen such a lovely ring."

Frank stood and, taking her hand, slid the ring on her finger. He held her for a moment and then murmured, "I'm completely committed. This is a forever and ever thing. Are you in?"

Reggie swallowed hard and blinked through the tears. "I'm in."

Violet was making herself at home. She already had Gayle trained to take her out in the fenced backyard and to praise her abundantly when she went to the back corner she now thought of as her private potty place.

Gayle had also bought her a lovely purple collar and affixed her shiny new tag. "Now you're legal, Violet."

Violet stared at her, her bright eyes peering out of the mop of white fur. When she fixed her gaze upon Gayle, this usually resulted in being picked up and cuddled. And when she was put down, Violet would roll over on her back, exposing her little pink stomach, begging for attention.

"Oh, I see. You need a good belly rub, don't you?" Gayle obliged, and every time she paused, the dog's paws flapped as though she was begging for more.

Gayle shook her head. "You are just a little love slut. Okay, more belly rubbing." She realized it was going to be difficult to hand her over to Paul.

Reluctantly, she picked up her phone and punched in Paul's number.

"Hello, beautiful. You made my day." His voice wrapped around her like an embrace.

"That's really sweet, Paul," she said. "I was wondering if you had time to run by my house. I wanted to ask your opinion on something."

Violet sat at her feet, her little puffy tail wagging hopefully.

"My lowly opinion? I would be happy to offer any assistance to the lovely lady... I can come right over."

"That would be great. See you in a few." Gayle hung up, grinning. She scruffled the patch of brown fur behind Violet's left ear. "Who's your daddy? Well, we're about to find out."

Violet stood on her hind feet and made the begging motion with her little paws together.

"Oh, you could own my heart." Gayle picked the small ball of fluff up and took her into the kitchen, where she had located Violet's food and water bowls as well as a cushy dog bed. "You stay in here until I introduce you to your possible daddy. Good girl." She closed the door to the kitchen and made a circuit of the living room, picking up a few things as she made her rounds. She spritzed a floral scent in the air, and by the time Paul knocked on her door, she was company-ready.

"Hi, Paul. I'm glad you could come over."

A wide grin spread across his face. "I'm glad you invited me."

She noticed that he had just shaved and smelled almost edible...something warm and spicy. "Come right in and have a seat. Would you like some coffee or tea?"

"Uh, sure. Whatever is easier." He took a seat on the sofa.

"I just made a pot of fresh coffee. I'll be right back." She made a twirl and went through the dining room and into the kitchen. She had prepared a tray for the occasion and just took a few moments to pour coffee into the cups. It looked nice.

Violet was curled up in her bed but kept watching her. "I'll be back in a little while, Violet." She picked up the tray and backed out of the room.

When she returned to the living room, she found Paul examining her books.

"You have quite a variety in your library."

She placed the tray on the coffee table. "I'm a voracious reader. What can I say?"

Paul joined her at the sofa and took a seat beside her. "Another thing we have in common. I haunt the library weekly."

Good man. "That's nice. We have a good library. How do you like your coffee?" She gestured to the cream and sweeteners on the tray.

He helped himself to a little cream and picked up a spoon to stir his coffee.

"And I made these cookies. Hope you like chocolate chip."

"Who doesn't?" He reached for a cookie and took a bite, making an appreciative noise. "What a woman. She reads. She bakes. And she's beautiful."

Gayle blushed at the compliments. "Thanks, Paul. Nice of you to say those things."

"They're all true. Now what is it that you want my opinion about? I'm always happy to help."

"Just enjoy the coffee," she said. "We'll get to that shortly. I was wondering when you first noticed me. When did you become aware of me as a person?"

He paused, the cookie halfway to his lips. "Aware of you?" He swallowed the bite in his mouth and set the cookie on the saucer under his coffee cup. "Are you serious? I've been aware of you forever." He shrugged. "Well, maybe not forever."

She gazed at him silently.

"Okay, it was when I first moved here. I had just gotten the teaching job, and I saw you at church. I wanted to get to know you, but I was too shy to just march right up and introduce myself... Did you notice me?"

"Hmm... Yes, I was told that you were the new history teacher at the middle school, and I think someone mentioned that you were single." She sipped her coffee thoughtfully.

"Well, I was aware of you, but I couldn't figure out how to meet you officially."

Gayle took a deep breath, ready to plunge in. She set the coffee cup back on the tray and turned to face Paul. "So you made up this story about a lost dog?"

"Okay, I am so embarrassed about that. Sorry. I'm normally a truthful person, but I couldn't figure out any other way to start a conversation with you."

Gayle noted that his face and ears had turned a bright pink. "I figured it out but kept having doubts. You could have confessed, you know?" She softened her question with a smile.

"I was trying to get up my nerve to admit my rotten behavior... but I was just ashamed. Can you forgive me?"

He appeared to be so contrite, Gayle couldn't help but smile. He had created this elaborate ruse because he liked her and was too shy to just move forward. She had to be flattered by his actions. "On one condition."

"Anything. What do you want me to do?"

"Simple. Never lie to me again. Just hit me with the truth, no matter what."

"Yes, I can do that." He was nodding.

"That's all I ask. Just be truthful." She finished off her coffee and set the empty cup back on the tray. "Are you finished with that?" She nodded toward his cup, and he drank the last of it, echoing her in placing it back on the tray.

She stood and reached for the tray, but Paul leaped to his feet and picked it up.

"I can take this for you."

"Thanks. If you don't mind bringing it to the kitchen for me."

He followed her eagerly, bearing the tray.

Gayle held the door open for him and gestured to the countertop by the sink. "Just set it over there, please."

When he had complied, he looked down at the small fur ball at his feet. "Hello. What's this?"

Gayle felt like laughing but held herself together. "This is my dog. Isn't she cute?"

Paul squatted down to pet her. "Cute doesn't half cover it. She's adorable. What's her name?"

Gayle leaned back against the counter. "Violet. Her name is Violet."

Paul rocked back in surprise and fell on his rear. "What?"

"I went looking for your dog…and I found her."

He sat on the floor looking up at her. "How can that be? I don't have a dog."

"I know. But now I do. You can pet her anytime you want."

Paul broke out in laughter, and Gayle joined in.

Violet's little head swiveled back and forth between her new mother and her mom's friend.

Chapter 16

Three months later…

"DADDY, ARE YOU CRYING?" REGGIE HAD APPARENTLY SUR-
prised him when she entered the living room soundlessly on her
bare feet.

Sure enough, Henry Stafford jerked upright in his recliner and
wiped his eyes with the back of his hand. "No, of course not." He
gave her a stern look as he lifted his newspaper higher to cover
his face.

A swell of emotion washed over her. Reggie had to blink back
her own tears. She completely understood how he was feeling. She
surveyed the cozy living room, took in her parents' portrait and
the other memorabilia arranged on the mantel by her mother's
loving hands. Her dad did not adjust to change easily.

She sucked in a deep breath and pasted a bright smile on her
face. "Tomorrow's the big day. You'll finally get rid of us and
have some peace and quiet around here."

The newspaper rattled, but Henry was silent.

"I know it was a big shock to your system when Shannon and
I had to move in with you." She shrugged. "I mean, you must
have rolled your eyes every time Shannon started wailing or you
stumbled over one of her toys."

"No, I didn't." His voice was raspy. "I was glad to have you
two here. I wanted to kill Kenny Landers for breaking his word
to you." He glanced up at her, his expression grim. "For breaking your heart, but I never begrudged you a place to live." He

cleared his throat and folded the newspaper, placing it on the table beside his recliner. "I'm your father. I have always loved you, and I always will."

"I knew that." She leaned down to place a kiss on his leathery cheek. "I love you too."

He snorted. "I knew that."

"I just wanted to let you know that I appreciate you taking us in. I was pretty much broken."

"Damned Landers. He may be in jail, but I still want to kill him."

"No need. Frank did a pretty good job of, uh…making an impression on Kenny." A giggle bubbled up from her chest as she remembered Kenny's expression when Frank was throwing him all over the *Gazette* parking lot.

Henry raised his brows. "He did? Good man. I always liked that Frank."

"Well, you should, because I'm going to marry him tomorrow. He promised me forever."

"He'd better live up to that."

"I have complete confidence in Frank. It's me I'm worried about." Reggie raked her fingers through her hair. "I'm so scared. What if I'm not capable of being the wife of a wealthy international businessman? I'm just a small-town girl. What if I let him down?"

"Don't be ridiculous. You're Reggie Lee Stafford. Smartest girl in the world." He did an elaborate eye roll. "You're editor of the *Rambling Gazette*. You're redecorating the Grady house." He gave a dry chuckle. "You and that assistant of yours…"

"Gayle?"

"Yeah, that'n. You two are making the upper floors of the *Gazette* building into new housing for Rambling. You're making things happen."

She smiled. "Well, I'm trying."

"You just be you. You can handle anything Frank Bell and the big wide world has to throw at you."

"Thanks. I needed a pep talk."

He heaved a huge sigh, his shoulders lifting and falling with the effort. "I just wish your mother could have lived to see you so happy." This time a tear rolled down his cheek and he made no effort to hide it. "I found this earlier. It was your mother's." He fumbled in the pocket of his bathrobe. "Aren't you supposed to have something old?"

Reggie's throat clogged with emotion as she gazed at the lacy bit he held out to her. "What...what's that, Dad?"

"This, young lady, is a hankie. It's something well-brought-up women used to carry. In fact, it's the very hankie your grandmother gave to your mother to carry during our wedding. I believe she said it had belonged to her mother." He tucked it in her hand and closed her fingers around it. "So, you see the importance of this little bit of lace. I think you will pass it along to Shannon someday."

"Oh, Daddy." Reggie's airway closed up, and her eyes filled with tears. She collapsed into the arms he held out to her. For a few minutes she silently sobbed against his shoulder while he gently rocked her as he had when she was a child.

"That's my girl. Don't worry about a thing." He patted her back rhythmically. "If this Frank doesn't treat you right, I'll kill him."

Evan straightened Frank's tie. "Man up, Bro. You look scared."

Frank released the breath he'd been holding. "Not scared. Just nervous. I don't want to screw this up."

Evan slapped him on the shoulder. "You'll do fine."

The knot in Frank's stomach twisted and tied another loop. "You got the ring, right?"

Evan grinned. "Sure do. You're not getting out of this one."

"I sure hope not." He straightened his spine. "I've never wanted anything so much in my life."

Evan stepped to the door and peeked out into the hall. "Looks like most everyone has gone into the chapel. We're supposed to get ourselves up to the front of the church before the bridal party starts down the aisle." He turned back to Frank. "C'mon, bud. Let's get it in gear." He motioned for Frank to follow and stepped out into the hallway.

Like a robot, Frank trailed after him, his insides still quaking.

The organist played some sort of light music that he recalled having heard somewhere in his past but couldn't place. They stood outside the doorway, and he glimpsed what seemed to be the entire town seated inside the church. He had expected to see the designated "bride's side" of the church packed with locals, but he was pleasantly surprised to find both sides equally full. *Probably overflow from the bride's side.*

He raked his fingers through his hair, but Evan slapped at his hand.

"Don't mess with your pretty 'do," he said. "C'mon, we'll go down the far aisle to the altar as soon as the Rev makes it up there. In the meantime, we can just chill out back in this corner."

Frank nodded and heaved out a sigh. "Nice music."

"'Jesu, Joy of Man's Desiring.'"

Frank swiveled to stare at him. "What are you talking about, Ev?"

"That's the name of the song she's playing…Bach."

Frank leaned back against the wall. "How did you know that?"

"Orchestra. I played cello in the high school orchestra."

"Really? I thought you were into football and all other sports."

Evan shrugged. "I was, but I was also really into music."

Frank reflected on how little he knew about the man who had been his best friend in high school. "I'm sorry. I didn't know."

"No reason for you to know. I was a little closemouthed about my musical interests." He shrugged. "Guess I thought orchestra was a little nerdy and I was a cool guy."

"Yeah. Listen, Ev... I really appreciate you standing up with me."

"What are friends for?" Evan nudged him when the pastor entered from the back and took his place at the altar. "That's our cue." He gestured for Frank to precede him.

Frank swallowed hard and made his way up the side aisle toward the altar, where he would promise Reggie Lee his fidelity for life. That part didn't scare him. He was petrified, but not of Reggie. He was scared he would mess it up.

He stepped up onto the riser, and Pastor Wilson reached to shake his hand, then Evan's.

"Man, just chill. You're Frank Bell. Mr. Cool. You got this."

Frank nodded. *Yeah, I'm Frank Bell. Mr. Cool unless it comes to Reggie Lee Stafford.*

There was movement at the back of the church. Several young women wearing fluffy pink dresses gathered in the open doorway.

His chest tightened when he saw Shannon, wearing a paler pink dress with a wide rose-colored satin ribbon tied around her waist. She looked adorable with a circlet of pink flowers atop her blonde ringlets. The woman who held her hand gave her a small white basket and whispered in her ear.

Frank could hear his heart pulsing in his ears. He hoped he didn't embarrass himself or, even worse, Reggie. He tried to breathe normally, but he wasn't sure what normal was anymore.

The first bridesmaid gave Shannon a little nudge, and she started walking toward the altar, occasionally throwing a fistful of petals on the carpet. When she spied Frank, she tossed the basket aside and ran toward him.

Frank scooped her up into his arms. He gulped back the sting of tears, his heart filled with emotion. Hugging Shannon, he turned back to the bridal procession.

There were three women wearing identical pink dresses. They

looked somewhat familiar, and he realized they were the same pack of girl nerds who had been Reggie's besties in high school. They walked slowly down the aisle toward him and lined up on the other side of the pastor. He vaguely recalled the brides-maids as being the ones who'd taunted him as "New Boy" and "Franklinstein."

Then he saw Reggie framed in the doorway, her hand tucked in the crook of her father's arm.

The music changed abruptly, the organist striking several chords and then sliding into the traditional wedding march.

His mouth felt dry. He tried to moisten his lips, but his tongue felt like leather.

If possible, Reggie was more beautiful than ever. She grinned when she saw him holding Shannon. Even her father looked pleased. They strolled toward Frank in time to the rhythmic organ music. When they stepped up to the altar, the pastor asked, in a resonant tone, "Who gives this woman?"

Henry let out a deep sigh and kissed his daughter on the cheek. "I do." He gave Frank his "I'm gonna kill you if you hurt her" look and reached for Shannon.

Frank gave Shannon a kiss on the cheek and handed her over.

Henry took a seat in the first pew on the "bride's side" of the church with his granddaughter in his lap.

Frank stared at Reggie. She smiled, but the corners of her mouth trembled. She must have been nervous too.

That gave him courage. *Can't let her down.* Reaching to take her hand, he brought it to his lips. "Love you," he whispered.

She flashed a smile and handed her bouquet to one of her bridesmaids. Taking a deep breath, she reached for his other hand.

"Dearly beloved…" the pastor began.

The words seemed to drone on. He talked about the meaning of marriage and the commitment and about the roles of the hus-band and the wife. Then he turned to Frank.

Frank held up his hand. "I—I'd like to use my own words, Pastor."

There was a hush, as though the entire church had drawn a collective breath.

"Reggie, you were my first love." He smiled when she blushed. "And you are my last love. I want to share my life with you and give you everything that is in my capacity to give. I don't have any family left, but you are my family from this moment on. We'll raise Shannon as our daughter. I want you both to live in my world, but I want to share in yours. What we create together will be our life, and I will be all the richer for it. Reggie Lee Stafford, I promise you forever. Please be my wife."

Tears ran down her cheeks in twin rivulets. She nodded wordlessly and then whispered, "I will." She melted into his arms, her face lifted for his kiss.

Frank kissed her passionately, pouring his emotions out for all the world to see.

The pastor cleared his throat. "Well, in that case, I now pronounce you husband and wife."

Chapter 1

"OH MAN! THIS IS GONNA KILL CADE!" TYLER GARRETT STARED at the television screen in disbelief. He felt as though he'd been sucker-punched.

Big Jim Garrett came into the den of his sprawling ranch house. "What's up, Son?"

Ty gestured to the video rolling across the screen. "It's bad, Dad. It's the—the airstrip. There was an accident."

Big Jim's jaw tightened as his gaze fell on the wreckage of a small plane. "The Canyon?" But in his heart, he knew the answer.

The nearby Palo Duro Canyon was where Jason LaChance, his niece's husband, often flew tourists over the nation's second-largest canyon for an aerial tour.

Jason owned a small airstrip just east of town. Mostly, he rented space to locals who owned small planes. A couple of companies that did crop-dusting also leased hangar space.

Big Jim prayed someone else had been flying the small plane, crushed like a toy at the bottom of the canyon, but somewhere in his heart, he knew the answer.

It was a prayer with no words but playing over and over in her head. There had been words, but now it was more like a scream of pain playing through every atom of her being. Please...please... Please, God... Where are they? Please...

But there were no answers yet. She had called every institution she could think of but had no substantive responses.

Maybe the Garrett family… Social Services over in Amarillo… Someone from the church, surely…

Where are they? The babies… My babies now…

Jennifer LaChance stood in line at the airport, waiting for the TSA to search her person. She had been relieved of her small suitcase but clutched her purse and a fold-over garment bag close to her chest.

"Next!" The security man waved her forward.

She placed her handbag, shoes, and garment bag into bins to be scanned on the conveyor belt, and then stepped up to be scanned herself.

"Raise your arms over your head."

She followed instructions like a robot, then stepped down and collected her items. It seemed as though everything was moving at warp speed except Jennifer LaChance.

Once on the plane, she donned her dark glasses and leaned her head back to indicate to her fellow passengers that she did not want to chat. Please leave me alone. I'm bleeding from every pore. Can't you see?

When she closed her eyes, puffy from endless tears, her brain was bombarded with images of Jason, her wonderful brother. The big brother who had led her on endless adventures, protected her and teased her… Her hero was gone forever. And Sara, his fun-loving wife…the mother of his children. They were dead, crushed at the bottom of a canyon. Pain sliced through her, causing her to wince. She opened her eyes to find the person in the seat next to her had drawn back and was giving her a derisive look.

She swallowed hard, hoping the flight attendant could bring her a water. Surely, given all the tears she'd shed, there was no more liquid left in her body.

She hadn't thought it possible that pain this great could hold her in its grip. Her mind and spirit were in ashes, while her body was in a state of rigor. Every muscle was tensed and ready to spring. When she tried to unclench her fists, they curled right back up again.

Jennifer exhaled and closed her eyes again. Please let the kids be okay.

———

Cade Garrett carried his niece and nephew from his truck up to his ranch house. Lissy's head was on his shoulder, while Leo gazed around with wide eyes. "We're home, kids."

Mrs. Reynolds opened the front door for them and stood back while he strode inside with his double armload. "I got their room ready."

"You're a blessing, Mrs. R."

"Here, let me take the little one." She reached for Lissy, and Cade let her ease the young girl from his arm. "Sweet angels," she murmured.

Cade watched her carry the sleepy one-year-old down the hallway to the room she had prepared for them.

"Hey, Leo. Are you hungry? Would you like a snack?"

Leo didn't respond but stared at him with his incredible blue eyes, almost turquoise and ringed with black lashes.

Yeah, your last name may be LaChance, but you're a Garrett through and through.

"Okay, let's see what's in the fridge. Maybe some ice cream. You like ice cream, don't you?"

The little head bobbed up and down.

"Okay, buddy. You sit right here and I'll get the ice cream." Cade placed Leo on top of the counter, fetched a half-gallon tub of vanilla from the freezer, and grabbed two spoons from the utensil drawer. "Here we go." He handed a spoon to Leo and removed the lid. "Dig in." He scooped a spoonful for himself to demonstrate.

Leo followed Cade's actions, as he scooped a much smaller

spoonful and got most of it into his mouth. He swallowed and licked the spoon. "My mommy puts my ice cweam in a bowl."

Cade's heart squeezed with sorrow. These were the first words Leo had spoken since the accident. Cade had no idea how he was going to take Sara's place. His baby sister had been a great mom to her two little ones and had mastered the art of dishing ice cream into a bowl.

Hell, he had no idea how he was going to tell the children that their parents were dead. He swallowed the wad of tears lodged in the back of his throat.

Cade had his own ranch to run, and now he would have to figure out what to do with the small airport Sara and Jason had owned. They rented storage space to a few area ranchers who owned their own planes, and they gave regular flyover tours of the nearby Palo Duro Canyon…the canyon where their own small plane had crashed, taking their lives and leaving behind two small children and their totally ill-equipped uncle.

He scooped some ice cream into a small plastic dish for Leo and put away the tub. Leaning against the counter to protect his young nephew from falling off, he reflected on how his own life had been shattered in the past twenty-four hours.

The minute Cade heard the accident involved his baby sister, he had jumped in his truck to drive to the County Coroner's office for the grisly task of identifying her remains. Tears running down his face all the way to Amarillo, he then had to track down the children. Social Services had taken them from their home, where a neighborhood teenager was doing her best to keep it together, to a children's facility in Amarillo. He had to prove his relationship and get a reference from the pastor and the sheriff before he was deemed worthy and they were remanded to his care.

The social worker would not release them until Cade purchased appropriate car seats, but finally, he was allowed to bring the children home.

He loved the kids, but he had been, up till now, a confirmed bachelor, and he didn't have a clue as to how he would become a substitute father. All the while, his own grief was burning up his heart. Not a problem, Leo. Uncle Cade is here for you and Lissy.

—◆—

Jennifer LaChance checked in at the small bed-and-breakfast, the Langston Inn. Her head throbbed, her eyes burned from crying so much. She felt exhausted and almost numb. Shoving her sunglasses up on her nose, she surrendered her charge card.

The woman at the desk was gracious enough, but Jenn just wanted to get settled and find out what happened to her niece and nephew.

"My name is Ollie Sue Enloe," the woman said proudly. "That's short for Olivia Susan. This is my bed-and-breakfast." She beamed at Jenn. "I call myself the innkeeper."

"Good to meet you, Ms. Enloe." Jenn adjusted Minnie in her arms, pretty sure dog hair was all over her jacket.

"Please, call me Ollie." One eyebrow rose as she glared at the dog. "Your dog is housebroken, isn't he?"

Jenn clutched Minnie closer to her chest. "Of course she is."

Ollie looked unconvinced but turned to run the card. "So you're from Dallas, huh? Big city?"

"Yes." Jenn tucked her credit card back in her purse and picked up her suitcase to follow the woman up a flight of stairs to a room across the hall from the bathroom.

"Um, are other people using this bathroom?"

"We don't have any other guests at this time," the woman said.

Jenn was relieved. She wasn't quite a germaphobe...but then again, maybe she was. She carried a small packet of sanitizing wipes in her purse and a larger tub of them in her suitcase.

She entered the room and set her suitcase on the bed. At least the room smelled like fresh linen. This was a corner room, so she had windows on two sides. Thankfully, the sun was setting, so she wasn't blinded by the light. Her eyes felt bruised from all the tears she'd shed over the previous forty-eight hours. She closed the drapes on the west side and went to stare out the back window at the scene below. She felt out of place, here in this rural town where her brother had made a home. She had visited once, after the wedding, but could not for the life of her figure out what the attraction was. It was probably what all of small-town America looked like, but Jenn had spent her whole life in cities and studying at various universities—a very well-educated woman with too many degrees. She couldn't seem to find a way to make a living with those degrees, and she feared she would be slinging hash in a diner soon.

Jason had loved to fly, and there was plenty of wide-open airspace out here in North Texas. Miles and miles of nothing but miles and miles...or so Jason used to tell her.

And then there was Sara. Apparently, the small-town beauty had been just what Jason was looking for because they meshed perfectly soon after he hit town. Of course, it was the opportunity to buy the airfield that had drawn him here. Jason loved to fly, and this was his idea of heaven.

Jenn swallowed a bitter taste in her mouth. "Well, I'm sure you really are in heaven, Jason. And now I'm here. I'm going to find out where the hell your kids are, and I promise to take them back to Dallas and raise them as my own." She brushed off a tear as it rolled down her cheek.

Sucking in a ragged breath, she leaned her forehead against the window frame and examined the scene below.

A sweet little yard contained a conversation area, a barbecue grill, and a gazebo, plus some neatly maintained landscaping. Gazing over the fence, she spied the spire of a church a block away. It looked like a painting. So peaceful.

A wave of nostalgia washed over her. When she was growing up, her family had always spent Sundays lying around in their pajamas, reading the Sunday papers and enjoying a late breakfast.

But Jason had turned over a new leaf when he moved to Langston.

Jenn had teased him, calling him "Saint Jason." He had gone to church on Sundays with Sara, and they had married in the church.

Jenn had attended their storybook wedding, meeting all of Sara's enormous clan. Apparently, marrying a Garrett meant you were annexed into this large and loving family.

Jenn heaved a sigh and turned around, ready to unpack and try to relax. She opened her suitcase and pulled everything out, arranging it on the bed. She shook out the garments and put them on hangers: one nice dress to wear to the funeral and a couple of more casual dresses. She arranged her shoes in the bottom of the closet: two pairs of heels and a pair of rubber flip-flops. She had packed hurriedly, anxious to find her niece and nephew, but at the moment had no idea what she had really brought with her.

She hadn't planned to stay in Langston that long, but she hadn't rationally been able to decide what was appropriate to take with her. She wondered how her whole family had evaporated in such a short time and how her own life had gotten so lost.

After she had earned her second master's degree, her parents' health had taken a downturn, or perhaps she had finally looked up from her studies to notice they needed her help. Jenn had dutifully moved back into the home she and Jason had grown up in and taken over the household duties, making sure her parents got to doctors' appointments and ate well-balanced meals. Now she was rattling around that big house all by herself, with very little in the way of funds to support it.

Her mother had passed away on hospice care just a few months ago, and her father had followed within weeks. It seemed he didn't want to live without his life mate.

Jenn huffed out a sigh. "Very romantic." But now Jenn felt even more abandoned. Her parents had small life insurance policies that paid off debts and burial costs. Now Jenn needed to find a job to pay the household expenses and support her brother's children...as soon as she could locate them.

Her savings were running out fast and her phone was not ring-
ing with job offers.

Something will turn up. Surely there is a job for a girl with a
couple of fine arts degrees and absolutely zero experience. She
had to stay positive. Otherwise, she might miss out on the great
opportunity she knew was just around the corner.

In the meantime, she needed to get something to eat. Ollie had
told her there were three restaurants in town, plus a Dairy Queen.
There was the Mexican restaurant, a steakhouse, and, across from
the courthouse, a small family-style diner with 1950s decor.

She locked Minnie in the room and went down the stairs. That
she was the only lodger at the Langston Inn didn't bother her at
all. Crowds bothered her.

Once in her car, she headed for the main street and decided on
the Mexican place. Jason had taken her and his family to eat there
a couple of times and she recalled that the food was excellent.
Tio's appeared to be doing well, if one could judge by the number
of cars outside. The parking lot was filled with vehicles, most of
them pickup trucks.

She parked between two large double dually trucks and went
inside. A sea of faces turned to stare at her. Yes, folks. Jason
LaChance's baby sister has arrived in town. She held her head
high and straightened her spine.

"Table or booth?" the hostess asked.

"Some quiet nook." Jenn followed the hostess to a back corner
and slid onto the plastic seat of a booth.

The hostess placed a menu on the table and brought her a glass
of ice water.

"I'll have the senorita plate." Jenn closed the menu and
handed it back to the woman. She sipped her ice water and surreptitiously scanned the patrons. A few were still gaping at her,
but most had resumed their conversations and gone back to stuffing their faces.

When the woman came back, she was bearing a platter of food that would have fed a small family.

"Oh my!" Jenn stared at the mammoth amount of food. "I forgot how huge your portions are."

"You've come in here before, haven't you?" The waitress was a pretty Hispanic woman in her early thirties. "I'm Milita Rios. This is my papa's restaurant. Are you visiting or just passing through?"

Jenn felt a rush of tears but managed to head them off with a paper napkin. "I'm just here to bury my brother, Jason. He brought me here a few times to eat with his family. It was always his favorite."

Milita's face morphed into sadness. "I'm so sorry about your brother. He was a great guy."

A clutch of pain prevented Jenn from responding.

"Such a lovely family." Milita walked away, shaking her head.

Jenn reached for her water and took a sip. Yes, Jason was a wonderful brother, and now he was gone, but where were the children? She ate as quickly as possible, and when Milita returned, she brought a Styrofoam takeout container. Jenn hadn't thought about taking the leftovers home, but Milita was scooping the food remaining on the platter into the divided container. The Spanish rice. The refried beans. And two enchiladas, one beef and one chicken.

"Aww, you weren't very hungry, were you?" Milita snapped the lid on the container. "I understand. Perhaps your appetite will return later."

"That was a huge plate. I ate two tacos and the guacamole." Jenn heard the defensiveness in her own voice. She sighed. "Sorry. My stomach has been in a knot since I first heard about Jason... The food was delicious."

"Glad you liked it. Hope to see you again soon." Milita put the Styrofoam container into a paper bag and slid the check onto the table.

Jenn did some quick math in her head to figure out the tip. Although she was low on funds, she couldn't bear not to leave an adequate tip for Milita. Jenn hated to be chintzy, but there was only so much money left in her account, and she had to stretch that until she got a decent job. Maybe something clerical or even retail. *I am not skilled in pole dancing.* She sighed. *Or much of anything, for that matter.*

Being an artist had only prepared her for being an artist.

Jenn paid the check at the cash register near the door. She was an object of interest again as she passed by. Gathering her credit card, she left without looking back and carried her leftovers to the car. Maybe there was a refrigerator at the inn. Maybe she would eat Mexican food again tomorrow.

Cade didn't sleep well. Hell, he hardly slept at all. Mrs. Reynolds made dinner and left. It consisted of things she thought the children would eat: macaroni and cheese and hot dogs. Just to be sure, she made scrambled eggs.

Tomorrow, Cade would have to shop for groceries…food the kids would like. And he needed to go by Sara's house to pick up clothing for the children.

Lissy sat on Cade's lap and he scooped in bites of mashed pasta, while she held a hot dog firmly in her fist. Her other hand was grasping the front of his Western shirt, grinding in the cheesy grease.

Leo sat on a chair at the table beside Cade. He was too short to reach the table, so Cade had placed a cushion from the sofa onto the chair to give him a little lift.

"How ya doin' there, buddy?" Cade asked, but Leo just looked at him. He was spooning food into his mouth though.

When the children finished eating, Cade had to get them cleaned up and ready for bed. He dressed both in his own T-shirts and tucked them into the bed in his guest room. Lissy whimpered, and he had to rub her back until she fell asleep. Just when he was tiptoeing out of the room, Leo's small voice cut through the silence.

"Unca Cade, where is my mommy an' my daddy?"

Cade froze in his tracks. He had no idea how to tell a three-year-old that his mother and father were dead...that he would never see them again.

"Um, your mommy and daddy had to take a trip, and I'm going to take care of you until—until they come back." Unable to speak the truth, Cade's chest tightened as he uttered the lie.

Leo's large blue eyes examined him carefully.

"Now, you get some sleep. Here, snuggle down." Cade pulled the quilt up under Leo's chin and gave him a pat. "Night, Leo."

Cade left the door open a bit and went to the kitchen. He grabbed a beer out of the refrigerator and carried it to his man cave: the den where his giant curved-screen television dominated one wall. He found the remote and flipped on the television, turning the sound way down. He was desperate to find something to occupy his brain besides the image of Sara lying in the coroner's office.

He watched a show without seeing it, and then the news came on. The anchor did a recap of the terrible accident that had occurred when a small plane took a nosedive into the Palo Duro State Park, killing both occupants. Just as the news anchor was wrapping up and the weatherman made an appearance, he heard a small voice.

"Unca Cade?"

He sat up and swiveled in his recliner. "Leo? What's wrong?"

A tear rolled down his cheek. "Lissy, she made pee-pee in the bed."

Cade stripped the sheets and bedding. He found an old plastic tablecloth and put it down over the soggy mattress. Then he made the bed with fresh sheets, put the children back to bed, and flung himself down on top of his own bed, exhausted but too tired to sleep. He lay awake in the dark, staring up at the ceiling, hoping the kids didn't wake up until morning.

There was a void in his chest. Every time he thought about Sara and her crumpled remnants lying in the coroner's office, he felt as though someone had ripped the heart out of his body.

Chapter 2

TYLER GARRETT CLIMBED OUT OF HIS BIG DOUBLE DUALLY TRUCK and rounded the cab to open the door for his lovely wife. He took the containers out of her hands and helped her slip down to the ground.

"Is he expecting us?" she asked.

Ty shook his head. "You know Cade doesn't stand on ceremony. Cade is all about family." He gave her a kiss on the cheek.

"Poor man," she said. "I haven't really accepted the fact that Sara is gone. I can't imagine how he feels."

Ty gestured toward the house. "Sara was a little brat when we were young, always tagging along…but she was sweet. Turned out to be really smart in school. When she and Jason LaChance got married, it was what everyone expected. She fell in love with the flyboy as soon as she set eyes on him." He shook his head. "Great couple. I guess I never thought anything could happen to them. I haven't really kept up with them lately, but they always looked so happy together when I saw them in church."

Leah made a scoffing noise. "You've been so wrapped up in your music, it's a wonder you keep up with anything."

He leaned against the doorbell. "I just try to keep up with you."

The door opened and Cade Garrett stood inside, appearing to be exhausted. He had always been a big, good-looking man, but sorrow was etched deeply on his face. Without speaking, he stepped back and gestured them inside.

"It's just me and Leah," Ty said, ushering her inside.

She took in Cade's appearance, obviously sympathetic. "Um, we brought you a little something."

"Hey, Leah. That's very kind." He shook his head. "I'm just overwhelmed at the moment."

"We're all just devastated about Sara and Jason." Ty reached out to Cade, wrapping his arms around him and holding him for a long moment. He felt a tremor ripple through Cade's body.

Cade drew back, his eyes lowered and lips pressed together. "Thanks, Ty. Let's go back to the kitchen." He led the way but turned and put his finger to his mouth. "The kids are here."

Ty and Leah followed Cade as quietly as possible. Ty set the container on top of the counter and Leah placed a paper bag next to it.

The kitchen occupied one end of a sizable combination family room and casual dining area. A large television was mounted above the fireplace mantel, and a big yellow SpongeBob image cavorted across the screen. On Cade's sofa, a tiny, diapered girl slept on her stomach, drooling. Fortunately, there was a small blanket under her.

Leah smiled. "Aw, Lissy's so pretty."

Leo had wedged himself under the coffee table, lying on his side with his knees folded up. He gazed at them with large blue eyes…as sad as Cade's own.

"That's where Leo has holed up," Cade said. "He's pretty confused right now." He shrugged his wide shoulders. "I guess I am too."

Ty felt his cousin's aching grief. "Dad wanted us to tell you, he's got your back. Anything you need." He spread his hands. "He figured you didn't need the entire Garrett clan to cluster around you right now, but we're all here for you."

"Thanks, Ty. Did you draw the short straw?" A wry smile lifted one corner of his mouth.

Ty grinned in return. "No, asshole. I got to come because you and I were in the same grade all the way through school. We're more than cousins, bro."

"I know, bud. Just giving you a hard time. What did you do with your kids, Ty?"

Ty removed his Stetson and tossed it on a side table. "Leah's grandmother is taking care of the kids. Gracie is helping." He had to smile when he thought about how much Gracie loved her brand-new baby brother. "She loves playing big sister."

Cade nodded, seemingly wrapped in emotion. "I hope I can be good enough to raise Sara's kids without screwing them up. That's my biggest fear."

Ty gave him a slap on the shoulder. "Oh, get over yourself. I've never known you to lack confidence about anything. In school you did okay, and you were a leader in sports."

Cade raked his fingers through his thick, dark hair. "I know, but this is different. More important."

"You can always lean on your family if you need a break. I know Leah and I can keep the kids for you."

Leah nodded, adding her support.

Cade took a wide stance and hooked his thumbs through his belt loops. "Thanks, man. That means a lot...but I think, right now, I need to keep them as close as possible. They need to know I'm doing what Sara would want me to do. I'm going to raise her children as she would want them to be brought up."

Ty realized Cade was just speaking through his grief. "You and the children are going to need all the family you can get. The Garrett clan is a formidable force around here." He turned to see his beautiful wife doing what Leah would always be doing: leading with her heart.

Leah was sitting on the floor, her back against the sofa. Leo had crawled out from under the coffee table and was plastered against her like a baby monkey clinging to his mom.

Ty swallowed hard, while Cade stared at her, openmouthed. "It's okay. She has that effect on kids... Heck! She has that effect on everyone."

When Jenn returned to the bedand-breakfast from her outing, she tip-toed into the kitchen to place her takeout container in the refrigerator. The house was dark and the innkeeper had gone to bed. It was kind of eerie, but she managed to creep up the stairs to her assigned room.

First, she gave Minnie half a cup of dog food and took her for a quick walk. Then she climbed the stairs again, this time with Minnie tucked under her arm. The children and her small dog were the only ones she would be responsible for now. She didn't have that much left to lose.

She was tired but probably much of her exhaustion resulted from her emotional chaos. This would pass, but in the mean-time, she thought she would take a bath and relax. The bathroom sported a real clawfoot bathtub and she wanted to try it out.

Gathering shampoo, bath gel, and her robe, she locked herself in the bathroom with only Minnie for company. She turned on the water and sprinkled in a handful of bath beads, while Minnie made herself comfortable on the bath mat.

While the tub was filling, Jenn placed a washcloth and a bottle of water on the bath tray that spanned the tub. She slathered an oatmeal mask on her face and slipped off the robe.

Jenn stepped into the tub and sank down into the warm, fra-grant water. In a few moments, she could feel the tension ebb and her body relax. She laid her head back and slid lower until only her neck and head were above the surface. She reached for the water bottle again, grasping it carefully so it didn't slip from her wet fingers. The ice-cold liquid rolled down her throat, cauter-izing a path to her gut, numbing her in the process. Exhaustion began to set in, easing the tension from her tight muscles. Her head throbbed in time with her heartbeat.

The next day she would have to show up at the funeral and watch the community mourn her brother and his wife. They would bury him in the dirt...forever entombed here.

A man who loved to fly would be interred in the earth. Grounded forever.

She had seen her brother in person as often as possible for the past couple of years. Most of their conversations had to do with finding someone to care for their parents and also the cost of such services. But they talked on the phone often and exchanged emails on a daily basis. Sometimes they Skyped. When she was down in the dumps, he was the one who could cheer her up, sharing a photo of the children or telling her about something they had done that day. He was also the one who would transfer money into her account when things were really dire. Now, she had no one. At least their parents had passed on and didn't have to mourn the death of their beloved son and his wife.

A tear rolled down her cheek. *How did I screw up so badly?*

Just a few years ago, Jenn LaChance thought she had the world by the tail. As a brand-new graduate with a master of fine arts, her future was bright. It had seemed like such a wonderful career path when ensconced in the comfort of the educational womb. However, in the real world, there didn't seem to be an abundance of eager employers waving job offers at her.

She expelled a deep breath and sank deeper into the water.

Now she had an ocean of educational loans to repay and no means to readily deal with her debt, although she had been able to earn a few scholarships and grants to lighten the burden.

"They can't squeeze blood out of a turnip, Minnie."

Minnie stretched and put her paws on the side of the tub.

"Sorry, kiddo. You have to stay out there." She reached out her wet hand to pat at the dog's little round head and received an affectionate lick in return. "I guess we're on our own. We have to be big girls now."

It wasn't that she expected Jason to bail her out. She just expected him to lift her spirits.

She accepted that she had been sheltered by the world of academia, but now she was getting acquainted with the real world, and it was not being kind. Okay, she had been wide-eyed, wanting to be an educated and sophisticated woman, her future firmly within her grasp. She wished she had been able to fight the aching loneliness instead of burying her head in her studies and the accolades from her professors.

For all the letters after her name, Jennifer LaChance was just a naive girl, ill prepared for the hard-edged reality of her new life.

But, oddly, it was her big, brash brother who had kept her on the straight and narrow. No matter what time of the day or night, Jenn knew her brother was always happy to take her calls or respond to her texts.

Having Jason available to FaceTime with gave her the confidence to get through whatever the day held.

We're all proud of you, kiddo, Jason would say. Just stay positive and keep your sunny side up. Yes, it was corny but remarkably comforting.

"No, Jason, I was an idiot with no idea how to live in the real world."

Minnie whined, gazing at her with an adoring expression.

"Now I have to find Leo and Lissy and figure out how to support us...and how to live without my guardian angel, Jason." A single tear rolled down to moisten the oatmeal mask. She scrubbed off the gummy mess, all the while wishing she had been able to learn the children's whereabouts. She would do whatever it took to provide for them.

She sank further down into the warm and comforting water. The forgiving water. The headache had eased a bit. She felt moderately cheered that at least she could provide her own consolation.

She closed her eyes and inhaled the fragrance of the bath beads. Lilac...

She took another long drink of the bottled water.

The next thing she knew, she felt someone dragging her out of the water by her hair.

Minnie was yapping rhythmically.

"Are you all right?" It was the innkeeper. "My goodness gracious! I thought you were dead." She was holding both hands over her heaving bosom.

Minnie's paws were on the edge of the tub, and she was whining.

"I—I must have fallen asleep." Jenn was flustered and she was suddenly aware of her own nakedness and tried to cover herself with her hands.

"I see." The innkeeper's lips formed a thin line. "Your dog was barking up a storm. You should get out of the tub right now."

Minnie gave a yip of agreement.

Jenn felt a little shaky. This woman was frowning ferociously, and her disapproval was evident. "Um, Ollie, isn't it? Could you turn around, please?"

Ollie huffed out an impatient breath but turned away. She took a towel off the rack and tucked it under her arm. "Now please get out of the tub. The water's cold and you're all pruney."

Jenn glanced at her fingertips, and indeed, they were wrinkled as prunes. She reached to pull the plug and tried to stand up, but the tub was slippery, probably due to the bath beads. A little whiny sound escaped her throat, causing Ollie to turn.

Ollie held out her hand and steadied Jenn when she attempted to stand. Jenn gave up and allowed the woman to help her climb out over the edge of the tub and then handed her the bath towel.

"Thanks." Jenn wrapped the towel around her torso and then took a second towel to drape around her dripping wet hair. She managed a weak smile. "Thanks again. I can take it from here. Guess I was just really tired."

Ollie crossed her arms over her chest, her face a picture of disapproval. "Tired?" she echoed.

"Look, my brother and sister-in-law were killed in an accident. I'm just here for their funeral." She paused as tears flooded her eyes. "It—it's hard."

Ollie's face morphed into an expression of concern. "Oh, you poor dear. Your brother was Jason LaChance? Such a nice young man. He and Sara were members of our church." She clucked her tongue a few times.

Jenn nodded, wiping her eyes on the edge of the towel. "I just need to get through the next couple of days. I need to find the children."

Ollie frowned. "The children? I understood a social worker had taken them to Amarillo."

"Oh, great," Jenn said. "I'm sure I won't be able to find them until they open on Monday. Poor kids."

"I'm going to the funeral... The whole town will be there. Everyone loved Jason and Sara."

Jenn nodded. "I'm just going to dry my hair now and go to bed."

"Yes. Yes, of course. You get some rest. I'll see you tomorrow." She patted Jenn's damp shoulder and left the bathroom.

Jenn still felt more than a little shaky. "Tomorrow," she whispered.

She wiped the steam off the mirror and peered at herself. Her eyes were red, but that was probably from the tears and getting no sleep. She slathered several layers of skin products on her face, neck, and body, hoping it would make up for her lack of rest.

She slipped her robe back on and tied the sash. Although she was twenty-six years old, she had never held a real job outside of academia, where she had acted as TA and tutor occasionally. She hoped to be able to get her butt in gear and find a job. Any job.

When she tiptoed across the hall to the room, she felt pleasantly relaxed. She locked the door behind her and let the robe slip to the floor before falling across the bed naked and instantly descending into a deep slumber with Minnie nestled against her side.

About the Author

June Faver loves Texas, from the Gulf coast to the panhandle, from the Mexican border to the Piney Woods. Her novels embrace the heart and soul of the state and the larger-than-life Texans who romp across her pages. A former teacher and healthcare professional, she lives and writes in the Texas Hill Country.

Also by June Faver